San Francisco, Paris, New York, Washington, Santa Fe

Betrayal / Battle / Storm

3 novellas

Larry Jay Friesen

firefall^{tm}

First Edition: January 2013

© 2013 Larry Jay Friesen, all rights reserved.
No part of this book may be used or reproduced
in any manner whatsoever without specific written
permission, except in the case of brief quotations
embodied in critical articles and reviews.

Cover Design & Inside Illustrations:
EB/BJR/NASA
Printed in the USA

hardcover: 9780915090891
paperback: 9780915090945

FIREFALL EDITIONS
Canyon, California 94516-0189
www.firefallmedia.com

SCIENCE FICTION BY SCIENTISTS-tm

BETRAYAL / BATTLE / STORM
Space mirrors Earth in the warp
of love and weave of war.

THE SEEDS OF ARIL
Earth reborn, 20,000 CE,
8,000 light years away.

A PLANET CALLED HAPPINESS
The sequel to SEEDS

magnetic levitation of a liquid

I would like to thank to Edgar Rice Burroughs, for inspiring so many of us to dream of Mars adventures, and Darrell Paiz, for helping me with the Apache language, to get the Apache name for D.J. right. He is an Apache and lives at the Jicarilla Apache reservation in New Mexico.

3 novellas

Buddy System
11

Sail a Dusty Sky
57

Armor in Aristoteles
160

Buddy System

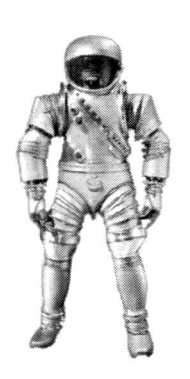

The first thing I became aware of was a smell. Faint, but odd and out of place. A pressure suit does not smell. When it's hanging in the locker, it smells. Even though you clean it thoroughly, inside and out, as part of regular maintenance, after you've had your suit for long enough, it gives off a faint hint of your personal aroma. Not too bad, but most of us in Timaeus Town can pick out our own suits from a locker in the dark.

But not while you're wearing it. The way the our suits work, the breathing mixture flows from pristine clean tanks first into our helmets, then through a check valve to provide cooling to the body, and finally through an exhaust valve to the recycling system. Carbon dioxide and excess water vapor are removed, and the rest of the mixture is pumped back into the tank. It's too precious not to be. But it's thoroughly filtered and scrubbed before it returns to the tank. There's no odor — your pressure suit *can't* smell while you're wearing it.

The scent was there all the same. Faint, but definitely present. One I had never smelled before. Slightly musty, like old books or unwashed clothes or very stale tea. But it wasn't any of those. Something different.

The second thing I became aware of was that I was coming awake. I had been sleeping or unconscious. How? What had happened? The last thing I remembered, I had suited up to go outside. I had closed my helmet and opened the valve to my air tank. I was still in my pressure suit. I could feel the underlayer pressing snug against my skin. My helmet was still closed. I was still near the airlock at the rear of the rover. Not knowing what had happened worried me.

I looked around. The rover was empty, except for me. Where was Rodney? Our pressurized rovers can sleep four comfortably, and they have plenty of cargo space, but they're not big enough to hide in. I picked myself up off the floor, opened my helmet, and looked out the windows nearest me to each side of the rover. I saw a dust coated landscape in shades of gray and brown. Crisp, inky black shadows cast by unfiltered sunlight. The rover hadn't moved in time I'd been unconscious. But no Rodney.

My worry was beginning to increase.

I went forward to the control cab. I scanned the moonscape all around the front of the rover, the empty terrain pocked with a few small craters. No Rodney. I noticed the chronometer readout as I glanced over the instrument panel. I had been unconscious for just under two hours. Two hours! How had I lost almost two whole hours?!

Then I noticed something on the computer screen. Not on the driver's side; the one for the right-hand seat. In the lower right quadrant of the screen, I saw the words:

> Jay, click on the blue diamond icon to read my message. R. Huffman

That *would* be the way Rod would leave a note. He's our top computer expert — hardware, and even more so, software. He's also a good all-around maintenance tech.

I looked around the screen's display. Sure enough, there was a blue, diamond shaped icon on the left side I'd never seen before. Once I got the pointer over to it, I clicked the left trackball key. Immediately the display cleared, and text began slowly scrolling up the screen.

> Read this very carefully, Jay, because this message is only going to be displayed once. Once it's complete, this program will wipe itself from memory, leaving no trace that it ever existed. If you hit the "escape" key or if you attempt in any way to stop this program, download the program, or attempt in any way to interfere with the program's operation, the display will blank, but the program will still wipe itself from memory, and you will never see the message.

I had no doubt that Rod could write a program that could do precisely what he described. I couldn't, but his programming skills are light years ahead of mine. Why would he write a program that would eliminate all traces of its own existence? That scared and worried me. But I had to put my fear and worry on the back burner for a second, because the message was continuing.

> Cynthia told me that she won't see me any more, because she intends to commit herself to you. I can't stand the idea of living without her. She's the one woman I've known that I really want. Not just for now, but for always. It looks like I'll never have her as long as you're in the picture.

Just what was Rod prepared to do, to gain Cynthia's affection? I recalled the first time I'd met her....

I had picked up my tray and found a seat which let me see both the outside view and the hallway entering from the main rover airlock. We'd built Timaeus Town into the north rim of the crater. Digging into the crater wall had taken care of half our radiation protection for us. With no solar flare activity in progress, the regolith-laden "storm doors" were wide open, giving me a clear view out the dining hall windows south onto the crater floor. I could easily see our launch/landing pads.

I also had an excellent view of a gibbous Earth, about twenty-five degrees above the horizon. Bright blue, with white cloud streaks and greens and browns of land masses, all against an inky black background scattered with stars. It is always in our sky, moving only a few degrees up and down in the course of a month on account of the Moon's librations, and likewise a few degrees east and west, but I don't think I'll ever tire of looking at it. Such beautiful colors, and not by any means a static view. It rotates before us at fifteen degrees an hour and changes phases through the month. The wind-blown clouds constantly shift patterns that never exactly repeat. At the moment, the line dividing night from day curved through eastern North America; the U.S. east coast and all of South America were lighted, but the Pacific just west of South America, and the western part of the Gulf of Mexico, including the Yucatan Peninsula, were still dark.

The light Earth casts gives a different mood to the scene than sunlight does by day. Dimmer than the sun, of course, but many times brighter even now than the most glorious moonlit night on Earth. A subtler effect is that it is bluer than sunlight. For me, this gives a moonscape a distinctly different emotional feel than daylight does. Several of my friends here have told me they have felt a similar reaction.

There were three dozen of us living at Timaeus Town. About a third performed mostly "housekeeping" functions to keep our base going: cooking, cleaning, tending the gardens, maintaining equipment, that sort of thing. Another third were technicians and construction workers laboring diligently to expand the base and to develop export products like oxygen and metals for rocket propellant. The rest of us were scientists: some were geologists and planetary scientists studying the Moon itself — like me; some were using the Moon as a platform for astronomy or space physics experiments; some were biologists studying how the lunar environment affects living organisms.

Cynthia Delany would make number thirty-seven.

"Town" may sound inflated for an outpost with so small a population. But we had chosen the name deliberately after a lot of consideration and discussion, to represent what hoped for the future. We didn't just expect the outpost to expand in size and population. Most of us were trying to build a lasting human community, one that would endure long after we left the scene. Even though most of us would return to Earth at the end of three or six month tours of duty, some of us had already signed up to volunteer for return trips after we'd spent a year or so back on Earth. I imagine that we shared many of the attitudes of the early settlers of Plymouth Colony, or the pioneers who went through the Cumberland Gap with Daniel Boone.

I'd read Dr. Delaney's electronic bio file. I suppose most of us had. The arrival of a new person is something most of us look forward to, and I, for one, can rarely resist the temptation to read a new person's bio to find out what sort of an individual we're getting. Dr. Delany would be another scientist — a biologist in her case.

I enjoy meeting new people when they come in, when my

duties allow. I'd timed my lunch to match the shuttle arrival from Selene's Sister, the staging base at the L1 Lagrange point between Earth and the Moon. It was due in at 11:45 Universal Time. The dining hall gives a perfect view of our landing pads, and people coming in from the landing field normally route right through the dining area. It is directly on the way from the embarkation area to the living quarters.

Lunar night would cause no hindrance to the incoming ship. We have found by experience that pilots can see quite well enough by Earthlight for launch and landing operations. We are at such a high lunar latitude, the shadows cast by Earth are always adequate for position recognition and obstacle avoidance.

We have helped nature out a bit. The lights installed in a great ring around the three pads were switched on. They are spaced sparsely, but they clearly outline the landing area. We're adding more lights to the ring, but shuttle pilots tell us that even as is, it's an immense help. In addition to the ring, floodlights were playing on Pad number Two, the one nearest the main airlocks.

I had hardly sat down to eat when I caught sight of the bright flame from the *Flying Fox's* rocket engines. While I watched, and began to taste the fresh flavor and crisp texture of the leaf lettuce, radishes, and bell peppers in my salad, she came down, slowing gracefully as she descended. Within two minutes, the shuttle's landing disks were touching the cast basalt and high-temperature glass surface of Pad # 2.

One of our pressurized rovers was already on its way out to the pad to meet it. I saw spacesuited figures coming down the shuttle's ramp. Some began unloading cargo from the hold. Debarking and cargo transfer were even more efficient than usual. In less than seven and a half minutes, the rover was rolling back toward the embarkation airlock. I hadn't even started my green peas and sweet potatoes.

Not quite fifteen minutes after that, Jackson Goldman, along with several of our maintenance and administrative crew, was escorting Dr. Delany through the dining hall. Jackson is Administrator of our outpost by appointment of the Diana

Consortium, and Mayor of Timaeus Town by our election.

Jackson is also a deputy United States marshal. We've had no crime at Timaeus Town as yet. Not surprising with only thirty-six people, carefully selected for personality as well as for abilities. But we're well aware that we can't count on that to continue if the town grows as we hope it will. We anticipated a need for law enforcement. Since the Diana Consortium is a U.S.-chartered entity, by treaty, in order to carry legal weight on Earth as well as the Moon, any officer needed to be someone appointed by the U.S. government.

A measure of our trust in Jackson is that the whole community — with the support of the Consortium — pushed for having him appointed marshal. A measure of the respect Jackson Goldman carries on Earth is that we got our wish.

When our population grows large enough, it won't be necessary for the Consortium's principle on-site commercial representative, the leader of the civil government, and the chief law enforcement officer to be the same individual. For now, a lot of us have to do more than one job.

Most of the people with Jackson were pushing carts loaded with cages holding various kinds of animals, plus crates and boxes which I guessed contained more living creatures and/or lab equipment. Everyone had doffed their pressure suits in the embarkation area.

I was the only person in the dining room besides the two on food preparation duty, and they were back in the kitchen and out of sight at the moment. Many of our base personnel tend to eat lunch a bit later and hadn't arrived yet. And apparently on this particular day, the people who like an early lunch were all still busy elsewhere. Jackson brought his procession near my table and came to a stop.

"Jay," he began with a smile, "I'd like you to meet our newest scientist. Cynthia Delaney, this is Jay Freeman. Jay, Cynthia Delany."

The picture in her bio file didn't do her justice. Must have been copied from a driver's license photo or something of the sort. It failed to convey the loveliness of her oval face. Nor did it give any hint of the lively spark in her green eyes. Her complexion would have been very fair if not for a light suntan that hinted she enjoyed outdoor activity. Waves of rich chestnut brown hair tumbled to her shoulders. I found myself wondering if she would cut it short, as many of the women at Timaeus Town do, to make it easier to tuck into the helmet of a pressure suit. No one was going to press her to do that, however. One of the unwritten customs that has grown up here is never to criticize or make fun of an individual's personal style, nor try to enforce any fashion, so long as that style doesn't create a safety hazard or interfere with their work.

Her bio picture was from the shoulders up, so I was not prepared for the trim figure and shapely legs which her traveling outfit of forest green, thigh-length shorts and bright blue, short sleeved blouse did so little to conceal. Flat-soled blue sneakers that matched her blouse added little to her height, but at 1.70 meters — only five centimeters shorter than I — she didn't need a boost.

Strong shoulders emphasized her slender waist, and I found myself wondering if she enjoyed swimming or rowing. That sort of information was not in her bio file. It isn't in anybody's. Career experience, education, publications, yes. But we've come to the conclusion after trying various approaches that people get more enjoyment out of discovering each other's hobbies, extracurricular activities, and personal tastes and preferences at bit at a time, as they get acquainted after they get here.

Her lips and eyes warmed with a smile as she reached out her hand. The clasp of her slim fingers was warm and strong as I told her, "I'm very glad to meet you, Dr. Delany."

"I am glad to meet you, too, Dr. Freeman. But call me Cynthia, please."

"If you'll call me Jay."

She continued, "I'm going to be doing research on how the lunar gravity environment affects organisms, including humans." She gestured toward the cages and boxes. I saw a couple of bushbabies, some mice, and a few turtles. I spotted what I took to be air holes. I guessed that those boxes, at least, held more organisms. "We've learned a lot about zero-g effects on humans and other organisms from space station research. But we still know very little about how low-g affects living creatures over the long term."

"Sounds fascinating." I meant it. We would need that sort of research, if we meant to inhabit the Moon for the long term, as much as we needed the studies presently under way looking at radiation hazards and how the lunar day/night cycle affects us. I waved an arm toward my plate. "As you see, I'm just at lunch. I'd love to invite you to join me and tell me more, but I'll bet Mayor Goldman, here, is anxious to get you settled in."

"Probably so," she agreed, "but a lunch break would be very tempting. The last time I ate was several hours ago on the shuttle, and that was only a snack of cheese and crackers and a few walnuts."

Jackson Goldman is not slow to take a hint. He nodded toward the carts. "Do you have anything perishable in this equipment?"

"No," Cynthia shook her head. Her chestnut hair floated beautifully in one-sixth g.

"Then if you're hungry, we can place your animals and equipment in the lab, drop your luggage off at your quarters, and get you back here in — oh, ten to fifteen minutes," he told her. "We'll finish installing everything later. Just come by my office."

"Thanks!" she said with genuine gratitude. I sympathized with her. I've been on long flights myself. I know what it's like to have my stomach grumbling. Not because the flight crew are being neglectful; just because the flight schedule isn't meshing with your body clock. "I can do most of my equipment setup. What I'll need most is some supervision to make sure I don't screw up anyone else's experiments while I'm setting up mine."

I admired her attitude. Self reliant, but not too cocky too accept help, and considerate of other people's needs.

She smiled at me again. "I'll see you in a few minutes, then.

I hope I don't delay your lunch too long."

"I'll have dessert with you," I told her.

Cynthia's first remark, after she reappeared a few minutes later and had set her tray down opposite mine, was, "Are you the Jay Freeman who designed the Mooncape?"

"Yes," I admitted, just before I sliced off a bite from my cantaloupe and put it into my mouth.

"I've been looking forward to meeting you," she said. "Do you realize that you have created a fashion craze on Earth? Capes of all sorts have come into style since Mooncapes began to appear, but someone who wears a Mooncape especially for dress-up occasions, and even more especially a woman really has things iced."

"Have things iced" was an expression I'd heard once or twice just lately, from other newly arrived personnel, and I'd started hearing on news broadcasts and entertainment programs beamed up from Earth. I had the impression that it was a fairly new slang term, equivalent to what used to be called "cool."

I was aware of that, rather vaguely. While we get television programs and news bulletins here on the Moon, most of us don't spend much time following clothing fashions. The kinds of personalities who are attracted to work on a new frontier tend to have other concerns uppermost in their minds. I know I do. I might not have been aware of the fashion effects my innovation had on Earth at all, had the Diana Consortium not taken out a trademark on it in my name, with themselves as co-owners. But I had no complaints about the results. My share of the royalties make a pleasant addition to my salary. Their larger share provides actual income to the Consortium, and will hasten the day when the Timaeus Town project is running in the black. The Consortium even earmarked a small percentage of their share of the royalties to my research budget, much to my delight. Their attitude is that if they allow individuals who come up with commercially valuable ideas or products to share in the rewards, they're likely to get more such ideas faster.

However, as I began to explain to Cynthia, fashion was a long way from my mind when I had developed the Mooncape. I had been trying to solve a thermal problem. When any of us have to do pressure suit work outdoors in the middle of a lunar day, we have to cope with a lot of solar heat. It doesn't get nearly as hot at lunar noon this far north, at sixty-five degrees latitude, as it does at the equator, but it gets hot enough. The cooling systems for our pressure suits can handle the thermal load, and keep us at a tolerably comfortable temperature while we work. They can handle the noontime temperature at the lunar equator, if they have to. But to do so, even at our latitude, they consume an awful lot of power. Even though our suits are light colored and reflective, temperature control at midday costs a lot of energy.

We found ourselves having to break from outdoor tasks and duck inside at much shorter intervals than we had anticipated. Not for lack of oxygen, nor for lack of water in our drinking tanks. We were simply draining the suit batteries to run the cooling systems.

This cut into operational efficiency in a major way. We had to break outdoor operations into shorter time steps. Each time we went in or out of an airlock, each time we had to take a rest break while we were otherwise still fresh, each time we had to change out a suit battery, consumed time. While we could schedule some outdoor operations away from the midday heat, this is not always practical. We'd have to avoid an interval several Earth days long each month.

I had been inspired with what had seemed to me a quite simple idea. A cape of white or silver material. It could be tied over the pressure suit — even over the backpack, with its air tanks, batteries, and air recirculation and temperature control systems — without impeding the use of arms and legs. An optional hood can be folded back when not needed, or drawn over the helmet.

This created an extra reflective layer a person in a pressure suit could put between him- or herself and incoming sunlight. It had worked. Power consumption during the hottest part of the lunar day went way down. Our limiting factor for vacuum work was no longer suit battery capacity but oxygen supply. As a bonus, the same capes that help keep us cool during the lunar day can help keep us warm during the lunar night. The light-colored cape surfaces that reflect incoming sunlight also reduce radiation of our own heat. The nighttime problem is not so extreme as the daytime problem; the human body produces a great deal of heat of its own, to add to what the suit heating elements can generate. But here, too, we found we could cut power consumption somewhat, and prolong suit battery endurance.

Another, less important bonus, is that the capes add extra protection against micrometeoroids.

After I'd finished my explanation, Cynthia responded, "I understand how you were focusing on a practical problem, and this fashion craze came as an unexpected spin-off." Then she laughed softly, and added, "But I still find it fascinating and a bit Alice-in-Wonderlandish that one of the Moon's first export products isn't rocket propellant or solar power, but fashion design."

"Well," I said, "Columbus came looking for a route to the spice islands. He had no notion of Aztec gold."

As we continued our conversation, I listened with genuine fascination as she described her plans for research into the biological effects of long term exposure to low g. I nearly always enjoy hearing someone who is enthusiastic about their work, especially research, even if that research is far from my own field. We also talked more about fashion in general and Mooncapes in particular. I discovered this was one of her hobbies. She enjoyed swimming and rowing, as I had guessed, and apparently enjoyed hiking as much as I do. But she was also fascinated by fashion. Not only current design, but the history and the sociology of it. She even designed clothes herself, for her own wear.

It occurred to me that if she really had been looking forward to meeting me, as she'd said, maybe she wouldn't mind an invitation for a date. So I asked her.

To my delight, and a bit to my surprise, she accepted.

I have never regarded my appearance as being especially

impressive. I'm not ugly, simply ordinary. At 1.75 meters, I'm a couple of centimeters shorter than the average 21st Century American male. My physique is so slender that some people call me skinny. I'm stronger than I look, and I take care to maintain my muscle tone with regular exercise while I'm on the Moon, but it's a wiry strength; my muscles don't bulge. My eyes are neither blue nor green nor brown, just gray. My nose is too large for my face. My hair is a nondescript light brown, and it's a thatch. It goes every which way. I comb it, and fifteen minutes later, it's back the way it was before. It is wavy, though, which I think makes it my best feature. At least, some women seem to like the waves.

Being in my late thirties, I am also several years older than most of the crew at Timaeus Town including Cynthia. I gained my position partly by virtue of a lifetime of studying everything I could about the Moon, and partly by sheer persistence. I applied at every opportunity, pushing myself forward every chance I got. I had to overcome my innate shyness to do it, but my desire to live and work on the Moon had given me the motivation.

My success with women had been rather hit and miss. More miss than hit, when it came to women as jaw-dropping gorgeous as Cynthia.

Nonetheless, it seemed as though Cynthia liked something about my personality. Or perhaps it was our shared interests that attracted her. Whatever the reason, I was immensely pleased.

I invited Cynthia out as often as I could.

Her looks hadn't given her a swelled head. She had a warmth that made it easy for me to open up. On our dates, I found myself telling her how I had dreamed of going to the Moon all my life, how I had wanted to study its rocks and craters and learn what events had formed its features. To learn what this could tell us not only about the history of the Moon, but about the Earth and the rest of the solar system. How I had studied every fact I could find about the Moon, how I had pored over every map, over photographs from every mission, at every available scale, dating back to the Rangers of the 1960's. I thought I could almost navigate the Moon *without* a map. I had looked at the ones I'd seen so many times, I'd practically memorized them. It may have sounded like bragging, when I got to that point.

Cynthia told me how she, too, had looked up at the Moon since childhood, and wondered what it might be like to be there. How after she had become interested in biology, she had begun to wonder how living organisms might be affected by different environments, not only different environments on Earth, but beyond Earth, as well. I quickly developed a huge crush on her.

It was often more than a week between dates. Like many of us at Timaeus Town, Cynthia wore more than one hat. While she was a Ph.D. rather than an M.D., she was a trained paramedic. So in addition to her own research into low-g biological effects, she joined the staff of our physician, Dr. Leroy Wyatt. She had to take her turns at being "on call" and manning the clinic. This included taking her share of late-night and graveyard shifts. Or I should say, the time slots that would have been "late-night" and graveyard" in the Greenwich time zone on Earth, since we have to accommodate the human twenty-four hour body clock, not the twenty-nine and a half day cycle of light and dark on the Moon.

My planetary science work caused its share of schedule conflicts. I would go out on field trips to collect rock and soil samples, or to set up or service instrument stations. That is one of my favorite activities. It is one of the main reasons I *came* to the Moon. But sometimes it took me away from Timaeus Town for days at a time.

Our social life wasn't as sparse as this sounds. We found opportunities to get together beyond formal dates. When our mealtimes coincided, we frequently chose to sit at the same table in the dining hall. We would "accidentally" run into each other in the exercise area, and join in games — or sometimes just conversation — in the recreation area.

Busy and sometimes conflicting work schedules weren't the only reason we went out together less than I liked. I had competition. Rodney Huffman had also been attracted to Cynthia.

I figured he had the advantage. To start with, at 1.80 meters, he is a good five centimeters taller than I, and one of the tallest men at Timaeus Town. Quite trim, but with broad shoulders for his height. On Earth, his height isn't exceptional. But big people mean more weight to lift to the Moon. Launch to space costs a fifth what it did a decade ago, but it's still a significant cost factor. When the Diana Consortium has its choice among comparably qualified people to send to the Moon, they tend to pick the lightest applicant. We have few really tall people at Timaeus Town, and no really plump ones.

Rod is also much nearer Cynthia's age than I, and a lot better looking. Where my hair goes in all directions, much as I try to control it, his is straight, jet black, and always neatly combed. He has intensely blue eyes, and if he hadn't wanted to work on the Moon, his face could have earned him a good living on Earth as a men's fashion model, or maybe an actor.

To top it off, he has a better knack for talking with women than I. He seems to know the right things to say, and the right way to say them. It's rare to spot him in the dining hall or the recreation area, and not see a girl, or two or three, next to him, their attention clearly aimed his way. Lately, Cynthia had often been one of them.

It was our third date…our fourth, if you count sharing a glass of fruit juice in the dining hall as a "date". Cynthia had greeted me at her door, looking stunning — as always — in bright colors. She had on the same blue blouse she had been wearing the day she arrived, and a sunshine yellow skirt she had designed and made. It was her version of the short, mid-thigh length flared skirts currently popular in Europe, Australia, and North and South America.

We had started with dinner: Rabbit roasted with carrots and mushrooms, accompanied by corn bread, lima beans, and a salad made with lettuce, red cabbage, cucumbers, yellow bell peppers, radishes, and a bit of rocket leaf. Honey made by the bees we keep to help pollinate our crops was on the table to spread on the cornbread.

Rabbit, and eggs from our small flock of chickens, are our main sources of animal food. We rarely eat the chickens themselves: the flock isn't large enough to spare many birds yet, and they're too valuable as a source of eggs. Plans are in the works to import some small goats so we can have dairy products, but they haven't arrived, yet.

The Diana Consortium had considered an all-vegetarian farm system, but ultimately rejected that option. It would have meant continuing to import nutritional supplements to the Moon forever, to meet our Vitamin B_{12} requirements.

As we gazed out upon an Earthlit moonscape through the dining hall windows, Cynthia tied into each dish with gusto. It was almost ten hours yet till sunrise at Timaeus, so Earth was just over half full. "Do you have any idea," she asked between bites, "how much I enjoy finding someone besides me who actually *likes* lima beans? A lot of people I know don't seem to care for them."

I responded, "Fortunately for those who don't, we also grow other legumes, primarily lentils and green peas. 'Course I like those, too."

She had wanted to try the vacuum-distilled "Moonshine" corn whisky a few of our enterprising base personnel have started to make. I managed to talk her out of that. Dave Boone, unofficial leader of that group, had informed me that all they have produced so far needs a bit more aging to smooth out the taste. The project is too new. He says his taste tests show considerable promise, but the beverage is still rather raw and harsh. I know he means it, because if it were ready, he'd be sipping it himself, and aside from his taste tests, he hasn't touched the stuff.

A different handful of hobbyist/entrepreneurs — well, not completely different; there is some overlap — have been making mead from part of the honey crop, and we did enjoy some of that.

In earlier conversations, Cynthia had told me that she had

not brought any insects or plants with her for her research project, because she had hoped that our gardeners would allow her to study their plants and bees. They were more than happy to oblige, especially since Cynthia volunteered part of her free time to help out with gardening chores.

The gardeners have no shortage of volunteer assistance. It's a task most of us are glad to take a turn at from time to time. I know I enjoy it. It's cheery to be working with living things, especially when you know you're going to be tasting some of the fruits of your efforts.

After supper, we took in a movie that was showing on the big-screen TV in the recreation center. It was the first of a planned science fiction trilogy called "Empire of the Galaxy". Third Millennium Studios had uploaded the full digital data to Timaeus Town without charge. In fact, Third Millennium was paying the Diana Consortium a fee; the publicity value of having the movie premier on the Moon the same week it opened on Earth was worth it to them.

Cynthia and I enjoyed the movie. So did the rest of the dozen or so in that night's audience. Up-and-coming director Lucia Spielman had done herself proud.

On our second date, Cynthia had given me a good-night kiss that had surprised me with its affection. Tonight she invited me into her quarters.

I soon found myself, somewhat to my surprise and much to my delight, seated on one of Cynthia's chairs, holding her on my lap, in the middle of a very passionate kiss. In the back of my mind, I was thinking how delightful it was to hold a girl on my lap in one-sixth g. I got the warmth and closeness without such heavy pressure as on Earth.

Another part of my mind was still in a state of wonder that a woman so lovely and with such a delightful personality as Cynthia would show such affection to *me*. But mostly I was absorbed in the intense sensory pleasure of the moment: The warmth of her body pressed close against mine, my arms around her waist and hips, hers around my shoulders, one hand caressing my back.

I felt the sweet, arousing pressure of a firm, shapely breast against my chest through her blouse and my shirt. I breathed in her scent as her face filled my vision, and her lips pressed softly, warmly against mine. Every once in a while her tongue teased my mouth; sometimes a brief flicker, sometimes slowly and gently.

I moved one hand from her hip to her bare thigh, just below the hem of her skirt. Her arms tightened as she pressed herself closer against me. Her kiss became more intense. I heard a "Mmm!" of pleasure from her throat. But when I moved my hand from her thigh to the top button of her blouse, she took that hand in hers and gently removed it. She moved off the chair and seated herself on a love seat just to the left of it.

The love seat and chair made a right-angle corner, half facing each other. The love seat's cushions, like the chair's, were inflatable plastic, covered by brightly colored fabric.

"Am I going too fast for you?" I asked her, "or too far?" The last thing I wanted to do was frighten her off; nor did I wish to alienate her by pushing her beyond her comfort zone or past what she felt right about. I had already learned she was a Catholic who took her faith seriously.

She took my left hand in both of hers, and with that gesture she assured me I hadn't offended her. "I have to confess I'm as hot blooded as you are, which is one reason I set pretty careful limits on how far I'll go with a man when I'm not in a committed relationship with him. I set even stricter limits when I'm dating more than one fellow at the same time. I suppose you're aware that I have also been going out with Rodney Huffman."

I nodded. "I'm aware. In a community as small as this, no one can keep that kind of secret, even if they want to. People may not know what goes on behind the closed doors of someone else's private quarters, but everyone pretty much knows who is spending time with whom. I can't blame you for going out with Rod." I couldn't suppress a soft laugh. "I considered myself fortunate to have you go out with me at all, with him in the picture. He's a lot better looking than I am, and probably a more charming conversationalist as well."

"Don't underestimate yourself," Cynthia responded. "You have your own kind of charm. You also have a kind of character I admire. I've talked to a few of the other women here. They tell me you're one of the most honest men they've ever met. Sandy Patterson mentioned to me that if you claimed the sun had turned green and Mars was blue, she'd believe you, because you wouldn't say so unless you'd seen it. Some of us women prize that kind of integrity.

"Rod *is* charming," she continued, "and I like him. But there's a difference in flavor between the conversations I have with him and the ones I have with you. When you talk about your work, for instance, your excitement about what you're doing is infectious. It feels as though you're sharing. When Rod does, it feels more like he's bragging. The conversation often seems to be more about *him* than about the work."

Cynthia paused for a moment, and a bit of a smile curved up her lips and lit her eyes. "In some ways, Rod makes me think of a peacock!"

I couldn't help but smile myself. "I have occasionally felt that way myself, but I feared if I told you that, if would sound like a cheap shot. I can't blame Rod. Isn't a peacock simply trying to display himself to best advantage, to try and attract a female? To be absolutely honest about it, I am trying to put my best foot forward, too, to gain your interest."

"I know," she answered, "but somehow there's still a different feel when I talk to Rod than there is when I talk with you."

The next moment I heard myself saying, "At any rate, if you want a commitment, I'll give you one. I will commit myself to you for the rest of my life, if you want." A part of my mind was experiencing a stunned surprise. Was this really me talking? I hadn't planned on saying anything of the kind. It seemed as though my mouth had spoken of its own accord.

Cynthia's eyebrows went up and her mouth formed an "O". After a moment, she asked in a hushed voice that sounded partly amused, partly astonished, "Is that a proposal?"

There were several moments of silence as I considered.

Whatever subconscious impulse had driven my voice, I had meant what I said. My feelings for Cynthia had gone far beyond a crush by now. I would be very happy sharing the rest of my life with this woman. At length I said quietly, "You can take it for one, if you want. I hadn't intended to say so, yet, but I am in love with you. If you want something phrased more formally, I'll try to find better words."

Cynthia's right hand let go of mine and reached up to touch my face. The heal of her palm gently cupped my chin. Her fingers lay warm alongside my left cheek and temple. "You can't do better than speaking from the heart, the way you just did," she said softly. Then she drew my face toward her, leaned forward, and softly kissed me. Not erotically, but very thoroughly. As if she were sealing something.

When she drew back, she said, "I haven't decided whether to marry you; I am going to need to think that over carefully. But I *have* decided you're the man I want in my life right now. I will tell Rod that I won't be going out with him any longer."

That had been five Earth days before the sample collecting trip Huffman and I had been scheduled to take. I was spending every opportunity I could in Cynthia's company, although those were few in those five days.

If Rod was upset by having Cynthia break off with him, he didn't show it. He was courteous, even cordial, on the occasions when we encountered each other. I was sure she'd spoken with him about it; she's the kind of woman who does what she says she'll do...but it wasn't obvious from his attitude toward me.

I didn't bring up the subject with him, fearing it would rub a raw nerve. I noticed Rod seemed to be avoiding me, but that could have been just a subjective impression on my part.

I did ask myself if it was a good idea to take Rod with me on this trip. I could foresee plenty of opportunity for tension between us. But who else was there? I had checked the work schedules. There was no one besides Rod who would be available at that time to go with me. If there had been, I'd have been glad to partner with them instead.

Nor was there another planetary scientist who could partner with Rod. I didn't necessarily have to go, but at least one person needed to know what kinds of samples to collect. Laurel Stone and Keith Walker weren't due back from their excursion to Protagoras for another week. Everyone else was tied up, one way or another.

I couldn't very well go by myself. It would violate our "buddy system" policy. The "buddy system" had been in effect from the foundation of Timaeus Town. No one goes outside in a pressure suit or away from base alone. We always have at least two people. Every one of us considers it an elementary safety rule for a raw frontier where the "great outdoors" can kill any of us in minutes. There are too many ways a person alone can get into trouble he can't get out of for anyone but a crazy person to consider breaking this rule.

I considered delaying the trip. There was no absolute requirement to pick up samples from the Epigenes area this week. It was on the schedule, but delay would be a relatively minor concern. Wait a few days, and I could go with someone else. There was plenty of work Rod and I could do on base in the meantime. Once out in the rover, there wouldn't be anywhere either of us could go to avoid each other.

On the other hand, we weren't going that far. Just a quick out and back. We didn't even have to overnight if we decided not to. (When I say "overnight" in this context, I mean the sleep period of an Earth day, not the two-week lunar night.)

I finally decided that I could stand it if Rod could. If he made any comment to me that suggested he would be uncomfortable in my company, or even that he had doubts, I would delay the trip until I could make it with another partner. But if Rod didn't like the idea of making the trip with me, he didn't say a word.

All the same, I put my mind on extra alert for interpersonal problems. I promised myself that I'd head back immediately if trouble started to brew. I would not wait until I was sure. At the first sign, I intended to start back.

The trip really hadn't seemed too bad. Rodney and I were polite to each other. Even friendly, in a distant sort of way…though neither of us mentioned Cynthia. Nothing dramatic had happened until we made the first to pick up samples, a couple of kilometers inside the easternmost rim of Epigenes crater.

Rod had taken my insistence that he drive *straight* up and *straight* down the slopes of the rim going in without complaint. That surprised me a bit, because he and I have gone round and round about the subject before. Left to his own devices, he has a tendency to take shortcuts, even if it means driving up or down slopes at a diagonal. He seems to forget that our rovers are a bit top heavy, and that taking a slope at a diagonal increases the chance of a rollover. He has occasionally called me an "old lady" for my caution.

I had suited up, connected the hose coupling on my air tank, and then closed my helmet and switched open the air tank valve to check the flow. That was the last thing I had remembered until I awakened on the floor.

> I planted a small canister inside your air tank. It was set to release a small charge of "Good Night, Gracie" into the tank as soon as you opened the valve. Not enough to do you any harm, but it should put you to sleep for a couple of hours.

Good Night, Gracie. The popular name for a knockout gas developed a few years ago. It puts people to sleep for short periods, from about fifteen minutes to six hours, depending on dosage but it is nonlethal, and very few people have reported any harmful side effects. It's been used on a few occasions for riot control, and once or twice in border skirmishes when tensions between nations got to the level of actual fighting. Police forces like it better than rubber bullets and some of their other nonlethal weapons, because it produces far fewer accidental casualties.

Must have been what I smelled when I started coming to. Where could Rod have gotten a supply? Or had he gotten instructions for synthesizing it? We have quite a variety of chemicals in our lab.

> The rover will not be able to move. When a rescue team arrives from Timaeus, the cause will appear to be accidental. Some dust getting into the connections between the fuel cells and the motors and shorting the circuits. Sadly, the backup circuits will be fouled along with the primaries.
>
> Heads will roll in maintenance for this, but mine won't. I've signed log entries to verify this rover was working fine the last time I had official access to it.
>
> A related dust foul-up in the same circuit box is going to freeze the rover's high-gain antenna in place, so you won't be able to communicate with Selene's Sister and call for help.
>
> I am taking the Scooter back to base. I will tell them that you insisted on remaining with the rover to give me the maximum chance of reaching Timaeus Town and bringing back help. You're going to be a hero. Trouble is, you're not quite going to have enough oxygen to make it until I get back.

The "Scooter" was the unpressurized rover we had secured to an external rack on one side of the pressurized one as a backup. It is larger and has much greater range than the rovers used during the Apollo missions, but its overall appearance is rather similar. Policy for expeditions going beyond walking distance from Timaeus Town is either to take two or more pressurized rovers, or — if the group has four or fewer people, and the destination lies within a Scooter's range — to take along a Scooter as backup to get you home in case the pressurized rover breaks down.

The Scooter should get Rod back to Timaeus Town. It

should have been able to get *both* of us back. But if Rod had planned this as carefully as he seemed to have, he would have some legitimate explanation to give everyone at Timaeus Town. The Scooter's fuel cells unaccountably low on power, maybe; just enough to require lightening the load by one person to make it back.

I was shaken. I had expected Rod might be jealous; I knew that he wanted Cynthia. But I had never, in my worst imagination, dreamed that he would resort to murder! It had never occurred to me that his mind would work like that.

I did my best to calm myself against the adrenaline rush of fear I felt. *Think, Jay, think!* I was glad training for lunar assignments included mind-calming and mental focusing techniques derived from yoga. That training was intended, among other things, to help focus the mind in just such life-threatening emergencies as this. Presently I had my fear sufficiently under control to evaluate possibilities.

I was still alive. The air inside the rover was still good, and with only me to breathe it, it should remain so for several hours, even if Rod had somehow jimmied the recycling system. What could I do to *stay* alive beyond that time?

First, check the vehicle systems. Find out if everything was as Rod claimed. Sure enough, the rover wouldn't move. Nor would the high gain antenna steer. And Rod had, as I feared, done something to the air recycling system, so that it wasn't removing all of the carbon dioxide. I would be good for seven to ten hours, depending on how much energy I used, but not much more. Everything else, however, seemed to be in working order. Even the computer. Rod's message program had disappeared, just as he claimed, but otherwise the computer was working fine.

There was one good air tank in the storage locker for my pressure suit, besides the one Rod had sabotaged. He had taken most of them. Maybe he didn't calculate he needed this one to get back. Or maybe he left it to support his story that he had tried his best to give me a fighting chance. He had also left my Mooncape.

There was one thing I could do, to create at least a chance that Rod might be brought to justice, even if I didn't survive this. I unhooked the air tank from the back of my suit. I found a utility knife in a tool drawer in the back of the rover, and laboriously scratched on the shiny metal surface "CHECK THE INSIDE OF THIS TANK". Wasn't easy: that alloy was hard. It had been formulated to resist abrasion. By the time I got done, the knife blade had completely lost its edge. But I got it done.

There ought to be some fragments of Rod's canister inside the tank, and probably some chemical residue from the "Good Night, Gracie" gas, *if* someone bothered to look for it. The message I'd scratched should bring attention to it...if Rod didn't get to it first and dispose of it.

While I had been scratching that message, I'd been thinking about possible courses of action. My subconscious was doing most of the work: I let my mind drift from idea to idea as I scratched. Some part of me almost wanted to try *walking* back to Timaeus Town. The odds I'd make it on foot were negligible, but the notion of simply dying where I was, without doing *anything*, was frustrating.

Wait a minute! There was a place closer, a place I *might* be able to walk to!

We have plans to send a rover expedition to the lunar north polar region. We want to get some "ground truth" about the water deposits spotted from orbit. How extensive are they? How rich? How far do we have to dig to reach them?

Our rovers don't have enough range to reach the pole and return to Timaeus without refueling. The Diana Consortium is developing new rovers with longer range. But it may be years before those are ready.

We don't plan to wait that long to explore the polar region. If those water deposits are as rich as we hope, we want to start making use of them. So we are setting up caches of supplies along the way: fuel for the rovers, oxygen, water, food, and spare parts. We've set up two caches so far. When we get the third one set up, we plan to make our first attempt on the pole.

The nearest of those caches was between Epigenes and Goldschmidt craters, just south of 70° latitude. I checked its distance and direction from the rover's present location with the computer. The cache was a bit over forty kilometers away, at a bearing of twenty-three degrees east of north.

If I could reach the cache, I could get plenty of air tanks. I could also radio for help. In addition to supplies, the cache was also equipped with communications gear. Including an antenna that constantly tracked Selene's Sister in its halo orbit around the L1 position.

The question was, could I make it? An air tank should last about six hours, give or take some depending on how hard I was working. I would have to average nearly seven kilometers per hour — faster if I wanted to have any margin of time left once I reached the cache, to change out my tank for a new one.

Earthside, I can maintain eight kilometers an hour for hours at a stretch without straining. Comes from trying to keep up with my dad growing up. Dad was taller than I, even after I reached my adult height, he likes to walk, and he walks fast.

Could I keep up that pace in a pressure suit? In suits from the Apollo or the Shuttle or the early Space Station eras, I probably couldn't have. But in the suits we use now, I ought to be able to. We only run them at 270 millibars pressure. And below the helmet, only half that is supplied by the gas. Gas pressure is stepped down to 135 millibars for the rest of the suit by a check valve. The other 135 millibars is provided by the "smartmesh" of the suit's undergarment. Once we put the underlayer on, we activate a control circuit that tightens the mesh until a feedback circuit tells it 135 millibars has been reached. The elastic fabric between the main mesh network allows the skin to breathe and sweat to evaporate. The low pressure gas cools the skin by convection.

This low gas pressure has allowed us to make suits much lighter and more flexible than past designs. I can bend, twist, and lift in my pressure suit with little more impediment than if I were wearing heavy winter clothes on Earth. I can't run as fast, but I can walk just as fast and just as easily as on Earth...when I take advantage of the low lunar gravity, maybe a bit faster.

We don't need a prebreathe period, because we only pressurize the rovers to 500 millibars. The pressure drop is not enough to cause the bends. That's based on all our experience since Timaeus Town was founded, not just theory. Those of us with some practice can get into a suit in ten minutes — counting the electronic and air systems checkouts — and cycle straight out the airlock. Getting the suit off takes a similar amount of time.

150 millibars of the 270 in the helmet is oxygen we crack from lunar rock and soil...about what airline passengers get at altitude on Earth. The rest is a mix of nitrogen with a small percentage of helium that we distill from the solar-wind implanted gasses of the regolith, plus a trace of water vapor to give our noses, throats, and lungs a little humidity. The air in the rovers has the same 150 millibars of oxygen, just more of the other gasses.

I ought to be able to reach the cache before I ran out of oxygen *if* I walked directly there, almost a straight line. Could I navigate well enough to *find* the cache, without missing it, and without wandering too far off track in the process?

The Global Positioning System that performs so brilliantly on Earth isn't very helpful here. We rarely use it. GPS gives our position with superb accuracy...in *Earth-based* latitude, longitude, and altitude. But we have to have a routine to track the Moon's motion, and another to transform to Moon-based coordinates. The computations require taking small differences of very large numbers, which means accuracy plummets.

We use primarily inertial and stellar navigation. They do quite well for us.

By night, I could have used stellar navigation. You have to get used to the fact that the Moon's North Star isn't Polaris, it's Zeta Draconis. But I'd been trained for that, the same as everyone at Timaeus Town. But right now, it wasn't night, it was late lunar morning. The sun was well above the eastern horizon, and climbing. Slowly, to be sure, but climbing. When your eyes adjust to the brightness of sunlight, they can't see the stars.

So inertial navigation it would have to be.

The rover's Inertial Navigation Unit or INU was working fine, but it was securely integrated into the instrument panel, and even if I could have freed it, it was too bulky and awkward to carry. The "Scooters" also have INU's, but Rod had the Scooter.

Our pressure suits don't have INU's. We haven't been able to shrink the size of them enough yet to fit into a suit. But every suit *does* have a gyrocompass, with a readout display in the helmet. And because the gyros are gimbaled to swing freely in the vertical as well as the horizontal axis, they not only tell you your heading relative to north, they tell you your lunar latitude as well. Could I find my way with a compass and maps? Did I know my way around the Moon, did I know the landmarks, as well as I'd claimed to Cynthia? It looked as if I'd be finding out. Having a latitude readout would help, because I knew the latitude of the supply cache very precisely. Once at that latitude, if I missed the cache, I would only need to strike directly east or west. But east? Or west? The catch was, I'd have to know my location on the Moon accurately enough to know which to choose. I didn't expect to have enough air for a second try.

Once I got within a kilometer, I would be able to *see* the cache. Not only is that within horizon distance on the Moon, we had built the cache next to a distinctively shaped boulder almost four meters high and seven across. We had erected an overhanging sheet of metal that formed a sort of half-cylinder about two and a half meters high to keep out the solar heat. A sort of open-ended Quonset hut. The only things we put outside this simple shelter were the solar cells to keep the power supplies charged up. Not content with that, we had marked the cache's location with a three-and-a-half meter tower topped with a reflective cylindrical banner.

I took off my pressure suit. I could do most of the tasks I was planning while wearing it, but the extra dexterity I'd get by handling objects with ungloved hands would save time.

I got the computer busy printing out hardcopy maps from its data base of lunar surface images. First an overall map of the entire region between Epigenes Crater and the cache. Then a series of overlapping maps of smaller areas at larger scale all along my intended route angled at twenty-three degrees to north. As each map came out of the printer, I slid it into a zip-seal clear plastic envelope. The envelopes were to keep dust from accumulating on the maps and obscuring them. One of the Diana Consortium companies developed this plastic. You can brush lunar dust off it fairly easily. Try brushing it off paper, and you get a gray-smeared mess.

    I scanned each map briefly as I zipped up its envelope. The terrain looked somewhat familiar. I guessed I really had almost memorized the maps of the Moon. The area around the cache looked especially familiar. The maps of that region I'd studied frequently, and in great detail, because I meant to be on the first attempt to go all the way to the lunar north pole. If I came anywhere near the cache, I could probably home in on it from the pattern of craters and other landmarks.

    There was one short stretch of terrain on the maps that did have me concerned. It was about three quarters of the way from where the rover now stood to the supply cache. We've nicknamed it the Rock Garden. It is part of the impact debris field thrown out by a small, nearby, extremely fresh crater. It is near enough to the crater that many large, angular rocks are close together. Sharp enough, perhaps, to pose a danger to a pressure suit, for there has been very little time since the crater's formation for smaller impacts to break the rocks apart or soften their edges. And close enough together, perhaps, to impede my normal walking stride. Would I be able to maintain the walking speed I needed in that stretch?

    My next step was to eat a substantial meal. We have managed to design pressure suits that allow the wearer to take a drink while fully suited up, but we haven't yet succeeded in finding a way to feed someone while his helmet is sealed. I didn't know how long it would take get help from Timaeus Town out to the cache, but it would be at least several hours, and perhaps a day, depending on rover availability.

The freeze-dried tuna I unwrapped from its plastic envelope was an import from Earth. But the corn, green peas, and strawberry preserves had been canned on the Moon, and the whole wheat bread was baked in our kitchen from wheat we had grown. It was surprising not only how much food production, but food preservation, had been developed in the short time since Timaeus Town had been founded. I savored the flavor of each item. I wasn't planning on dying…but you never know. This *could* be my last meal, so I let my senses make the most of it.

While I was eating, I took some notepaper and wrote a brief description of what Rod had done and where I was heading. We don't have much paper on the Moon; it's an expensive import, and we don't have fiber crops to produce our own, yet. But we need some to make hard copies of text and images…and tissue for sanitary purposes. In fact, I wrote three copies of those notes. When I'd finished, I posted two copies with adhesive tape: one on the driver's instrument console, the other just inside the airlock door at the rear of the rover. The third I was saving to post outside. Rod might dispose of those messages if he found them before someone else did…but I was going to make the attempt. I wasn't going to make things any easier for him than I had to.

Before I suited up again, I used the rover's commode to take a dump. Had to wait half an hour or so before my bowels were really ready to, but I figured it was worth it. One aspect of pressure suits we still haven't managed to improve much is solid waste collection. We still use "diapers" much like those dating back to Apollo. The urine tubes in the crotch of the suits seal well and fit comfortably. But nobody I know likes using the "diapers". Cleaning 'em afterward is a mess, so we try to avoid the problem whenever possible.

It isn't as though the suit designers haven't tried to come up with better systems. But the engineering has proved tougher than people expected.

When I suited back up, I checked every fitting, and my one oxygen tank, very carefully. I also strapped a utility belt around the suit's waist, and selected the tools I might need to unfasten oxygen bottles from their storage racks, once I got to the cache, and swap them for the one on my back: a couple of screwdrivers, a pair of wrenches, and a vice-grip. I shouldn't need *any* tools; the cache had been designed to enable people to gather oxygen bottles and other supply containers with nothing but their suit-gloved hands. But I was taking no chances. What use reaching the cache, if some hand-grip knob got stuck?

I loaded the tools into loops on the utility belt and clipped my maps together. I made sure my suit's drinking tank was full. I made a final check of every system in my pressure suit, and tied on my Mooncape. Then I picked up my maps. I also picked up one of the meter-and-a-half long walking sticks we always carry in the rovers. Some of us like to use them on rough terrain, some of us don't. I don't usually use one...except to steady myself on steep slopes. And I knew from my maps that there were slopes in places along my route. Starting with the rim of Epigenes Crater itself.

I stepped into the airlock at the rear of the rover. I closed the airlock inner door, and started the pumps to take the air from the lock into the rover. We can never get completely down to lunar-surface vacuum, but we scavenge as much air as we can every time we use the locks. Recycling our life support supplies is second nature for us on the Moon.

Once the lock was ready, I opened it and stepped down the short stairway — four steps — that led to the surface. That was still down from Rod's departure. The rack that had held the "Scooter" had been swung down to its horizontal position and was empty. I could see the tracks from the "Scooter" leading in the direction of Timaeus Town, roughly paralleling the Rover's.

First thing I did, once on the surface, was to tape the last copy of my note to the outer surface of the outer airlock door.

Before I set out on my walk, I made one try to call the L1 station. "This is Lunar Rover Four calling Selene's Sister. Lunar Rover Four calling Selene's Sister."

No answer. I hadn't really expected my suit radio to have

enough power to reach the Lagrange point station…but it was worth a try.

I checked my suit compass and took a bearing of twenty-three degrees. I used the top of the walking stick to help me sight along that bearing toward the horizon. That spot on the horizon would be my first aim point. I picked a boulder just my side of the horizon, and a tiny fraction to the left of my aim point. I would go until I reached a spot just to the right of that boulder, then pick another aim point.

I began to walk. Not run. That would work up a sweat. Worse, it would make me use up oxygen faster. I'd cover ground faster, too, but my speed wouldn't go up as much as my oxygen consumption. Just a brisk, steady walk. A cruising speed for me, but my cruising speed eats up ground. Especially when I could take advantage of the extra "bounce" the Moon's low gravity gave my step.

I could feel the faint crunch as my feet pressed into the ground at each step, leaving imprints of my boot sole treads behind me. I could even hear the crunches, but only through the air in my suit and the solid-body conduction of my body, so that they were muffled to a faint whisper, almost lost in the sounds of my breathing and the whirrs of the pumps and motors in my backpack. I could feel an extra resistance every so often. That would come when a rock lay just beneath the regolith surface.

I balanced the walking stick in one hand. On level ground I didn't need it. I carried my maps in the other.

Without my Mooncape, I would have been warmer than I preferred, with the sun this high in the sky. With it, I was comfortably cool, even with the exercise I was doing.

It wasn't long before I reached the inner slope of the Epigenes Crater rim. There my pace slowed noticeably, and I needed the walking stick several times to keep my balance steady. When I reached the rim crest, I checked my suit chronometer. It looked as though I was still on track to reach the cache with oxygen left in my tank.

Before I started down the outer slope, I turned back for just a moment to see the line of my boot prints leading down and back. I couldn't see the rover from where I stood. It was beyond the horizon, even with the extra height above the crater floor given by the rim.

Then down the outer slope of the crater rim. It was just as difficult, in its own way, as the upslope walk had been. It didn't require as much muscular effort, but it was just as awkward to keep my balance. I made even more use of the walking stick to keep myself upright than I had on the upward climb. I resisted the temptation to run, to let gravity help speed me on my way. If I tripped and fell here, if I cracked my helmet or tore my pressure suit, I was dead *now*, not a few hours from now.

When I reached the plain outside Epigenes, I once again balanced my walking stick in one hand and resumed my easy stride in the direction of Goldschmidt, following the bearing on my compass of twenty-three degrees.

Oddly enough, I was enjoying the walk. I was keenly aware that my life was at stake, that I very well could die. That made me all the more ready to savor what pleasures I could for as long as I remained alive. And for me being out on the surface of the Moon, walking in one-sixth g, was most definitely a pleasure. Whatever came, I had achieved my lifelong goal to get here, and to explore this world.

I was enjoying the moonscape I was walking through, even while still aware I was in a struggle for my life, and a part of my mind held worry and fear. With the mental training we all have taken, I was able to hold that fear at bay. But it was there all the same. If I knew the Moon as well as I thought I did, I should be able to do this. But did I? Was I really as good as I thought I was? Or was my opinion of my abilities an excess of optimism on my part? There certainly couldn't be any more serious test of that than now.

Every once in a while I had to walk down into a small crater, then up and out the other side. Or go around, in cases where that looked safer or quicker.

The rim shadows of the craters, and of occasional boulders I encountered, were stark black against the brightly sunlit browns and grays of the rest of the terrain. Nearly as black as the sky above a horizon only half as far away as it would have been on Earth. No atmosphere to soften their sharpness, and only a faint amount of light scattered into the shadows from the terrain around them. And long, like shadows of early morning or late afternoon on Earth, because this far north, the sun would never get even as high as thirty degrees above the horizon, even at noon.

Every once in a while I'd see a particularly interesting small crater, or a good size rock sticking up from the regolith, and wished that I had my rock hammer and could afford to stop to pick up samples. If I survived this, I planned to retrace the tracks I was laying down, and come back to some of these spots.

I found myself getting warm. My Mooncape was doing a good job and so was my suit temperature control; I wasn't hot, really, but unfiltered sun is plenty strong even with a Mooncape to reflect it, and I was exercising. So I was getting a bit warm.

From time to time, I grew thirsty, and took a sip from my helmet's water tube.

The next checkpoint I had my eye out for was a crater about four hundred meters across I'd noticed on my maps. I hoped my horizon sightings were accurate enough to keep me on track.

When I looked at my back trail, as I did every so often, it wasn't a perfect straight line. I'm only human, and I can't quite manage that. But it was mighty close. By following the bearing of twenty-three degrees and checking my maps, I was keeping the deviations mighty small.

After another forty-five minutes or so of easy striding, I saw I was approaching what looked like the rim of that four hundred meter crater. I checked my maps, and looked not only at the crater, but the rest of my surroundings. Yes, that looked like it.

By my chronometer, I was also still on the schedule I needed. I might even have gained a little time; it looked as if I had made slightly better speed than I had expected.

I guessed I'd covered about half the distance to the cache when I noticed I was getting a bit tired. Not exhausted...but it had been quite a while since I'd hiked this far without a break. I was in no danger of collapsing. But I would have to watch myself, and make a conscious effort to keep up my pace. I didn't want to eat away my margin for error by taking longer than I'd planned to reach the cache.

If I really knew the Moon as well as I thought I did, I should be seeing other landmarks I'd studied from maps and orbital photos. Next on my right should be the "Bathtub". Not an official name, just our nickname for a small elliptical crater about thirty meters across on the short axis, about a hundred and ten the long way. Probably caused by a very oblique impact.

Sure enough, about the time I thought I should see it, there it was, about halfway to the horizon. I began to have a little more confidence that I might, after all, make it. Not that I wasn't still worried — I was. And I still felt a little afraid. But the worry and the fear were a little weaker than they had been.

With the Bathtub behind me, I began looking for what we had nicknamed "the Audi Quartet" — a string of four small circular craters almost in a straight line. About eighty meters across each, and so close together their rims overlapped. It was that "togetherness" that had reminded us of the German auto maker's logo. We guessed that they were a string of small volcanic vents, probably from some ancient lava tube. But no one had yet investigated them closely to check whether that hypothesis was true.

It was not long before I spotted the foursome, about four hundred meters off to my left...just where they should be. Another mental sigh of relief. My confidence level lifted one more notch.

Soon I should be reaching the Rock Garden, if my estimate was right. And in a couple of minutes, it was in sight. Shortly I was among the rocks thrown from that very young crater...assorted shapes and sizes, from dust up to basketball size, some even larger. Not all were sharp edged, but enough were that I must be careful where I stepped, lest I cut my suit.

The rock field didn't stop me from walking through it. What it did was to slow me down by messing up my rhythm. Up to now in my trek, I had for the most part been able to swing my legs in an even, steady stride. Yes, there were small craters and the odd boulder to dodge, and climbing into and back out of larger craters changed my pace. But those were occasional minor adjustments to an otherwise steady rhythm. Here in the Rock Garden, there *was* no steady pace. Not for more than two or three steps in a row, at any rate. I found myself shorting my step to miss a rock, or stepping over a rock or between rocks, requiring me to lift my foot much higher, with much more knee action, than my typical swinging stride on level, even ground.

I dared not leap over the rocks, as I might if there were only one or two. I couldn't guage my landing spot well enough to be sure I'd avoid landing on another, or trip on the landing and go sprawling on top of some sharp edge.

In some places, it was simplest to step from the top of one rock to the top of another. My walking stick got plenty of use, steadying me as I stepped over, between, or atop.

Up to now I had traveled faster than I needed to, building up a reserve of time, a cushion against whatever delays I might encounter once I reached the cache, changing out air tanks. The Rock Garden was seriously eating into that reserve. It extended so far to my right and left that I judged it would cost even more time to walk around it. Not to mention how walking around it would screw up my navigation technique, which depended on keeping a steady bearing.

Finally I was through it. My sigh of relief might have been quiet in most circumstances. In a pressure suit helmet it was distinctly noticeable.

Five hours and twenty minutes into my walk, I guessed — that's all could do, was make an educated guess from my estimate of my pace and the elapsed time — that I had covered thirty-seven or thirty-eight kilometers. I should be getting close enough to the cache to start recognizing landmarks. I scanned the terrain ahead, and checked it against my maps and my memory of orbital photos. I was looking for two craters which ought to be visible to either side of my path ahead, if I were on the right track and the cache were within my horizon distance. One should be about a hundred and fifty meters across, and on my left. The other should be larger, about two hundred and fifty meters across, to the right of my path ahead, and further from me than the first.

Ah! There was the one on the left! Then I saw the larger one…almost dead ahead. I must be a bit too far to the right. I adjusted my path several degrees leftward, and began seriously scanning ahead for the boulder I knew must be there, and for the cylindrical shelter and the banner that marked the cache.

After another couple of hundred meters, I saw the glint of the shiny cylinder, sunlight reflecting brilliantly, even uncomfortably, from what was at that distance a very small spot. It was still distinctly to the left of my path, so I adjusted my direction once again.

I could feel a smile growing on my face. My heart felt very much lighter, and worry began to melt away. It was one thing to believe, intellectually, that I had an excellent chance to survive if I could reach the cache. It was quite another to see the source of supplies that could save my life within visual range.

I resisted the temptation to break into a run. But fifteen more minutes of walking brought me to the shelter.

I quickly found the supply of spare air bottles. Didn't need my tools. It was easy to unfasten the clamp that held the first one I tried to its storage rack.

The next steps were trickier. Thank God the people who designed our lunar pressure suits put the connections between the air bottle hoses and the helmet inlets on the *front* side of the suits. And left enough hose section on the helmet side to get a grip on.

Even so, once I closed off the valve from the old air bottle, on my back, I'd have about five to seven minutes of breathable air in my suit. I'd have to do things right, and I couldn't afford to waste time. I thanked God again...this time for the mandatory suit drills we have, every month. My fingers had experience changing air bottles in vacuum.

Before I did anything else, I put the fresh air tank within handy reach, so I wouldn't have to fumble for it once I started the switch.

Okay...now! Touch the switch that closes the exhaust valve from the suit body, where the used air goes back into the backpack for recycle. Close the helmet air intake valve. Reach down to my side to release the latch that holds the air tank in place on the backpack. Pull down the air tank from the rack on my back. Uncouple the hose from the inlet on the front of my helmet, to the right and below my chin...a mirror image to the one on my left. This two-valve arrangement allows us to carry two air tanks and breathe from either, if we have the extra tanks available.

Now grab the hose from the new tank and couple it to my helmet's inlet. Couple my suit's exhaust valve to the other end of the tank. Open the tank's valves, and my suit's inlet and exhaust valves. I heard and felt the air flow start. I checked the suit's pressure system readouts...everything was fine. Man, what a feeling of relief!

Now that the hoses were coupled, and air was coming in, I could fit the tank into position on my back rack at my leisure. Didn't take long, but it was much less nerve racking than trying to fit the tank into position first, *then* fitting the couplings would have been.

Next thing I did was to find the cache communication system controls. I turned on the power and switched the mode setting so the cache com unit would relay the output from my suit radio to Selene's Sister. I selected the emergency frequency that Selene's Sister is always supposed to be monitoring.

"This is Jay Freeman calling Selene's Sister," I began. "Jay Freeman calling Selene's Sister. Come in, please. Over."

Two seconds later, I heard a reply. "Dr. Freeman, this is

Selene's Sister. Nathan Armstrong here. Do you have an emergency? Over."

"Yes, I do. I am calling from the Supply Cache Alpha, between Epigenes and Goldschmidt Craters. Rodney Huffman sabotaged our rover and left me to die. I managed to hike here. I want you to relay this message to Timaeus Town and ask them to send a rescue vehicle to come here and pick me up. I can keep myself alive with the air supplies at the cache until someone gets here. I also want Huffman arrested and charged with sabotage and attempted murder."

Armstrong whistled. "I will relay your message," he replied. Then he added, "Good luck and stay healthy till they get there."

"Thanks for your good wishes. I will stand by on this frequency for any return messages," I told him. "Freeman out."

Perhaps ten minutes later, Armstrong called back. "Jackson Goldman told me that a rescue party will be out as quickly as they can make it. He also told me Rod Huffman hasn't showed up yet."

"Very curious," I responded. I did not say aloud what we both knew: on the scooter, Rod should have been able to get back to Timaeus much sooner than I could reach the cache on foot.

The cache was about a five hour drive from Timaeus at the average speed of a rover, allowing for craters and other uneven terrain. Allowing the people at Timaeus some time to get a vehicle organized and a crew equipped, I figured on maybe six hours of waiting. I mentally prepared myself to watch the clock, and to be ready to change air tanks again should that be necessary.

I spent time watching the lunar landscape. I don't seem to tire of it. The view may bore some people. Not me. I enjoy woodlands, seashores, mountains, prairies, and gardens on Earth. But I also enjoy visiting deserts. I think of the Moon as a most fascinating sort of desert. And somehow, for me, the fascination of *this* desert never seems to become dull.

From time to time, I also contemplated some of the samples I had gathered at various locations on the lunar surface in the last several weeks, and the analyses I had made of them in the lab. I spent even more time contemplating Cynthia, and my feelings for her.

I spent a lot of time thinking about Rod. I felt a cold anger. I wondered how it was he would go to the point of attempting murder. My mind just didn't work like that. Jealousy over Cynthia I could understand. If she had picked Rod over me, it would have hurt like the very devil. But I felt it was up to her to decide who she wanted to spend time or share her life with. Whether Rod, or me, or neither. I could never have brought myself to harm anyone to get my way, no matter how much I wanted someone or something. So I was ill prepared to understand someone who would.

I was a bit surprised when I noticed a glint of sunlight reflecting from a rover on the horizon only four and a half hours after I'd radioed Selene's Sister. Somebody must have pushed their speed.

A few minutes later, when the rover reached the cache, I recognized the triple shoulder bands — one red, one blue, one green — of Jackson Goldman's pressure suit, as he came down the rover's exit stair. So he had led the rescue party himself. "I'm glad to find you alive!" came his voice over the radio.

"Not as glad as I am!" I returned.

Right after him, another figure bounced down the rover's stair. This one was feminine — you can actually see something of an individual's shape in our suits — but with a double orange shoulder stripe I hadn't seen before. This person also moved like someone who isn't very used to pressure suits, especially to moving in one under lunar gravity. Those of us who've been on the Moon awhile can spot that subtle unsteadiness of a newcomer almost instantly.

Unsteady or not, the second figure bounded over to me in

a rush. I heard Cynthia's voice over the radio, exclaiming, "Oh, Jay, I've been so worried for you!" and then her arms were around my shoulders in a hug.

I was surprised enough that I almost failed to notice the third spacesuited form exiting the rover and approaching us. The blue over yellow shoulder stripes told me that it was Luke Edmunson. He is almost as good a programmer and maintenance tech as Rod Huffman. I guessed his task would be to lead us in undoing the sabotage to the other rover when we returned to it. I could see Luke's dark-complexioned face through his helmet faceplate.

"She wouldn't let us leave her behind," Jackson told me as I returned Cynthia's hug. "By the way, Rodney Huffman still hadn't checked in when we left. I left word with the people on duty to detain him when he shows up."

Jackson then radioed Selene's Sister and had them patch through a link to Timaeus Town. After a few minutes of exchange, he turned to the rest of us, and with a puzzled voice said, "No one at Timaeus has seen Rodney yet, nor the Scooter."

I spoke aloud what I'm sure everyone was thinking, "If he isn't at Timaeus Town by now, where could he be? Could he have doubled back to the rover maybe, to make sure of me?"

"We'll have to start there, anyway, to track him," said Jackson. "I sure didn't look forward to start exercising my position as marshal." He shook his head — we could barely see the gesture through his helmet. "I expected I'd have to, some day, but I did not think it would be so soon, and I wasn't expecting my first case to be criminal abandonment and attempted murder."

We boarded the rover they had brought, and started back along my trail toward the one where Rod had left me. The distance that had taken me more than five hours to walk we drove in less than two.

Wherever Rod was, he hadn't returned to the rover he'd left. When we reached it, we saw no trace of him nor the Scooter. Only the lowered boarding stair and Scooter rack, and the open outer airlock door with my note taped to it. That and three trails:

the rover's wheel tracks leading up to the point where it had stopped, the Scooter's tracks leading away back toward Timaeus Town, and my footprints leading toward the cache.

Using my description of Rod's computer-screen note, Luke Edmunson had had a good idea what tools and parts he needed to bring. His trouble shooting located the source of the problem in less than fifteen minutes…in the circuit box where Rod's note had indicated it should be. If we ever caught Rod, it looked as if he would be convicted based on his own statements, together with whatever evidence we found in my sabotaged air tank.

Under Luke's direction, Jackson Goldman and I simply replaced the entire box with a spare that Luke had brought. When we got back to Timaeus, we would try to clean out the dust and salvage what circuit boards we could. For now, we just wanted to get this rover up and running and back to base. We couldn't afford to be without it; we don't have vehicles to spare.

Fortunately, we could access this circuit box from inside the rover, and Luke gave clear directions. He had tamed the Alabama black accent he'd grown up with so that we hardly noticed it — except when he got really excited about something. So the replacement went quickly. No more than twenty minutes from start to finish. Then another twenty to power the rover back up, and check that everything was working again. Motor drives, steering, computer, communication antenna everything was working fine once again, after the new circuit box was in place and connected.

We decided that Cynthia and I would drive this rover back to Timaeus Town while Jackson and Luke took the rescue rover. On the way, we would follow the Scooter's tracks, and try to find out where Rodney Huffman had gone. All of us were still quite puzzled, because he had still not checked in at Timaeus. Angry, too. From remarks Jackson and Luke had made during our return trip to the sabotaged rover, and during the repair operation, I gathered that the news had already spread across the base by the grapevine of person-to-person conversation. I further gathered that feelings were running quite high against Rod. On the Moon, you need to be able to trust the partner you're working with, because your life quite literally depends on them. I hadn't realized just how angry people could get toward someone who violated that trust. I suspected they hadn't realized it themselves, any more than I had...because it had never happened before.

But on top of the anger was great puzzlement. Neither Jackson Goldman, nor I, nor anyone else could think of any place Rodney could hide out. Not on the Moon. Timaeus Town is the only place on the Moon currently populated. There have been other human landing sites, and two other bases where small research stations had been crewed for short periods of time. Oh — and an astronomical observatory on the far side. But crews only visit the observatory on occasion, to perform maintenance or install new instruments. No one was there now. And none of those bases were within a Scooter's range, nor did any of them have resources Rodney could use: no spare oxygen, water, or food.

Nor could any of us think of any reason why Rodney *would* try to hide out. He should still believe his scheme was working, and should have checked into Timaeus Town by now, with his cover story all ready.

Those questions were much on our minds, as we followed the Scooter's tracks. Not at top speed, more like two-thirds. About the usual cruising speed for the pressurized rovers. We didn't want to go too fast; we didn't want to miss any change of course, nor any other clue that might have been left.

About a third the way back to Timaeus, I heard Jackson Goldman's voice over the rover's radio, "Do you see that?"

I had indeed seen what Jackson had. The Scooter's tracks had stopped paralleling the pressurized rover's outbound wheel marks. They had split off to the right at about a twenty degree angle. "He's taking a short cut back to base," I responded.

Jackson had already figured that out. A quicker, more direct route back to Timaeus Town than the somewhat roundabout way Rodney and I had taken on our outbound path. It should make his story about trying to give me my best chance to survive more believable. Or would have, if I hadn't been around to say otherwise.

It was about another four kilometers when we caught sight of the Scooter. Its tracks led at an angle across a sixty-meter crater. It had almost made it out. Just inside the top of the rim, we saw the Scooter overturned, wheels up.

It looked as if Rodney had tried to "cut the chord", to take the shortest route instead of driving around or directly across the diameter. And instead of driving *straight* down the slope and straight up again, he had taken the slopes at an angle. On the downward slope, he had gotten away with it. Not coming back up the rim.

We sped up our rovers. As we grew closer, we saw a space-suited figure beneath the overturned Scooter.

When we reached the Scooter, we were able to figure out what must have happened. The track from the Scooter's left front wheel ended at a basketball sized boulder. Before the encounter, the boulder had been completely — or nearly completely — buried beneath dust, so Rodney would not have seen it. The impact had caused the Scooter to roll completely over, pinning Rodney beneath it. He was face up, not moving.

Under lunar gravity, he should have been able to push the Scooter off himself and get to his feet. Why was he still pinned?

Looking closer, we saw. The steering wheel had partly broken away from the control column when the Scooter had fallen on its back. A sharp corner of a broken spoke had scraped across the left arm of Rodney's pressure suit. It had made a slight tear in the fabric, just enough to make the tiniest of leaks. The control column and broken steering wheel were pinning the arm to the regolith. And from the look of things, the impact might have broken that arm.

All four of us suited up and exited the rovers. Cynthia hurried to Rodney's form and knelt down to examine him. As I approached from behind her, I heard her take a ragged breath and say, "No sign of life." It was obviously hitting her hard.

It was hitting all of us hard. Even me. I wanted Rodney brought to justice...sent to prison for the rest of his life, maybe. But I didn't want him dead. It must have been a slow way to die...air leaking out, little by little, and unable to move.

Jackson called out on the radio, "Look over here!"

Rodney had still had the use of his right arm, and he had written something with his finger in the dust. We looked closer, and read, "I sabotaged the rover. I'm sorry, Jay. Forgive me, Cynthia."

Cynthia stood up and came close to me, pressing her suited form against my side. She welcomed the arm I put around her shoulders, and she put an arm around my waist. Or tried to, as best she could around the backpack of my pressure suit, beneath my Mooncape.

I spoke aloud a thought that had occurred to me. "If I had been with him, I could have taped up that leak. Could have gotten the Scooter off of him. And somehow, I think we could have made it home."

Jackson spoke his own thoughts with a somber voice. "But you weren't with him. He left you. Then he took one chance too many...and the Moon killed him."

Sail a Dusty Sky

— CHAPTER ONE —

I WISH SHE WERE on board the *Hesperia*. Or that I were on the *Xanthe*.

"She" is Dr. Diana Jane Thorsen..."Diana" or "D.J." to her friends. She's Principal Investigator or "P.I." for meteorology and atmospheric sciences on the mission.

She is also P.I. for the Propellant Production Test Unit. We want to investigate how much the cost of future expeditions can be reduced by producing propellant *at* Mars for the return journey, rather than hauling it all from Earth. The Test Unit or PPTU ("TwoPeeToo" we call it) is a laboratory scale "suitcase" operation to try this out.

Old hat, you say? Didn't a probe or two use Mars-made propellant to get mineral samples home for analysis, years ago? Sure did. One used hydrogen brought from Earth to make methane and oxygen from carbon dioxide in the Martian atmosphere.

But with the PPTU, we will try to *produce* hydrogen from Martian resources. We hope to separate ground ice or water of hydration from soil samples, then electrolyze the water into hydrogen and oxygen. In production scale, hydrogen and oxygen would be supplied for landing craft, and liquid hydrogen would be ferried to orbit for the nuclear engines of Earth-Mars deep-space craft.

We know from unmanned missions that Martian soil *has* significant amounts of ground ice near the surface in some places. We are also aware that soil with hydrated minerals exists in some locations. The Unit is also equipped to test other possibilities. The two other chief concepts are to use imported hydrogen to make methane and oxygen from atmospheric carbon dioxide the way that unmanned probe did years ago, and to crack carbon dioxide into carbon monoxide and oxygen.

My sadness about our separation is because I've really fallen for D.J. My feelings for her run deep, although finding words to express them is not easy.

It isn't just that D.J. is beautiful...beautiful though she is. Five feet two, superb figure. First time I saw her in a swimsuit, I almost forgot to breathe. She got her Norwegian last name from her grandfather. She owes her raven-black hair and the coppery red complexion I admire so much to her Cheyenne grandmother and her Apache mother. In addition to her English name, Diana also carries the Apache name Náaki Tle'na'ai, which she tells me translates into English as "Two Moons".

But there is much more to her than just her good looks She's bright, which I like in a woman. She is also very warm, thoughtful, and considerate. And courageous; she proved that more than once in our training exercises on the Moon. I know I can count on her when the going gets tough. She's someone I really like to spend time with. I'd like to spend the rest of my life with her.

One or two reporters looking for controversy tried to suggest that D.J. owes her position on this expedition to her father, Morris K. Jackson Thorsen, who was head of the National Science Foundation at the time the crew was being selected. (Yes, her father is *that* Morris Thorsen.) But I know better. So does anyone who knows her. She's diligent, enthusiastic, and damn good at her profession. Like many on the crew, she has more than one area of expertise. Besides her Ph.D. in meteorology, she has an M.S. in geology. She's *earned* her position.

I forgot to introduce myself. Major Jonathan Wagoner, United States Army Reserve.

So what is an Army man doing on the first expedition to Mars?

I started out in the air cavalry. That was the branch of service I requested when I got my aeronautical engineering degree and my ROTC commission from the University of Virginia.

It was just a couple of years later that I took part in the South American Expedition. You remember — it was all over the news at the time. You certainly remember the New Day movement that was operating along the border between Peru and Bolivia. They claimed to be a guerrilla army carrying out a struggle of liberation on behalf of the Indians living in the area. It is true that plenty of examples of corruption could be found in the governments of both countries. But none of us who went down there thought of the New Day as liberators. When we saw a few examples of their handiwork, we concluded that they were just a gang of bandits, using the term "guerrillas" in an attempt to gain international respectability and sympathy. They'd hit targets in both countries, and when pursued by the forces of one, they'd retreat across the border to the other.

You remember how they had captured a group of tourists and were holding them hostage for a ransom of money, supplies, weapons, and the release of some of their buddies from jail. This startled the governments of both countries into putting their heads together, and issuing a joint request to the U.S. and U.N. for police and military assistance. The President's response, with U.N. agreement, was to send the Expedition to Lima: a few units of U.S. forces including our air cavalry troop. Other U.N. members, primarily Mexico and Argentina, contributed smaller numbers of troops.

In the meantime, the Spanish ambassador to Peru offered to go up to the Altiplano area where the hostages were being held, to try to negotiate their release. He was a member of the House of Bourbon, a cousin to the king of Spain, and a widely respected diplomat. Three years before, he had successfully mediated a dispute between Peru and Bolivia over revenues that should be paid by a company with mines on both sides of the border. I learned from him later that part of his motivation for volunteering as negotiator was that the tourists included some Spanish citizens (along with people from the U.S. and several other countries).

The U.N. agreed to let him try. But as soon as he arrived at the New Day encampment where the tourists were located, the bandits took *him* hostage.

Colonel Edward Lee, the Expedition commander, decided at that point that if we were to do anything at all about the situation, we'd better act fast. The President and the U.N. Security Council had already authorized him to act according to his own best judgement. G Troop was by far the most mobile of his units. So we got a cram course with the best maps and satellite photos available of the bandit area. Then we went in.

I didn't like the way our aircraft were handling as we neared the location of the New Day encampment. Our scout helicopters, gunships, the tilt-rotor transports for our airmobile infantry platoon and to carry the hostages back — *none* of them were performing well. Everything was flying with that mushy, wallowing feeling you get in flight training, when your instructor has you fly at minimum controllable airspeed.

The helicopters and VTOL aircraft we were using had all been designed and selected for Army transport and close support. So they had been optimized for low altitude. No one had paid attention to high altitude performance. Engines couldn't generate adequate power, props and rotors couldn't get enough bite, wings couldn't get enough lift in the thin air of the Altiplano. Especially with the amount of ordnance and equipment we were carrying.

A few of us were making extra effort to catch our own breath, in spite of a few weeks of high altitude training.

Too late to change that now. We'd just have to make do with the machines and troops we had.

We came over the last ridge, a sort of lip between two high peaks leading to a high valley. There was the encampment. We slanted down. The transports tilted rotors to hover configuration. The rotors from our machines began to kick up dust as we neared the ground.

Captain Putnam had deployed us so that our airmobile infantry platoon was landing as near as possible to the old mine tunnel opening, where recon photos suggested the hostages were being held. Most of the gunships were to stay airborne but at low altitude, interposing themselves between the transports and buildings we believed to be weapon emplacements, storage areas, and living quarters. A few gunships and lightly armed scouts would remain higher, in criss-crossing patrol patterns.

As a platoon leader, I was in one of the "semi" gunships, the Pawnee model that could be outfitted with gunship weapons, but could also carry five or six troops in addition to the pilot and gunner.

As soon as the transports touched down, the bandits opened heavy fire from all the buildings we suspected. Not just rifles; machine guns and rockets, too. That didn't surprise us. We knew that the New Day had raided military arsenals on both sides of the border on several occasions.

Captain Putnam was already yelling, "Third platoon, out of the transports! Out! Out! or you'll be hit like sitting ducks! Get to the tunnel! Find those hostages!"

But our gunships were slow to respond. The ones near the ground were sluggish on the pick up. Those at higher altitude, at the ends of their patrol runs, were mushy on the turn-around maneuvers to come back.

While all this was going on, we were taking hits. Radio was crackling with casualty reports. I saw one 'copter from my platoon take heavy machine gun fire. The rotor slowed, and the machine settled to the ground. Pilot and gunner got out, the pilot limping, blood coming from one leg, the gunner holding a bleeding left arm.

As soon as they were out, they hit the ground flat, making as small a target as possible for the incoming fire. A medic started to worm his way toward them.

A rocket hit a gunship from First Platoon just below the engine. The explosion made a ball of fire through the cockpit and sent the main rotor flying. I felt grim at the sight.

Normal tactics were too slow with our impaired maneuverability. It was time to try something else. I told my pilot and gunner, "Let's stop trying to get up speed for a normal firing run. Just hover in ground effect, and pivot her in place with machine guns firing. Like we were a turret. Rake the buildings to our front. Pass the word to the rest of the platoon to do the same."

Hardly had the platoon started to carry out those orders when Captain Putnam was on the radio. "I've been hit, Wagoner!

Bad! Chest wound!" His voice was weak, but clear. "Lieutenant James and Lieutenant Powell have also been wounded. You and Lieutenant Rice are my only two platoon leaders still unhurt." It didn't take a genius to deduce what Captain Putnam was going to say next. Al Rice was only a Second Louie, the ink hardly dry on his commission papers. The only other officers in the troop were some warrant-officer pilots. So I was senior. "I am placing you in command of the troop."

It had to be a bad hit, for Captain Putnam to relinquish command. He was not an officer to shirk responsibility. He would not be handing the troop over to me if he had any other choice. I swallowed hard.

But there was no time to waste. The battle wouldn't stop to let me gain my composure. I felt an adrenalin surge, but I had to keep my head.

"Medevac!" I ordered, "As soon as you have a full load, evacuate Captain Putnam and as many other wounded as you can! Take the most seriously wounded first!"

I needed to take charge of the hostage rescue portion of the operation. Third Platoon was being held back by fire from the tunnel mouth. New Day guards with the hostages were the source of the fire.

My pilot was senior warrant officer of our platoon. "Craig," I told him, "you have charge of the platoon. Keep the bandits pinned down as best you can. Tell the other platoons about our little spin-and-fire maneuver. I'm joining Third Platoon."

I ducked out of the 'copter and sprinted for a boulder, then dropped to the ground and wormed my way as fast as I could to where Third Platoon was pinned down. Although Lieutenant Powell had been hit, as Captain Putnam had said, he was still conscious and in command.

"George", I told him, "I need a couple of your grenadiers."

He hand signaled two over from his First Squad, nearest us. As they crawled over, I was glad to see that they had plenty of 40 mm grenade cartridges in the loops of their special jackets. Did they have the right *kinds* of grenades for what I wanted to do?

"Do you have any tear gas grenades?" I asked them, "and do you have smoke grenades?"

"Yes, sir," they chorused.

"All right," I said. "Private Jenkins, when I give the word, I want you put tear gas into the tunnel mouth. Corporal, as soon as he does, I want you to lay down a wall of smoke to the left of the tunnel, between it and the rest of the encampment, to screen us. Pass the word to all squads to rush the tunnel as soon as you fire. Except you two; you'll stay here and continue to lay down smoke."

"But sir," Jenkins protested, "we don't have our gas masks out —"

"And we don't have time to get them," I finished. "The wind's blowing from us toward the tunnel. And there'll probably be time for the gas to disperse by the time we reach it. But we've got to chance it. I don't want to give the bandits time to start killing the hostages — if they haven't started already."

In less than a minute, the word came back: "All set!" The grenadiers had already loaded the launchers slung beneath their rifle barrels.

"Fire!" I told them. As soon as the first puff of white smoke billowed out, I yelled, "Third Platoon! Follow me!"

We sprang up and began running. It was just over a hundred and fifty meters to the tunnel mouth, but it seemed like a kilometer. Although our enemies couldn't see through the smoke, they were still firing blindly, and we still had the occasional bullet whining through. Two more men dropped as we ran toward the tunnel.

No more firing from the tunnel itself, though. The tear gas was having its effect. As we neared the tunnel, two of the bandit guards were stumbling out, coughing and choking, in no condition to fight.

When we entered the tunnel, we found that the hostages were indeed inside our intelligence had been right. Thank God for small favors! Some of them were coughing and weeping from the gas, but they were alive!

But wait. As we came further into the tunnel we discovered two New Day guards still in there with them. Each bandit had one arm around the neck of a hostage, holding a pistol to their head with the other hand. One guard held a man, the other a woman.

What to do? Think fast, I told myself. To the bandits I said, "You can get out of here, but you have to let the hostages go to do it."

They weren't relaxing. Perhaps they didn't speak English. "Anyone here speak Spanish?"

I was looking around at the Third Platoon when I said it, but a tall, slim, dark-haired man among the hostages responded. He wore a thin moustache and despite the surroundings, had a look of elegance about him. "I believe I can help you señor," he said. As he spoke, I recognized him from a picture we'd been shown during our briefings. He was the ambassador from Spain.

"Can you tell these men what I said?" I asked him. "Tell them we'll let them go unharmed, but only if they release the hostages."

He nodded and turned toward the two gunmen, taking a slow step toward the one nearer to him as he did so. He began translating my offer into Spanish.

They weren't buying it. "No!" yelled the nearer of the two to me, the one with the male hostage. That was one Spanish word I didn't need translated. He was panicking. I saw his finger start to tighten on his pistol's trigger.

I quickly dropped to one knee and lined up my rifle, trying for a head shot that — I hoped — would miss the hostage. But not quickly enough. He fired a fraction of a second before I did, hitting the man he held in the temple just before my bullet went into his eye.

The Spanish ambassador used the distraction to close the distance to the second gunman, and struck up the barrel of his pistol. The pistol went off as he did so, hitting the woman hostage in the head; how badly I couldn't immediately tell. The gunman managed to throw off the ambassador and line up his pistol on the Spaniard. My second bullet took him in the chest before he could fire. He went over backward, the pistol flying from his grip.

"I owe you my life, señor," the ambassador declared, as our medics checked the two hostages.

"I wish I'd been able to save theirs, too," I replied. I felt awful. The man was dead; the woman barely alive. She *might* make it...*if* we could get her to a hospital quickly enough. But I had no time to sit and feel miserable over my decisions. There were still other lives at stake, and more decisions I must make as best I could - and quickly.

"Okay," I said, "back to the transports. On the double!" I assigned troopers to carry the wounded woman and the dead man. We double timed it back to tilt-rotors through the smoke screen being laid by my grenadiers, assisting the hostages as we hustled. I returned to my copter.

"Do we have everybody aboard?" I yelled. "Wounded included?" I had no intention of leaving anyone behind to the mercies of the surviving New Day members. They'd be very angry over this raid, and they had a bad reputation about treatment of prisoners. The hostages had been an exception, because the bandits knew that any possible ransom depended on them being in good condition.

"Everyone still alive is aboard aircraft, sir!" came from the platoon sergeant of Second Platoon.

"All right!" I called. "All aircraft, back the way we came! Transports first, then scouts, gunships last! Stay in ground effect until you're over the lip, then drop to get out of the line of hostile fire! Gunships — we'll back out and maintain suppressive fire as we go!"

Despite our losses in men and aircraft, we left in good order. Those of us in gunships kept our machine guns firing until we were over the lip, then turned about and escorted the formation back to base. The woman hostage who'd been shot died on the flight.

By the normal standards of a military engagement, we took a terrible licking. We took heavy casualties: we lost 30 percent of our troops, dead and wounded, and 40 percent of our aircraft, while inflicting little damage and few casualties to the bandits. But we fulfilled our mission. We got all of the hostages but the two who were shot out alive.

That action got me my captain's bars. The Army decided I'd done a good enough job to rate a promotion. It was in that same action I won my Distinguished Flying Cross. And because one of the people we got out alive was the Spanish ambassador, I found myself in a ceremony at the Spanish Embassy in Washington, D.C., receiving the Spanish Order of Military Merit from his own hand.

The major reason we had taken such heavy losses was the poor high-altitude performance of our aircraft. Because the helicopters and VTOL aircraft we had used had been designed for Army transport and close support, so much design attention had been given to *low* altitude performance that no one had given much thought to what they would do at *high* altitude. The possibility of deployment in high mountainous terrain had simply been overlooked. After the Expedition, I made a vow that never again would American troops be sent into action with inadequate equipment. So I got into aircraft acceptance testing and from there into test piloting.

As a test pilot, I have flown every model of helicopter and VTOL aircraft in the U.S. inventory. Not just Army aircraft but Marine, Navy, Air Force, and Coast Guard as well...and quite a few foreign machines to boot. I've flown everything from light observation helicopters to heavy tilt-rotor transports to supersonic jump jets. I have even flown a few lighter-than-air machines, mostly hybrids combining blimps with helicopter blades.

So when Mars Mission crew selections were announced, and they tried me out on the Mars Lander simulator, I performed better than anyone else who had been on it. To me, it was just one more VTOL flying machine.

That will be my main job, piloting the *Phobos*, the landing craft carried by the *Hesperia*. That, and flying the *Coprates* once we get down. The *Coprates*? That's the giant blimp intended to let us range over the Martian surface, to see and sample more than just the immediate area around the landing site.

I have some doubts about exploring an unknown planet in such a frail-looking machine. But the designers have convinced me that the safety margins are adequate. I still feel some trepidation about the plans to go so far from the landing site. Especially when we only have one blimp. Weight limitations prevent us from carrying a second.

Despite my fears, there's nothing you could pay me to get me to give up the chance to see so much of Mars. Especially since Diana will be coming along.

— CHAPTER TWO —

I SHOULD INTRODUCE the rest of the crew. Once upon a time, when America started Project Mercury, there were only a handful of astronauts, Soviet and American together, and everybody knew their names. They were household words. And while some of you born in recent years may not believe it, in those days, Soviets and Americans were the *only* astronauts. But these days, with so many people flying, it's hard to keep up. The twelve of us *will* be household words *if* we make it to Mars. Or better yet, if we make it back, and spend some time on TV talk shows. But for now, most of us aren't well known.

My best friend on the *Hesperia* — on the expedition, if you don't count Diana — is our flight engineer, Terence Tarkhan. I'm convinced he got under the 6'5" height limit only by stooping and having a sympathetic doctor when he was measured. I threatened to call him the "green Martian" when we were doing Earth-orbit and lunar-orbit rehearsals, because he always gets space sick at the start of free fall. Fortunately his stomach and vestibular system always calm down after a few days, just like everyone else's.

Terence's wife is expedition biologist Teresa Sola. Even with the findings of the Curiosity rover, the answer to the question: did Mars have life at some time in the its history? remains a strong "maybe". This after analysis of several meteorites thought to have come from Mars and all unmanned orbital and surface missions to the red planet, even returned samples brought back by some of those probes. I gather from Teresa that estimates by most members of the planetary science and biological research communities range from 60 to 80 percent likely. The question of *present* Martian life gets much more widely scattered answers. Estimates for *that* range from less than 30 percent to more than 70.

So Teresa plans a very intense research program once we're there, to look both for fossils and for evidence of present day life. She admits that we will have to get lucky to find evidence of either on a first expedition. But she is going to try.

Teresa will also be monitoring our bodies' responses to the trip, and to Mars' gravity once we arrive. She is a trained nurse and paramedic, and the ship's medical officer. Not only will she monitor our condition, she has been trained to deal with most medical contingencies. For any situation she can't handle on her own, she can at least stabilize a patient until Tell Packs can come over from the *Xanthe*.

She is also an expert computer programmer, and Terence calls on her help from time to time in his engineering duties.

Captain of the *Hesperia* and commander of the expedition is Captain Kent S. Kent, U.S. Navy. Or as we sometimes call him, "Kent Squared". I expect it will be Rear Admiral Kent, if we are successful. He came to the astronaut corps by way of test piloting, as I did. If there's any one person I'd as soon trust my life to in a flying machine as myself, he's the one.

Some would-be wit among the crew — I don't recall who — started playing on his name and referring to him as "Captain Can't". The term started to spread and catch on. Kent's response when he first overheard it showed his leadership ability. A lesser man might have ranted and raved and issued an order prohibiting use of the phrase. Instead, he turned things about with his own brand of humor.

"No," he said, "Captain *Can*. We *can* make this expedition a success. We *can* get to Mars and back, and bring back enough knowledge to earn our place in history."

Captain Kent's enthusiasm has been contagious. Because he has believed so strongly in the expedition and in us, the rest of us have grown more enthusiastic than ever. So now, when we're not calling him "Kent Squared", he is indeed "Captain Can".

Kent's wife is Tara Halley, astronomer and planetary scientist.

The final member of the *Hesperia* crew is Dr. Fay Adair. She is a geologist — and ice specialist and hydrologist. Five feet six, lovely face, beautifully curved figure. Blue-eyed, with hair as blond as D.J.'s is dark.

Captain and flight engineer of the *Xanthe* are the same man: Xavier Buthelezi of South Africa. His presence is proof to me of the wisdom of opening crew selection to world-wide application.

Xavier is a prince, I understand, among both the Xhosa and Zulu peoples. While his father was a member of the family of the traditional hereditary paramount chiefs of the Zulu, his mother was likewise a Xhosa princess. Their wedding had been something of a national event in South Africa.

In school, Xavier discovered early an aptitude and liking for engineering. And by the time he was in college, he was attracted to flying. So it was aeronautical engineering and flight school for him, and after graduation, a tour of duty in the South African Air Force. After that, he turned his hand to designing aircraft for South Africa's airplane manufacturers. He was working on some engine improvements when the selection for the Mars crew was announced.

The pilot for *Deimos*, the *Xanthe's* landing craft, is Captain Carter Horace. He's another test pilot, from the U.S. Air Force. You might remember him from his Air Force Academy days, when he was an Olympic silver medalist in both long jump and high jump.

I've done a little track and field myself, but my best sport is fencing. While we were training for this mission, I learned that Terence Tarkhan also enjoys it, and we had a match now and then, when we had some free time. Which of us is better? Depends on the weapon. With epée, I win more often. But with saber, where Terence can use the slashing attacks he favors, he more frequently has the edge.

Carter's wife is Dr. Ruth Vivian Dean. We call her the "Beastmaster", because she has the job of monitoring and controlling the fleet of mini- and micro-rover robots that will be fanning out from our landing site to augment our human exploration. They are multilegged devices that look like nothing so much as small mechanical animals, or giant insects or spiders. Her favorite model is a 10-legged type she calls the "little lion", because the cluster of instruments and antennae at its forward end resembles a mane.

Physician for the *Xanthe*, and chief medical officer for the expedition, is Telemachus (Tell) Packs. He was a surgeon on the organ transplant team at the University of Kansas Medical Center in Kansas City before he was selected for the Mars crew.

His wife, Valeria Diaz, originally from Durango, Mexico, does double duty. She is a psychologist, observing crew reactions on the voyage, and hoping she can help everyone keep their mental balance during the long period in a confined space at close quarters with each other. But she also has training in cartography, and once we reach Mars, she will be P.I. for mapmaking.

I was supposed to be assigned on the same ship as D.J. I had hoped we would be married before the trip started. As you've gathered from the list of crew members, NASA, ESA, and the other space agencies involved decided early in planning that the best crew mixture for sustaining mental and emotional health on such a long voyage would be even numbers of men and women, and best of all would be husband-and-wife teams.

Mission planners realized that they wouldn't necessarily be able to achieve that mix and at the same time have the mix of crew *skills* the mission required. So they expanded their selection search beyond the then-existing astronaut corps. And when they couldn't find husband-and-wife pairs with the sets of skills needed, they did their best, with psychological and personality profile tests, to pick pairs of men and women who would find each other attractive and compatible, and who, with a little bit of luck, might marry one another before launch.

That selection criterion was never a secret. It was made quite public, so that anyone applying for the voyage was well aware what the mission planners were aiming for.

D.J. and I were just such a pair who were selected with each other in mind. Each of us was fully qualified for our place in the crew on our own merits. But the fact that each of us was also compatible with another selectee was one more point in our favor.

I had no objection to the idea; the thinking behind it made sense to me. I especially had no objection once I'd met Diana, started training with her, and had dated her a few times. She has all the qualities I admire in a woman. Beauty, intelligence, determination, strength of character, and warmth of personality. The more time I spent with her, the more attracted I became, and the better I liked her.

About six weeks before launch, I proposed. I didn't get quite the reception I'd hoped for.

We were at the Cape, preparing to launch in a few days to the Moon for one of our low-gravity spacesuit training exercises. I had taken Diana for dinner at the Santa Fe, a restaurant that featured southwestern style cooking, one we had both grown to enjoy.

After dinner, we went for a walk on the beach. It was warm enough to dress lightly — short sleeve shirt and slacks for me, light blouse and skirt for Diana — yet pleasantly cooled by a breeze blowing salt scent softly in from the sea.

The Moon, not quite full, was already high in the night sky, shining brightly down upon us. We could also see the red spark of Mars in the east. It had risen not long before. Seeing the two worlds that awaited us, one in a few days, the other in a few months, seemed a fit setting for saying what I had in mind.

I have little gift for fancy words, and by now Diana knew that. So I did not try. I simply asked, "Diana, will you marry me? You may have guessed I've been thinking about it for a while, and now I'm sure you're the woman I want."

Diana's face grew soft, and she put her hands upon my chest as she looked into my eyes. She had to reach up to do it; I am a full foot taller than she is. "Jonathan," she said, "I am truly touched. I really like you. But I've had trouble from the start with the idea of marrying someone just so we can satisfy each other's needs for the duration of the mission. That part of the selection process has bothered me, although I didn't dare say so for fear of not being selected…I really want to go to Mars."

"That way of looking at the crew selections makes it sound really cold," I responded. "I just don't feel that way about it. And if you think I'm asking you to marry me just to satisfy my needs, I haven't made myself clear at all. I'm not just hot for your body. I'm in love with you."

"I have to confess," she admitted, "that I love you, too. But I am old fashioned enough to want a marriage to last a lifetime. And for that, I want to be sure, really sure, that I am committing myself to the man I want to spend the rest of my life with."

"I am already sure that you are the woman I want to spend the rest of *my* life with."

"I think that you may be the man for me," said D.J. "I really hope so. But I am not one hundred percent sure, yet. I need some time to make sure. I want to be certain that I'll still want to spend my life with you *after* the trip. Can you please allow me that time?"

"There isn't a lot of time left before we launch," I pointed out. "And most of what there is going to be pretty busy."

I already knew there would be no sex until we were married. She was an old fashioned girl in that respect, too. She enjoyed making out, apparently as much as I did. But there was a limit to how far she would go.

That was fine with me. I wanted her on *her* terms; I wanted her to remain true to herself. I didn't just want someone who looked like her, who would do what I wanted. I wanted *her*. I'd known other women, but this was the first time I had actually been in love, unless you count a couple of brief high school and college crushes. I liked the feeling.

"I know," she conceded. Her eyes began to light up with an idea. "How would this be? Have Captain Kent marry us on the voyage. He has the authority to; the mission planners had such situations in mind. If we can still stand each other after a few weeks in close quarters, I'll *know* we're right for each other.

"I realize it's asking a lot," she went on, "to make you wait like this. It will be hard on me, too. Even if it doesn't sound like it, my emotions are running just as high as yours. But I want to take the time to make sure of myself. Will you allow me that?" she pleaded.

I shook my head in resignation. "All right. I'll wait if I must. I'm not eager to; it will be frustrating. But you are worth waiting for."

We'd made that decision expecting that we'd make the trip aboard the same ship. That was how we'd originally been assigned, and we anticipated we could complete our courtship shipboard, even if that was not quite how either of us had envisioned wooing a mate.

But that wasn't how things had worked out. William Hood, who had *originally* been selected as the expedition's chief medical officer, was injured during an EVA while on a lunar surface training exercise. By the grace of God, his space suit wasn't ruptured, but he broke his left leg.

The break would not likely heal before launch date, and we've learned from space station experience with test animals that low or zero gravity impedes the healing of broken bones. So Tell Packs had to be called in from the backup crew to replace him. That meant that Tell's wife had to be included in the crew. Since Bill Hood was a bachelor, that meant dropping a woman from the crew. Who turned out to be Lana Gauthier. *That*, in turn gave Captain Kent and the mission planners the headache of reevaluating the psychological compatibilities and skills mix needed aboard each of the two ships, and some major reshuffling of personnel assignments. A real chain of dominoes.

Which is how D.J. and I have wound up on different ships, all the way to Mars. Courtship has sort of been put on hold. There would have been little enough privacy together on the same ship. There is none at all when our communication has to be by radio or television, ship to ship. The crews of both ships understand and sympathize with our situation, and allow us as much comm time as they can. But neither of us feels like saying the personal things we really want to, on an open line.

Arrangements may be different, on the trip back. One thing the long voyage allows us is lots of time on simulators. Not only does that help us cope with boredom, but it is enabling us to cross-train for each other's jobs. Which is a benefit to the safety of the mission...and may permit us to rearrange accommodations on the return flight.

One bright spot in this frustrating picture is that the trip, long as it is, is much shorter than it would have been without our ships' nuclear engines. Nuclear propulsion has permitted us to use "fast track" trajectories, out and back, and still keep propellant mass down to something reasonable. The choice to send an unmanned tanker ahead, so that our return propellant is waiting for us in orbit around Mars, also helped.

This choice of propulsion and mission strategy is keeping the trip time on the outbound leg down to four and a half months. This will give us three months at Mars before another four and a half month trip home.

It is not a bad trip, though. When I stare out a window into space, and I do that often, it's wondrous. Watching the sun, the stars, and the planets, seeing Earth growing dimmer behind us and Mars growing brighter ahead is truly beautiful. Those sights give me a sense of awe and wonder. Tara Halley is teaching me to appreciate the stars and constellations as more than navigation aids. But gazing at them does *not* make the time go faster. Rather, watching the sky around us makes me feel that the time spent is worth while. When I am watching the stars, or — as I do more and more as the voyage goes on — looking at Mars, I can lose myself in wonder. If it weren't for how much I miss D.J., I wouldn't mind how long the trip takes.

But a complicating factor has arisen, and it's just as well the trip won't be any longer. I became aware of it a few weeks out from Earth.

Fay Adair approached me one day while I was at my regular exercise routine. That was in the Utility section of the ship, where we keep the exercise equipment, as well as laundry equipment, sanitation facilities, shower, and many of the consumables. I was doing arm-presses at the time on a spring-loaded resistance machine.

That was another reason the mission planners had preferred a fast-track trajectory. Not just to minimize the psychological and social stresses among the crew, but to keep our bones from deteriorating too much. And minimize exposure to cosmic rays and solar flare particles.

Fay had on her own very attractive exercise outfit, snug to her curves. She had also made sure no one else was in this section of the ship. I wasn't surprised at that Fay was dressed for exercise. We all need to keep fit. What surprised me was what she said and did next.

"I've been wondering why you spend so much time at this," she said, "and why you spend so much of your time at the strength-building exercises." She looked pointedly at the resistance machine. She was heading for the treadmill. "Not that you're cheating any of the rest of us out of our time. But you certainly put in more than the minimum daily recommended allowance."

"Well," I grunted as I did another press, "It's a way to pass the time. And when we get to Mars, I want to be in shape to work. Long-duration space station microgravity experiments indicate that exercises that put stress on the major bones not only help maintain muscle tone, but reduce bone calcium loss as well. The biologists say that the final answer isn't in yet, but it does look like a good bet."

Fay realized that I hadn't tuned in to the fact that she was trying to talk about more than mission requirements and muscle tone. She stopped and took a breath. She said, "I was hoping to run into you, and I guessed this would be the most likely place."

I stopped, too. I disengaged myself from the resistance machine and looked directly at her. She was acting as if she had something she wanted very much to say, but couldn't quite work up the nerve. I hoped it might help if I gave her my full attention.

Fay seemed to take encouragement. She continued. "I...I've

fallen in love with you. I was hoping, wondering if... if you...might marry me."

I was dumbfounded. I've always been slow on the uptake reading other people's emotions. I knew Fay liked me, but I'd missed this entirely! I blurted out, "But I thought...from what I knew about the personality profiles...you'd be falling for Xavier Buthelezi!"

"That's what the crew selection board were hoping when they picked us," Fay agreed. "It might have worked out that way if ship assignments had remained as originally planned. But he's over there, and I'm here."

I nodded. There has to be a qualified deepspace ship commander and a qualified engineer aboard each ship. Which meant that Xavier has to be on one ship, Captain Kent and Terence Tarkhan on the other.

Fay went on, "With his duty load as a ship's captain, we never had as much time to get to know each other as you and Diana did. And here you are, close by all the time, and I don't think you realize what a gorgeous hunk of man you are."

I was beginning to feel embarrassed, and Fay sensed it. She laid a hand on my arm. "I know you feel awkward when people talk that way about you. But I've gone this far I had to let you know how I feel. The fact that you're *not* a boaster, but modest, courteous, so much the gentleman, makes you all the more appealing."

My answer to her was one of the hardest things I'd ever had to say. Nothing in my experience had prepared me for this. In my career as an army officer, I'd dealt with a lot of interpersonal situations. But nothing like this one.

"I am deeply sorry," I told her. "I don't feel toward you the way you do toward me. I am so much in love with Diana that there is no room in my heart for anyone else."

"I was afraid of that," Fay admitted. "I know you care a lot about her." But she hadn't quite given up. "If you really can't stop loving Diana, okay. But you wouldn't have to marry me. We could..." she hesitated, and lowered her eyes from mine. Did I detect a blush? Not like Fay. She is usually bold almost to the point of being brash. She was really keyed up over this. "...share accommodations."

"I'm sorry, Fay," I said. "I can't say I'm not tempted. Very tempted. If I hadn't already fallen for Diana, I might accept. But now...I'm so much in love with her that I just don't want anyone else. Physical satisfaction just wouldn't be enough for me any more."

Fay's face showed hurt, then almost anger, then sadness.

I don't relish the thought of facing her, day after day, for the rest of the trip. But our duties require us to work together from time to time. And the small volume of the ship makes it nearly impossible to avoid each other for long.

This is a very new situation for me. There have been a time or two in my life when a woman has been more strongly drawn to me than I to her, and a time or two the other way around. But not a time when the woman's feelings were as intense as Fay's apparently were now. I do not like hurting other people's feelings. This is not comfortable at all.

— CHAPTER THREE —

Is the voyage really over? Are we really in orbit around Mars? We had gotten so used to the slow rhythms of the deepspace trip, that getting our minds in gear for the rapid sequence of events required to enter Mars orbit and prepare for descent to the surface was quite an adjustment. Our bodies had some adjusting to do, too. A G and a half of braking acceleration felt like quite a kick after four and a half months of weightlessness.

Before we actually entered Mars orbit, we had deployed two satellites to assume polar surveying orbits around the planet, one from each deepspace ship. If we had waited until our ships were in orbit to deploy, the satellites would have been confined to the same 25-degree orbital inclination as the ships. That's better for starting the return trip back to Earth, but poorer for observing the planet. The ships will return to Earth with us. But the satellites will remain, continuing to relay data from our ground stations and rovers, and continuing to monitor Mars with their cameras.

Now is when all my flight training and skills pay off. I have to take the *Phobos* down along a carefully designed profile of altitude and speed, reach our chosen landing site north of Valles Marineris, and set her down gently, without damaging cargo or injuring anyone in the crew. The *Deimos* will follow us down later, once we are safely on the surface. I've managed it well in simulations; now we'll see how well I do it for real.

Before we separated from *Hesperia*, we set chronometers on both deepspace ships and on both landers. One chronometer on each ship will remain on Earth time, Universal Time (UT), to be precise. A second chronometer on each will be set to track the Martian day at the Mars longitude of our intended landing site.

Because a Martian day is so closely similar to an Earth day, we have chosen to treat it as 24 "Martian hours", allowing each such hour to be slightly longer than a terrestrial hour. We'll refer to clock times on Mars much as if we were on Earth. Each of us also has an individual watch especially designed for Mars day tracking. These have display switches that can allow us to read either Earth Universal Time or Mars local time, whichever we need. Our space suits are likewise equipped with similar dual-mode chronometer readouts. Once Terence Tarkhan had set the shipboard chronometers on the *Hesperia* and *Phobos* to the appropriate landing site Mars time, he set and synchronized each individual watch and suit chronometer Mars mode readout. Xanthe Buthelezi had done the same aboard the *Xanthe* and *Deimos*.

"*Phobos* is on internal power and life support." That was Captain Kent. He was acting as my copilot for the trip down. He was in command during the voyage from Earth, but for this leg, we've agreed I will be.

"We have separation from *Hesperia*," I announced.

"Confirm sep," he agreed.

Looking down on the ruddy Martian landscape, I saw that we were passing over Syrtis Minor; we should be starting our descent shortly. It was difficult to see Syrtis Minor. We were on the night side of Mars, and the only significant light was dim moonlight from Phobos — Mars' inner moon, not my landing craft — just rising over Syrtis Minor's horizon. But a scan of my instruments and displays confirmed our position. "One minute to de-orbit burn," I told everyone. "All hands prepare for acceleration." The rest of the crew were already strapped into their seats.

"Thirty seconds to de-orbit burn," said Kent.

"Ten seconds," said I.

Kent counted me down. "Five...four...three...two...one. Ignition!"

Though my hand was poised at the throttle, the autopilot had already started the engines. What a kick! Not as strong as the orbit entry burn, but for a body unused to weight, even half a G comes as a surprise.

Now we were on our descent trajectory. Before long, I felt the beginnings of deceleration as the *Phobos* encountered the upper reaches of the Martian atmosphere.

I was watching the outer hull temperature indicator. Heat was starting to build up from the shock wave we were creating as the kinetic energy of our orbit was converted into atmospheric heat while we decelerated.

Captain Kent was monitoring the angle of descent at the same time. "Descent angle as planned," he reported. With angle and temperature profiles both within tolerances, it looked like our flight path was as it should be. But I was still keeping a close eye on the accelerometers, because we didn't know the atmospheric density profile as well as we would have liked, despite the unmanned probes that came before us, and it is changeable, from one Martian season to another.

I watched the awesome immensity of Olympus Mons, topped with its volcanic caldera, pass by to the left of our ground path. Its height wasn't obvious from our altitude, but its vast area certainly was. Then we passed over the only slightly less impressive Pavonis Mons and Ascraeus Mons, with Pavonis Mons a little to our right. I heard Kent telling me, "We're drifting off track."

"I see it," I agreed. "It looks as though a strong high-altitude wind is blowing us slightly northward." Fortunately *Phobos'* aeroshell has plenty of lift and control for the corrective maneuver I put in. "We'll be reaching parachute deployment altitude shortly."

"I'm on it," Kent called out. His hand was at the parachute deploy lever, his eyes scanning the elapsed-time clock and the altimeter. But as with me at the de-orbit burn, the flight control software did its job and popped the chute just as he was about to; first the drogue chute, then the main trio.

We were still drifting eastward over the ruddy landscape, as intended, approaching our intended landing zone in Lunae Planum. Shortly it would be time to jettison the parachute and complete our landing on *Phobos'* engines. "Stand by to release chute," I told Kent, as I placed my hands on the engine and attitude controls.

"Standing by."

This time I counted him down. "...Three...two...one. Release chute!" At the moment he did so, I ignited *Phobos'* rockets. I took her in manually. We could see, confirming what *Hesperia's* radar had told us from orbit, that the landscape beneath us was too rocky, too boulder strewn for the automatic landing system to bring her in safely. If there was a space flat enough and clear enough to set *Phobos* down, I'd find it. I wasn't confident that the computers could.

We were getting pretty close now. "Two hundred meters," Kent called out the altitude for me. I saw that the place we were heading for was too rocky. We'd have to shift to somewhere else.

"One hundred fifty meters," came Kent's voice.

I changed attitude and *Phobos* began to head further east. After translating about eight hundred meters, I saw a better place. Still rocky, but the rocks were smaller — none much larger than twenty centimeters, with plenty of space between them for *Phobos'* footpads. Better still, I saw it was the edge of a much larger area of similar terrain, so that *Deimos* could comfortably set down here, too.

I adjusted attitude again. Now we were coming straight down.

"One hundred meters," said Kent, then briefly later, "fifty meters."

"When we get to twenty-five meters, count me by fives," I told him.

"Roger. Five meter increments, starting at twenty-five meters," he assented. While he monitored altitude levels, I watched rate of descent and engine thrust levels. We both glanced back and forth between the direct outside view through our ports and the closed-circuit TV monitor, which actually gave us a better view of what was directly beneath us.

"Twenty-five meters," came his voice.

"Twenty meters." Our engines were starting to kick up some of the ruddy dust from the surface.

"Fifteen meters." The dust did not simply arc and splash as it would on the Moon, but billowed in the Martian atmosphere. Not quite the way it would in the thicker atmosphere on Earth, but we were forming a dusty reddish haze about our landing point that was beginning to obscure our vision slightly.

"Ten meters."

"Descent rate slowing to 1 meter per second," I reported back to him.

"Five meters."

"Descent rate 30 centimeters per second and maintaining."

"Two meters." A pause. "One meter."

"Descent rate to 15 centimeters per second," I informed him.

Another six and a half seconds, and we chorused together, "Touchdown! All stop!" I throttled back the engines and cut the ignition. I felt the thrust go off, and sensed only my weight from the Martian gravity. Only 3/8 that of Earth, but it still felt heavy after four and a half months of free fall. I was glad I kept up my strength-building exercises.

Together Captain Kent and I breathed a sigh that was a mix of relief and satisfaction. So did the other crew members of *Phobos*. Then, as if motivated by a single mind, all six of us gave a simultaneous shout of triumph. "Yes!"

I looked out the viewport at the red, rocky, sandy, dusty landscape around us. Everyone was looking out some viewport, and no one was complaining about crowding. In a moment, I turned to the communication controls. "Message to Earth and to *Xanthe*: *Phobos* is down and safe at Redsand Landing One. Repeat, we have landed successfully on the surface of Mars." Earth would not receive our message for several minutes, but *Xanthe* should be above our horizon.

That was confirmed immediately by Xavier Buthelezi's booming, "Congratulations!"

I quickly added to my message, "*Phobos* to *Xanthe*. *Deimos* can come on down. There is plenty of good landing area near us. Once we get our beacon unpacked, we'll set it up slightly north and east —" I looked a question at Kent Squared, to see if he agrees with my selection. He nodded. "— of our location."

After receiving *Xanthe's* acknowledgement, I look around me at the rest of the crew. "Captain," I said to Kent, "we're all suited up." (It been decided that for the landing, everyone would be in space suits.) "Shall we go out and have a look around? See what this part of our new world is like?"

"Absolutely," he affirmed. He reached to a storage drawer where we had stowed some small items, mostly games and entertainment equipment for times when the work schedule might be a little slack. From it, he pulled a deck of playing cards that we had shuffled beforehand, while we were still in orbit. We'd agreed to cut for high card for the privilege of being first out on the surface. Yes, handling cards is a bit difficult when wearing space suit gloves. But we were all practiced enough by now that we could play cards while suited up.

Each of us in turn took our try. Terence Tarkhan drew the jack of spades, Teresa Sola the eight of clubs. Captain Kent pulled out the king of hearts. ("Good for him!" I thought to myself.) Tara Halley's card was the ten of diamonds, Fay Adair's the queen of hearts. Without much hope of beating the high cards already showing, I reached for about the midpoint of the deck and turned it over. As my card came into view, I took a start. I wondered if the shock I was feeling showed in my face. I was staring at the ace of spades!

The first human to set foot on Mars! I had wanted this. We all did. I'd kept silent about it, figuring that the others in the crew were as eager for the privilege as I was. I'd mentioned how I felt to D.J. during our training, but not to anyone else. But they all knew.

How luck or the good Lord had picked, I had no idea. But I was glad for my fortune. Quietly, exultantly joyous.

When I looked around at the others, I saw no grudges in their eyes. I saw that all wished they could be in my place. Yet I saw that at the same time, each one was glad for me.

Because the airlock was constructed to pass sizeable pieces of equipment, it could allow two of us at a time. "Then Captain," I said, "will you join me?"

We closed our helmets and checked our space suits. I had Terence Tarkhan double check my hoses and connections, while

Tara Halley checked Kent's. No sense coming all this way, only to be asphyxiated because we didn't check our equipment.

We wouldn't need a prebreathe period. Years of human experience in space and on the Moon had shown that going from the 500 millibar shipboard pressure level to the 300 millibar suit pressure would cause no problems.

"Communications check," I announced. "Alpha, Bravo, Charlie, Delta. How do you read?"

"Read you loud and clear," Terence reported from the *Phobos* console.

"And how about you, Captain?" I asked.

"I read you loud and clear on my suit receiver," Kent reported. "Now my turn. Echo, Foxtrot, Golf, Hotel."

"I read you loud and clear," Terence reported.

"Loud and clear," I agreed.

We were ready to pass through the airlock. Fay Adair opened the inner hatch. I stepped in, then Kent Squared followed. We both fit, but it was pretty close quarters. Fay closed and sealed the hatch.

I closed the pressure reduction control, and heard the pump starting to pull the air out of the lock into storage tanks. I watched the pressure indicator, and saw it begin to go down. The pumps are efficient; in only a few minutes, I saw the indicator drop to 5.4 millibars — a match to the outside pressure. Yes, I know that Mars surface pressure can approach or exceed 9 millibars. But only in the lowest elevations, not at the altitude of this part of Lunae Planum.

Landing site selection had been a compromise between the need to be smooth enough to set down safely, and the desire to be in surface transportation range of several targets the scientists wanted to look at. The scientists would also have liked a low altitude location, but the planners couldn't satisfy all their desires on this first trip. The scientists consoled themselves with the knowledge that the surface transport we carried and our blimp would enable us to reach and study low-altitude areas.

I stopped the pumps. From the ship's console, Terence Tarkhan confirms: "Airlock pressure is matched to external pressure. You are go to open the outer airlock hatch."

"All right, Captain Can," I told Kent, "Let's go see what's waiting for us."

I swung open the hatch and stepped out onto the "porch" from which a metal stairway sloped down to the surface. But I hardly looked at the ladder, and I was only half aware of Captain Kent stepping out beside me. I was transfixed by the landscape in front of me. All my imagination, all the photos, all the simulations did not have the impact of the reality.

I could not speak. I could only gaze in silence on this desert landscape, with rocks of various sizes — none larger than 20 centimeters nearby, of course, but car and even house-sized boulders off to the west — down to gravel size pebbles, and sand. And dust. Some places drifts of it, often against boulders. Other places just a thin sprinkling atop the rocks. And atop our landing pads now, I noticed.

The porch faced west and a bit south, toward a horizon only seven-tenths as far away as it would have been on Earth. Between us and the half of that horizon within my view, I noticed three small, weathered impact craters, none of them more than a few dozen meters across.

And everything in shades of red: some darker, some lighter. Here modified with some orange tones, there with a hint of brown. All beneath a butterscotch colored sky, heavy with airborne dust. In that sky, the sun on this Martian morning stood only two-thirds the size it would have seemed on Earth, giving less than half the light.

I could even see, looking up almost to zenith, a tiny spark of light that was the further moon Deimos, although it was not easy to spot with the sun in the sky and the yellow-brown haze in the atmosphere. I have better than average vision, but even so, I could barely make out a disk, in crescent phase. Phobos was still on the night side of the planet.

Our suits have microphones to pick up sounds that might

be carried in this thin atmosphere, but at the moment it was quiet. There seemed to be no wind.

I found my voice at last, but could only say, "What an incredible sight!"

Kent was equally moved. He could only add, "Amen!"

If I lacked words, I at least had a means to create a record of this experience to share with the people back on Earth who were awaiting word from us. Our space suits were each equipped with a miniaturized chest mounted camera, capable of taking still pictures or video. I reached up and switched mine on to video mode. Kent did the same with his.

I started a voice-over recording as I did so. "This is Jonathan Wagoner, on the first human expedition to Mars, beginning descent of the stairway from the landing craft *Phobos* to the Mars surface." I grasped the stairway's handrail and started down.

The designers of the stairways for the Mars landing craft had learned a valuable lesson from the Apollo lunar lander ladders. Once the lander was at the surface, the foot of the stair had extended well away from the base of the lander's hull. This gave the stair a shallow enough pitch that, with handrails, a space-suited human could comfortably and safely walk down the stairs *forward*, and not have to back down.

As I descended, I could hear very faintly through the thin atmosphere the clump of my boots on the stairs. When I was about halfway down, Captain Kent started down behind me.

I felt some resistance to my movements from the suit, but nothing like the old Shuttle and early Space Station days. Not only do we use lower pressures these days, but suit design and construction is much improved as well, allowing far greater mobility. We *have* made some progress over the years.

The remaining suit restrictions on mobility were more than compensated for, to my mind, by the lightness I felt in Mars' low gravity. Even so, I was glad for the handrail. It was the only thing that steadied me and kept me from falling twice, when I missed my step. I was having to learn to walk all over again in this gravity field. Yes, I've walked on the Moon, but that's only half the gravity on Mars. And yes, we've constructed simulators on Earth, with counterweights and such, and the simulations had been useful, but they were far from perfect.

By the time I reached the bottom of the stairway, I felt like I had the hang of it.

I paused and took a breath. I didn't know what my heart rate was, but I was feeling more adrenalin than when I'd fought in that mountain battle to rescue the hostages in South America, those years ago.

I stepped off the bottom stair onto the Martian soil. Now, in place of the dull metallic clang of the stairs, I heard a faint scrunch of sand and fluff of dust beneath my boot. I saw some of that dust rise and drift in the air, as my feet disturbed it.

What to say, for such a historic occasion? I hadn't really anticipated being first, much as I wanted to be, so I had not prepared anything. What was the real significance of this event?

"This new world," I began, "is now our world. A human world. From now on Mars and Earth are both parts of the human environment. As we on this expedition and others that follow it explore this new planet and study it, and grow to understand it, Mars, like Earth, shall become a place where people can build their hopes and dreams and futures."

I wondered if I'd said too much. Perhaps it would have been better not to try to say anything at all. But as I doubted myself, Captain Kent said, "I didn't know you had such a gift for words."

"I didn't know it, either. Perhaps I was...inspired by the occasion."

"It sounded to me," he said thoughtfully, "as though you spoke from the heart, from the spirit."

Shortly the other members of the crew came out to join us, two by two, like a disembarking Noah's ark. Sunlight reflecting from helmet visors made it difficult to see faces, but I observed from pauses during their descents, and from body postures, that each one, like Kent and me, were taking in the rocks and dust, with their pallets of reds, oranges, yellows, and browns. I saw each bend back at some point to look up at the dusty sky, the shrunken sun, and the spark of Deimos. When each one reached the foot of the stairs, he or she stood awestruck for a few moments.

After everyone was down the stairs, I simply had to see how well I could jump in Martian gravity. I'd done leaps and hops in the Moon; how similar would it be here? I gathered myself and made a standing leap, leading with my left foot and pushing off with my right, as though I were making an extra-long step. I did not put forth my maximum effort. I was not trying for distance this first time; just to find out how it would go.

I sailed much farther than a similar effort would have taken me on Earth, but less than half as far as I would have gone on the Moon. I didn't land well, however. I could feel my momentum start to carry me beyond vertical, and it required much flailing of arms to keep myself from toppling over. It was clear to me that I still had a way to go to fully master Martian locomotion.

I heard Tara Halley's voice on my radio. "Glad it was you who tried that! I was about to, but I think you just saved me from landing on my tush. I think I'll work up to jumping cautiously."

After several minutes we were able — not to ignore our surroundings, but to concentrate enough to get to work. The first work was to unload the equipment bay of the *Phobos*.

We opened the bay door wide and extended a broad ramp. We all pitched in and lifted off instruments, supplies, and other assorted cargo that was stacked atop two slate gray vehicles folded in their storage configuration. Once they were cleared and had sufficient headroom, Terence Tarkhan pressed a large button on the side of one. The control cab at the front lifted from horizontal to its upright operational position. It gave me an impression of the head of some enormous beast. The vehicle stirred and unfolded all its appendages, stretching itself up to its full height. When it had completed this reconfiguration, the top of the cab stood a good three meters above the floor of the bay — almost hitting the ceiling.

Terence climbed up into the cab. While we were in space, he was the *Hesperia's* engineer. On Mars, he is lead driver for these monsters. He took his seat, put his hands and feet on the controls, and engaged the motors. The vehicle began to walk down the ramp. That's right, I said walk — on 8 legs. We could not know ahead of time precisely what kind of terrain we'd find at the landing site. Trials on Earth and the Moon led the designers to conclude that with current microprocessors and software, legs can give a vehicle acceptable performance on a wider variety of surfaces than either wheels or caterpillar treads. Eight was the number they arrived at by trading off redundancy vs. complexity of programming the control software.

As the vehicle trod down the ramp, we could hear through Mars' thin air a faint "clop clop" as each foot hit the ramp surface, deeper than the sound of any Clydesdale.

Never let it be said that the NASA engineers who pick out names for such things — and their acronyms — don't have a sense of humor. The official designation for these vehicles is Transport, Heavy, Over All Terrain.

Terence had gotten his vehicle to the bottom of the ramp, and he was walking it further out onto the Martian surface to make room. His wife Teresa was following him down on the second THOAT. Once off the ramp, the "clop clop" softened and became nearly inaudible. Each foot left an oval print in the sand and dust when it lifted, a print marked with wavy crosswise tread marks.

Once both vehicles were down, Terence radioed to us, "I've pressurized the cab. I am going to test the brainwave pickup system." Through the cab windows, we saw him remove his helmet and put on a headset he had picked up from its overhead storage rack. He took his feet from the pedals and rested them on the floor of the cab, and placed his hands on his knees.

With not a hand at the controls, the THOAT went through a series of test maneuvers. Walk forward. Speed up. Slow down. Steer left. Steer right. Stop. Back up. Kneel the legs, as if in preparation to load cargo onto the broad, flat back; then raise them again. All in perfect response to Terence's will.

The headset is a second control system, in addition to the ordinary hand and foot controls. It was monitoring Terence's brain activity for certain key configurations and translating them into vehicle commands. These types of control systems have shown high reliability in Earthbound testing. Mostly in laboratory situations so far, but they're beginning to show up in engineering and commercial applications in the last few years. A few have been incorporated into machinery intended to aid individuals with disabilities. Mission planners felt that they were far enough advanced to include in the design of these vehicles.

Not just anyone off the street can manage such a system. The operator has to be trained, as some of our crew have been, to signal his or her intentions to the vehicle with specific thought patterns, just as someone has to be trained to operate the hand and foot controls. If the operator doesn't watch what he is thinking, the pickup processor, like all computers, will do what it was told, not what the operator intended.

We had some pretty hilarious episodes during training with this system on the Earth and the Moon, from operator inattention or straying thoughts, and a few dangerous ones. No one was killed, by the grace of God, but those episodes instilled mental discipline in us while using the headsets. By now, some of us, myself included, have it down to a science. Terence and Teresa have it down to a fine art. In either hands-on or hands-free mode, they can almost make the THOATs dance.

Kent Squared said, "If the vehicles are operational, we need to get the landing beacon deployed."

"Right," Terence agreed. The *Deimos* crew would want to home in on it. "We'll only need two people and one vehicle. Teresa, you'll be with me." He removed his headset and sealed his helmet so that he could depressurize the cab to allow her to enter. The cab isn't big enough to allow room for a separate airlock.

Teresa climbed up to the right hatch of Terence's machine. She dusted her boots off with a whisk broom stowed in a pocket alongside it before she entered. It brushed off fairly easily, not clinging as tightly as Moon dust would have. But I could see we'd have to take precautions against dust here, as on the Moon, to keep it out of our living spaces and our machinery.

Terence could probably deploy the beacon without a second person. But while we're on the surface, we plan to operate on the "buddy system". The rule is, no one goes anywhere alone. Always bring at least one other person with you to help in case you get into trouble. And always at least two people stay at the lander. Once *Deimos* was down, we could relax that rule to say that two people should stand by either lander — it didn't matter which one. Each lander could lift all twelve members of the expedition back to orbit, if need be.

Once they were both aboard, Terence resealed and repressurized the cab. He steered the THOAT over to the open bay, not up the ramp but beside it. Then he put the headset on once again, and turned his seat around to a second set of controls.

As soon as he began to operate them, even someone who did not know the THOAT's design could see that the jointed appendage at the rear that resembled a tail was in fact a crane. A crane to load cargo on and off the long, broad, flat bed between it and the control cab. A bed well equipped with clamps and tiedown fixtures so that a load could be held securely in place against any tilt of the bed, even if the vehicle should have to negotiate slopes or rough terrain. We had many sorts of cargo, with or without container modules, that we could load onto a THOAT's bed. Even inflatable passenger modules to carry extra riders, which could be connected by tunnel to the rear hatch of the control cab.

Just now, the only cargo Terence needed was the meter-high pyramid with antennas and light fixtures atop it...the homing beacon that would help the *Deimos* find our landing site. Kent and I had walked over to the bay to help Terence load the beacon onto the central axis of the bed. I would spot him from one side, Kent from the other, and Teresa from her vantage point inside.

Here is where the true value of the brainwave control system became apparent. Terence saw that he was too far from the beacon; the crane would not quite reach. Without having to take his hands from the crane controls, his thought-instructions caused the THOAT to side-step closer to the bay (a maneuver that would have been tough to do with wheels or treads). With the help of a few words and hand signals from us and Teresa, he lifted the beacon, guided it carefully to the spot where he wanted it, and lowered in gently to the bed.

Off they went to the northeast. They selected a spot about eight hundred meters from the *Phobos* with plenty of level ground around it, and set the pyramid down. We knew they'd switched it on when we saw the pair of green and white lights at its top began to flash brightly. It had been decided during mission planning not to use red lights. That color might offer insufficient contrast against the surface to be easily spotted during Mars daytime operations.

We heard Teresa Sola's voice on our radios. "Are you receiving the beacon radio signals?"

Tara Halley, who had gone back aboard the *Phobos* while Terence and Teresa were moving out to the deploy point reported, "Yes, on all five frequencies."

While we were waiting for the planet's rotation to bring our landing site into proper alignment with *Xanthe's* orbit plane, so that *Deimos* could descend, we unloaded some more of the expedition's equipment from the bay. We unloaded Tara Halley's seismic sensors, gravitometers, magnetic field measurement devices, and the drilling and excavation devices she and Fay Adair will both use. Actually, we'll all use them, but those two would direct us. They understand planetary science better than the rest of the *Phobos* crew, so they know what they are looking for.

We also unloaded Tara's telescopes. She has two 10 centimeter scopes: one primarily for ultraviolet observations, the other mostly for visible and near-infrared wavelengths. They are small partly because of the mass limitations on our total payload, and partly because they are along only for initial tests of what can be observed from the Mars surface. Tara has told us frankly that she does not expect much from these instruments. She anticipates that dust suspended in the atmosphere will cause very poor seeing. Any real astronomical results from this expedition she expects to come from the instruments on board the *Hesperia* and the *Xanthe*. But she, we, and the committee of astronomers who recommended the instruments are all agreed: we'll never really know what observations can be made from Mars' surface until someone tries.

The analysis equipment to determine the chemistry and mineralogy of Martian dust, rocks, air, and (if we find any) water or ice we don't have to unload. That is built into the *Phobos*, in a small lab bench on the interior, and in a series of boxes on the exterior just adjacent to it. One box is rigged as a glovebox that can be used by people standing inside at the lab bench. The others are equipped with various remote manipulation devices. All have microscopes and a battery of analysis equipment that will enable us (Tara and Fay, primarily, plus Ruth Dean when the *Deimos* lands) to study samples we collect without ever removing them from the Martian environment.

This will allow comparison with samples we *do* bring inside, to see what difference, if any, exposure to the shipboard atmosphere and all us humans running around makes to the analysis. Matter of fact, we will analyze some samples in the external boxes *before* we bring any inside the lander. We want to find out if any substances that may be present are toxic to us or hazardous to our machinery, before we allow any in.

We had hardly opened those sample analysis boxes to their operational configuration when Tara and Fay began gathering samples to put in them. And were commandeering the rest of us to help them. Teresa Sola had already brought five carefully marked plastic bags of samples she had picked up near the beacon site, and on the way back to the ship.

First, they wanted an immediate set of contingency rock and soil samples, some from right next to the lander, others further away for comparison, to see how much the exhaust gases from our descent engines had affected the chemistry of the local area.

Then Tara said, "Kent, would you and Jonathan go with me

in one of the THOATs to pick up a series of samples from the nearest impact crater to our west?"

"Aye, aye," I said. While we were in space, we pilots and engineers were in charge. But now that we're on Mars, the P.I.'s call the shots.

Kent is still in overall command of the expedition. He can overrule their decisions. But he's smart enough not to. Unless it's necessary. "Tara," he reminded her gently, "maybe you're not hungry. But have you considered that perhaps Jonathan might be? And maybe some of the others? I'm beginning to have an appetite myself."

"Oops!" she replied. Her hand moved toward her mouth in a gesture that had become familiar to us when she was mildly chagrinned. It smacked into her helmet, of course. She laughed at her mistake as she continued, "I'm so excited that I forgot we haven't stopped for lunch."

"We're all excited, my dear," Kent said, "but we'll work better if we stop to resupply our energy." Then he made a general call on the radio. "Lunch break, everybody! Rendezvous at the ship."

Once we were all there, he offered, "I think we all deserve a treat. It won't be a fancy lunch. We still have a lot to do, and there's the *Deimos* landing to get ready for. But what say we break out some red salmon?"

That brought unanimous approval. The salmon was freeze dried, but it would still be a treat we'd all enjoy. We'd been saving it for just such an occasion.

It may puzzle some of you back on Earth that we relied on stored food for this mission, rather than growing our own. You must understand that while the deepspace ships recycle their air and water, they do not have space station or moonbase style food growing equipment. It's a matter of arithmetic. The mass of equipment to grow food exceeds the mass of stored food for a mission of this length.

Each lander had a well equipped, if extremely compact, kitchen. With gravity again, we could use a wider variety of cooking techniques than in free fall. But Kent was right; for this meal we didn't have time for fancy cooking. We didn't even have time to take off our space suits. In spite of the lunch's simplicity, it seemed a wonder, after four and a half months in free fall, actually to *sit down* to a meal.

So it we celebrated our landing with a cold platter of red salmon and beets with crackers, washed down with reconstituted fruit juice (cherry flavored, for me). Salmon and beets tasted great, even reconstituted from freeze drying. All seasoned to delight with conversation. Now bantering, now serious, the words weren't what really mattered. It was simply a way to share our joy, to express a companionship among shipmates.

— CHAPTER FOUR —

THE *DEIMOS* LANDED THAT AFTERNOON. Carter Horace brought her down one hundred fifty meters this side of the beacon. Just about where I expected. Close enough for easy contact between landers, but far enough beyond the *Phobos* and to the side to make quite sure his exhaust flame missed us. And to make sure the *Deimos* missed us, if anything went wrong. But nothing did. Carter brought her in easily, smoothly, cutting her engines just as she kissed the ground.

With twelve pairs of hands to help instead of only six, and the THOATs already deployed, we got quite a lot unpacked from the *Deimos's* equipment bay that afternoon, even though less than three hours were left till sunset by the time her crew debarked. We pulled out D.J.'s weather instruments: wind speed and direction indicators, pressure gauges, thermometers. Her balloons that would be released to get both meteorological data and high-altitude aeronomy data from as wide a range over the planet as they could travel. Ruth Vivian Dean's little "beasties", her mini- and micro-robots that would carry their own sets of instruments over the surface of Mars, and remain scuttling about on the planet even after we left, continuing to collect data. Surveying equipment for Valeria Diaz.

D.J.'s Propellant Production Test Unit we did not unload that day. That would wait until tomorrow. So would the very large package, larger than a van, smaller than a city bus, that held something much larger than her weather balloons.

Supper would be an even bigger celebration than lunch. We'd be trading visits between ships' crews for the meal. Fay Adair and the Kents would be dining aboard *Deimos*, while Tell Packs and his wife Valeria Diaz would be visiting *Phobos*. So would the person I was really looking forward to seeing...D.J. The unloading during the afternoon had been all business, with no time for social conversation. I hoped that this evening, things might become a little more personal.

Teresa Sola took charge of the meal preparation on board

Phobos. Unlike lunch, we were taking time for this meal to make use of the tiny kitchens on the landers. All of us on the expedition have some modest culinary skill (I can open a package and reconstitute and heat the contents with the best of them). But Teresa is perhaps the best of the *Hesperia* crew. If she hadn't picked biology as a career, she might easily have become a chef.

I wasn't sure what tonight's menu was to be aboard *Deimos*, but for us Teresa converted some multicolored fuselli, tomato sauce, dried onions, and a few well chosen seasonings into a pasta dish that was out of this world (Earth or Mars, take your pick). D.J. pitched in (when there was elbow room at the counter, which was only part of the time) to combine a few preserved vegetables to make a surprisingly appealing salad.

Terence had unfolded the small dining table while this was going on, and set the places, couple by couple. He made sure that my place was just to D.J.'s right. Terence doesn't always say much...but he's one of the most thoughtful friends a man could ask for.

As we approached the table, I whispered to D.J., "I've really missed you." For answer, she took my hand in hers and squeezed. She let go so we could get to our chairs. But once seated, she reached her hand beneath the table to clasp mine again. She still had not spoken a word, but she punctuated her handclasp by looking my way with a gaze filled with joy, affection, and warmth. When I saw that look, I understood how a glance from Helen of Troy could have launched a thousand ships.

Supper tasted better than any food I had had in four months. Better even than lunch. Its best seasoning, of course, was the company. My dear friends Terence Tarkhan and Teresa. Tell Packs and his lovely wife Valeria Diaz, whom I hadn't seen face to face in those four months. And best of all, sharing the meal with Diana. Even after she let go my hand so we could eat, the simple joy of within reach of her sang within me. One thing was sure — our separation hadn't made me fall out of love with her.

I couldn't bring myself to speak of something as personal as my affection for her in such close company with the others. So conversation revolved around our tasks for tomorrow, and the sheer wonder of our being here, and what we had thus far seen and experienced.

After supper, Tell and Valeria started on back. Valeria had suggested that I see D.J. "home" a bit later, and return with the *Phobos* crew members who were enjoying the hospitality of the *Deimos*.

When D.J. and I had donned our space suits and exited the airlock, we could see walking in the distance Tell and Valeria — or rather the backs of their suits, well on their way back to the *Deimos*. When we reached the base of the stairs and stepped out a few paces, stopping next to one of the THOATs, we looked around us to take in the wonder of the Martian landscape by night.

In addition to the lights from the ships, and others we'd installed around the landing sites during the day, the scene was illuminated by moonlight. Not as bright as moonlight would have been back on Earth, but easily enough to light our walk to the *Deimos*, even without the flashlights we had clipped to our suit belts. We looked up.

Despite Mars' dust haze we could see stars. Amid them, Deimos was still high in the sky. Although it had gone down almost thirty degrees toward the western horizon, that still meant nearly sixty degrees' elevation. It was much brighter now, not only because the sun was no longer in the sky to overwhelm it, but in addition from change of phase. In the hours since I'd first stepped out onto the porch and looked up at it, Deimos had gone from waning crescent to new moon to waxing crescent, and now was almost at first quarter.

But Deimos wasn't the source of most of the moonlight. That was Phobos, already well above the western horizon and climbing rapidly toward its further companion. Crossing the sky at thirty degrees an hour, or the apparent width of Earth's Moon every minute, we could *see* it move across the stars, if we watched closely. And see the shadows it cast move upon the ground.

The moment moved me to place an arm around D.J.'s shoulders and breathe her Apache name. "Náaki Tle'na'ai!" I spoke softly.

It is hard to embrace in a space suit. She tried to reach her arm around my back, but the breathing tanks in the life support backpack got in the way. So she reverted to her earlier gesture; she placed her hand in mine. She gave it an affectionate squeeze as she responded, "'Two Moons' does seem very appropriate for the occasion. Makes me wonder if my mother was a prophet when she chose it."

Then I saw through her faceplate a smile start to spread over her face, and a note of amusement came into her voice as she added, "*Phobos* and *Deimos* are both down —" a sweeping gesture of her arm indicated our two landers "— and Phobos and Deimos are both up!" at which the arm pointed to the sky.

After we'd shared a laugh, I gestured to Diana to switch off her radio; as she did, I did the same. We leaned toward each other to touch helmets. This way, we could have a very private conversation. I had to speak up to be heard via the helmet-to-helmet sound conduction, and so did she, but neither of us minded. "I've been missing you terribly," I began. "There are some things I need to talk to you about."

I told her how Fay Adair had fallen for me, how awkward I'd felt when I rejected her, how even more awkward I'd felt since, being around Fay, aware of her feelings, but unable to reciprocate.

"I think," Diana said thoughtfully, "that if Fay has truly accepted your turndown, what we need is to arrange duty rosters and schedules so that she and Xavier spend a lot of time together. My bet is that over time, with enough contact, her affections will turn to him. My sense is that they really are well suited for one another. Captain Kent will probably think of this on his own, but it won't hurt if you and I mention it to him. And the rest of us P.I.'s can put our heads together and work out experiment schedules with that in mind."

We began walking toward the *Deimos*, with our heads bent toward each other so that our helmets were still in contact. "Well, my Two Moons sweetheart," I told her, "you've got the matchmaking for Fay and Xavier pretty well figured out. How about *us*? Can you and I match ourselves up, now we're at last on Mars?"

"I'll try to arrange for us to have as much time together as possible while we set up the landing site — on and off duty," Diana responded. "But I think our best chance will be on our trip."

"You mean on the blimp?"

"Yes."

"Then," I told her, "I'll be looking forward to when you come fly away with me.

— CHAPTER FIVE —

The next morning we continued unloading instruments and equipment from the *Deimos*. The first item out was D.J.'s Propellant Production Test Unit.

Then came the very large package I described. It looked like we might have a little trouble with the wind when we tried to open this. Yesterday, when we landed, was an almost perfect calm. Today, though, D.J.'s instruments were showing a definite breeze. Not enough to kick dust up, yet, but enough to blow it when *we* did. Could cause a bit of awkwardness.

I thought it was actually a good test. My opinion was, if we couldn't handle this thing in a gentle wind, we'd better find out about it now, because in that case it would be no use to us whatever.

We loaded the package aboard one of the THOATs. On the other, we loaded several ropes, a stiff mastlike pole many meters long, and five more packages. Four of these, instead of being bus shaped, were flat, about two and a half meters across each way, but only a fraction of a meter thick. The fifth was smaller, boxier, and heavier. Then we tapped *Deimos'* propellant tanks for some hydrogen, transferring it in gaseous form into some high pressure storage tanks. The hydrogen transfer was the lengthiest part of our loading operation. Finally we loaded the hydrogen pressure tanks, along with some pumps and hoses, onto the second THOAT.

With the THOATs we carried the package about midway between the two ships and placed it on the ground. We would need plenty of space.

Kent, Terence, Carter Horace, and I each grabbed a portion of the first opening flap, Terence and Carter on one end, Kent and I on the other. This was definitely a four person job. Not because any part of this was heavy, but because the whole package had such an unwieldy scale. Xavier Buthelezi braced one corner of the package to steady it, Teresa Sola and Tell Packs another.

Ruth Dean, standing a few meters away, gave us the arm signal we'd agreed on, and the four of us at the flap lifted together, folded it back, and laid it flat on the ground.

We repeated this procedure with the opposite flap, then the two end flaps, and cleared away some bracing and some padding. When we were done, we saw before us, resting on the bottom of the package, a mass of thin, smooth, neutral gray, flexible synthetic, all folded together, hanging over and masking some supporting structure. At this stage, it looked like nothing so much as the solar system's largest garbage bag.

Having gotten the package out of the way, we next had to begin to unfold the synthetic. This required even more hands, and just as much careful coordination, as opening the package had. So we began step by step, fold by fold, to open out the shape, careful not to tear or puncture the thin stuff. Our job was made a bit easier by the fact that this synthetic had much less of the static cling that makes separating trash bags or plastic wrap on Earth such a nuisance.

I wasn't terribly worried about punctures. I knew this crew was careful. I also knew how tough this material was, despite how exceedingly light and thin. I knew from *trying* to puncture samples of it on Earth. The mission planners had had a real selling job to convince me that it was rugged enough to risk my life with. So they'd demonstrated by asking me to puncture it. I'd attacked samples with knives, with ice picks, with sharp rocks. It *could* be cut or punctured, but only with a lot of effort. It usually took a combination of a sharp object and a high speed impact.

After a time, we had gotten the synthetic unfolded to a point where it covered an area of ground well over a hundred meters long, and more than twenty wide. Near the center of this area, we could still see the bulge where it draped over the supporting structure beneath it. By this time, we were able to see several flexible but sturdy plastic loops securely fastened along the edges of the gray material. Captain Kent signaled us with a gesture, and we fastened tiedown ropes to six of those loops with quick-release clips. We secured the other ends of the ropes to the cargo beds of the two THOATs, which were parked on either side of the limp mass of material.

While Terence, Xavier, Kent, and I were securing the ropes, Carter Horace was connecting a length of hose to one of our compressed hydrogen tanks. He attached the other end of the hose to a pressure regulator. He connected a second hose to the other side of the regulator, and finally, to a valve near one end of the synthetic material.

Once the ropes were secure, Kent looked at Carter and gave him another gesture. Carter opened the valves, and hydrogen began to flow. Slowly, the material near the valve he'd linked the hose to began to swell. As it inflated, it began to lift, a bubble of hydrogen-inflated synthetic trying to pull the weight of the rest of the material up.

After a few minutes, that segment had filled, and Carter closed the regulator valve. The envelope is divided into eight separate gas-tight cells. What impressed me most about the new carbon fiber synthetic the envelope was made from was not simply that material so thin had been made so tough — though that was impressive enough — but that it had been made hydrogen tight! More precisely, the diffusion rate of hydrogen through the material is so low that the half-life against leakage from each cell is measured in decades.

Besides the eight hydrogen cells, there are four ballonets connected to the outside air, two forward and two aft, to control the volume of the lift cells for ascent and descent, and to adjust for changes in air density, for example due to temperature changes from day to night, while maintaining the ship's shape. In addition, we can pump hydrogen from the cells into reserve pressure tanks, if need be.

While Carter was filling the first cell, I had gotten a remote control from one of the THOATs. A remote that could be manipulated easily even by a hand in a space suit glove. This remote controlled the internal valving in the tubing that led from the external fill valve Carter had connected the hose to, thus controlling which segment would be filled by the incoming gas. With it, I changed the selection and informed Carter, "You may begin filling the next segment."

As he did, I noticed the first segment drift slightly, lazily, first one way, then another, as gusts of the thin Martian wind blew past at various speeds and sometimes from slightly different directions. The tiedown ropes were a very good precaution.

After the two cells furthest aft were filled, we filled the two furthest forward, then the two amidships. Then the final two, filling in the spaces between the amidships and the fore and aft sections.

At last the full figure of this huge inflatable form stood before us...a giant blimp, 150 meters long, 27 in diameter, with an internal volume approaching 2300 cubic meters. What had appeared to be a "support structure" when the uninflated material had been draped over it, masking it, was the crew and payload gondola beneath the envelope. In blue letters along the side near the nose, and again on the vertical tail was the name *Coprates*, and in red, MAS-1 (for Mars Air Ship).

There is no danger of fire using hydrogen as the lifting gas in Mars' CO_2 atmosphere, of course. But even with that, and for all *Coprates'* huge size, her gross lift in the Martian atmosphere is just over 2 metric tons of mass. The result is that besides her own structure and propulsion equipment, she can manage to carry just two people, their life support equipment and supplies for several weeks, and a very modest scientific payload.

The wonder is that a structure of such large dimensions could be kept light enough to carry even that. Only the new carbon-fiber synthetic fabrics could be made thin enough, and still strong enough and puncture resistant enough, to serve as the containers for the lift hydrogen we would be using, and not add too much weight from their own structure to prevent *Coprates* from flying.

She won't even lift herself now. We had adjusted the ballonets so her lift was less than her empty weight. We weren't ready to fly her yet. There was a lot else to do first.

Including opening those four two-and-a-half meter flat packages. In them were the propellers, which we attached to their shafts via geared joints that would permit them to rotate ninety degrees, which would allow *Coprates* to take off and land vertically, as well as fly forward or back. These propellers were optimized for the thin, cold Martian atmosphere. We didn't actually have to have four. Two would have sufficed. Having two extra is for backup. And they do improve maneuverability.

Once the propellers were installed, we opened the last, heavy package. In it was a metallic cylinder, which we lifted with great care and with the assistance of the crane on one of the THOATs, and placed in into its receptacle on the *Coprates* with equal care. This was the power plant, the radioisotope battery that would supply the energy to turn those four props, and all other electrical needs on board *Coprates*.

Now that the *Coprates* was assembled, we needed to install the long, stiff metal pole near her nose to make a mooring mast. That proved not to be easy. Drilling into the Martian soil gave us some difficulties. Not as bad as trying to excavate more than a half-meter or so on the Moon, but tough enough. Not only were there rocks strewn about on the surface, but we kept running into them below. And there were patchy distributions of soil with enough moisture content to act like permafrost in the cold Martian temperatures, even though there seemed to be some thawing by day. We'd run into a frost-stiffened layer, then it would be looser below, then another stiff layer, now a rock, and on it went.

Our P.I.'s D.J., Teresa, Tara, and Fay were delighted, of course, with the rock and soil samples we were bringing up in the process of this, in spite of the wear and tear Tara's and Fay's drilling machines were being subjected to.

Although *Coprates* is puncture *resistant*, she is not puncture *proof*. Despite my own tests of the material, I am uneasy that we are planning to go halfway around the planet to the Elysium region, alone. The fact that we'll stay in communication with the main landing site with the help of our deepspace ships and satellites left in orbit helps not much. If we get into trouble, the rest of the expedition will *know* about it. But there won't be anything anyone can *do* about it. We'll be on our own — survive or die.

At least I managed to convince the project managers to develop patch kits capable of repairing punctures or rips in *Coprates'* envelope or gas bags. Patch kits that will work, even in very dusty conditions. I tested them myself, in the New Mexico desert and on the Moon, with me working in a space suit. Neither location is a perfect analog for Mars, but they were the best tests we could devise until we were on Mars' surface.

Despite the risk, there is nothing you could pay me to pass up this chance to see so much of Mars. It isn't just the chance to see more of Mars that I'm looking forward to. It's also that the other person on this trip will be D.J. As atmospheric scientist, she is to make surveys of pressure, temperature, winds, dust content, moisture content all along our route.

We will also be picking up samples of soil and rock — and ice, if we find any — along the way. We'll be guided in that by telecommunication with advice from Tara Halley and Fay Adair. And we will deploy a few small sensor packages containing atmospheric and seismic monitoring instruments.

And I hope — oh, how I hope! — that this time together will give me opportunity to pursue my courtship of D.J.

We wouldn't be going off into the dusty wild yonder right away, though. First there was a lot of work to be done around the landing site. Terence Tarkhan and Teresa Sola, and sometimes Carter Horace and me, were taking instrument packages off in the THOATs and setting them up in locations beyond easy walking distance from the ships, and bringing back samples. Tara Halley and Fay Adair were still directing the collection of rock and soil samples, including a few drill cores, and I occasionally helped with that.

D.J., to no one's surprise, wanted to put many of the soil

samples through her PPTU. I assisted her whenever I could find an excuse.

We were all pleased to find that some soil samples had a detectable frost content, and others had minerals with significant amounts of water of hydration. This meant that one of our hopes had been fulfilled. We would be able to produce hydrogen propellant at Mars for the return legs of future missions. This would improve the odds that Mars exploration would not be just a one-mission affair but an ongoing activity, perhaps (I dreamed) eventually leading to large scale human settlement.

I was less pleased that the busy schedule and a lack of privacy prevented me from doing much in the way of courting D.J. I consoled myself with the thought that once on our distant air mission, I would have the chance I wanted.

I observed some of us beginning to adopting a unique gait, as we got used to moving in Martian gravity. We were all now able to walk steadily, without stumbling every few steps; our muscle and balance systems had figured out how much vertical force to use with a horizontal step. But when we wanted to cover distance a little more quickly, some of us, myself included, were starting to use a sort of loping leap. It wasn't the "kangaroo hop" some people use on the Moon, similar to the way some of the Apollo astronauts moved. It wasn't quite a walk, nor quite a run, nor quite a jump. We would set one foot after the other, as though we were walking, but with extra force, so that we would leave the ground before putting down the next foot, and for an interval in the step, neither foot would be touching the ground. Each step then became a short jump, one after another. We bounded over the ground almost as fast as if we were jogging, but with much less effort than jogging takes on Earth.

One morning we were treated to "Beastmaster" Dean setting her "critters" out on their explorations, which they would continue even after we humans packed up and went home. Literally dozens of mini- and microrovers, of four different models, looking like nothing so much as a menagerie of multilegged animals and insects. These have far more autonomy than any previous rovers that have been deployed to the Martian surface, and more ability to cope with Martian nighttime and winter conditions. We helped her unpack them and set them down upon the Martian surface. Then she went to a control panel on board *Deimos* to send the signals to start them on their way.

She returned from the *Deimos* to watch with us while they began stepping and skittering out from our base in all directions, their electric motors buzzing and footfalls clattering ever so faintly in the thin Martian atmosphere — almost like whispers. Every so often, one would stop and scan a rock or a patch of soil at various wavelengths, or "sniff" it with chemical sensors. They would continue their robotic explorations until they ran out of power or received enough wear or damage to incapacitate them. This could be as long as several years; some were powered by radioisotope batteries, others had chemical batteries rechargeable from solar cells they carried. All were designed to resist the cold of Martian nights and the abrasion of the ever present dust.

All the while, at intervals, Kent Squared, Xavier Buthelezi, Carter Horace, and I were checking out all the *Coprates* systems, and making preparations for the air voyage. We were loading provisions and instrument packages. Not to forget high pressure tanks of extra hydrogen, and into which we could pump hydrogen when we wanted to reduce buoyancy, rather than valve it off to the atmosphere and lose it. We couldn't afford simply to throw hydrogen away. And patch kits, don't forget patch kits.

We began taking *Coprates* on short test hops. First a few kilometers. Then a few tens of kilometers.

We became aware, as we made these preparations and test flights, that the weather was becoming more and more windy, day by day, with more dust blowing. Nothing drastic. Each day, the gusts blew just a little more frequently and a little harder. But we could see the trend. It wasn't just locally, either. We were getting images from the *Hesperia* and the *Xanthe*, in orbit, and from the two satellites we had deployed before we landed. Their cameras showed the same thing happening all around the planet: winds and blowing dust gradually picking up.

We'd known when we started that our expedition would arrive in a season when dust storms could occur. We still don't understand the Martian climate and weather system well enough to predict whether a *planet-circling* dust storm would definitely happen. But we knew it *could* happen. We had anticipated the possibility during mission planning, and we felt that we could cope with it. As if we had a choice. If we got dust storms, we'd damn well *have* to cope with them.

To keep within our payload weight limit as we've loaded equipment onto the *Coprates*, I've been trying to keep D.J. from bringing along the kitchen sink. "Do we really need the TwoPee-Too?" I asked her. "I'd like to keep us a lift safety margin for the unexpected."

"Yes," she insisted. "We can leave behind some of the sensor stations if weight really becomes critical. But we don't know if the program managers will decide to put a permanent Mars base here, at our initial landing site, or if they'll choose somewhere else entirely. It's important to find out what the propellant production possibilities are not only here, but as many places as we can around the planet, by providing that information. That's one of the reasons I'm the P.I. who's making this trip."

I couldn't argue with her logic. "You win," I assented. "We'll take it."

— CHAPTER SIX —

On the ninth day after our landing, the *Coprates* was ready to be taken out on its long-distance voyage. The last supplies had been loaded; all instruments were on board. The short distance shakedown flights had given me confidence in the ship and in my ability to handle her under actual Martian conditions.

Those flights had also demonstrated that a couple of tiedown ropes and stakes each fore and aft could hold her steady on the ground. This would allow us to stop for rest, for sensor deployment and sample collection, and for weather. Which we would need to do if the wind speed exceeded the *Coprates'* maximum airspeed — something we knew could occur under Martian conditions. It doesn't matter how thin the air is...if your airspeed is slower than it is, you will make no progress against it.

D.J. and I had done a walkaround of the ship, and now we were aboard. We had removed helmets and space suits. We had decided that flying the ship would be much more convenient if we wore our pressure gear only when we went outside, and the risk was minimal. While it might be possible to puncture the gas cells, the gondola was pretty well armored.

We were going through the preflight checklist. "Motor number four", she read off to me.

"Prop is rotating," I confirmed to her.

"That's the end of the list," she said. "We're ready to go."

"Stand by to cast off!" I radioed our crewmates on the ground who were manning the tiedown ropes. I rotated all four propellers to the vertical takeoff position. I revved each one up to liftoff rpm. The downdraft from them began to blow dust about on the ground.

"Cast off!" I ordered. All ropes released, including the one at our nose securing us the mooring mast. We began to lift majestically into the sky.

"Bon voyage!" came Kent's voice. He was monitoring the launch from the instrument panels on board *Phobos*.

"We'll see you in five weeks, Captain Can!" I assured him.

"Godspeed!" I recognized Terence Tarkhan's voice. He had been one of our ground crew.

D.J. sent him a heartfelt "Thank you!"

Once aloft, I tilted the propellers from vertical lift to forward thrust configuration. Our first direction was south. The destination for this leg was the place for which our ship was named: the Coprates Chasma section of Valles Marineris. Nearly twelve hundred kilometers from our landing site…a good nine hours' flying time at cruising speed.

The THOATs, *Phobos* and *Deimos*, and the rest of our encampment began to dwindle behind us, and finally disappeared below our horizon. I gazed with a quiet awe at the ruddy Martian landscape passing beneath our ship. I could hear a soft hum from the electric motors, and a bare whisper from the propellers driving through the thin air.

I shifted my gaze for a moment to Diana, seated next to me in the copilot's chair. She was more than a bit distracting, for her choice of cabin wear was a well-fitting sleeveless blouse and an equally well-fitting pair of brief shorts. On her figure, the combination was dynamite. It didn't hurt that both garments were a shade of blue that suited the red-brown complexion of her skin perfectly.

As long as I had been concentrating on checklists and launch procedures, I had only casually noticed her appearance. Now I ran my eyes over the graceful curves of hip and leg and breast, the trimness of her waist, and felt a surge of hunger for her. It was going to be a long nine hours.

She felt my gaze and turned hers toward me. As I looked at her lovely face, it hit me once again how much in love with this woman I was.

"It is going to be a bit like an ocean cruise," I suggested.

"Yes, we can think of it like that," she agreed. "The pace will be leisurely, and we'll have frequent stops to see the sights and collect souvenirs." As she said this, she smiled. That smile lights up my feelings the way a sunrise lights up my eyes.

We turned our faces forward again, to watch Mars pass beneath us once more. I reached out and put my arm around her shoulder. She leaned a bit toward me and placed one hand atop mine.

We made an overnight stop at Ophir Chasma. We could have pushed on to Coprates before dark, but Ophir was scarcely out of our way, and D.J. and I agreed that it would be a shame not to stop and collect some samples, to compare the floor and wall compositions of Ophir and Coprates. Was the Valles Marineris system pretty much alike all the way through? Or were there important differences between one canyon segment and another?

We were both in awe of Ophir's breadth and depth. We knew the dimensions, we had seen stereo projections based on orbital pictures taken by Viking, by Mars Global Surveyor, and by subsequent probes. It was quite another thing to see it full size, in person, up close. Neither of us had much to say as I took *Coprates* out toward the center of the gap, then began a descent toward the floor. We could not seem to find words to express our emotions. As I took the ship down, we watched silently as the floors of both canyon walls disappeared below our horizon. We could still see the red-brown rims, though, forty or so kilometers away.

I wanted to approach a wall to get photographs and samples. But I didn't know how tricky the Martian winds might be within the canyons, and I didn't want our ship smashed against wall or floor by some sudden gust or downdraft. So my plan was to reach the floor near the center, then approach a wall along the *bottom*.

We stopped at the center long enough for us to put on space suits and for D.J. to dash out and get a soil sample, and one rock. We both had to put on suits, because the *Coprates* cabin is not large enough for a separate airlock. We have to depressurize the entire cabin, pumping the precious oxygen into storage tanks, before we can enter or exit.

It was near enough to sunset that the south wall of the

chasm was already in shadow, so once D.J. had collected those first samples, I headed toward the better lit north wall. As we neared it, D.J. and I could see layering. We'd expected this from images taken by Mars Global Surveyor and other unmanned missions since. Perhaps this would enable us — or future researchers — to learn something of Mars' history in the layers of rock — sediment? lava flows? some of each? — laid down over time. We also saw a talus slope at the bottom the bottom of the wall, pieces of rock that had broken off and fallen down the chasm wall. Over how much time? We could not begin to know until we collected some, and took them back to base — and some to Earth — for analysis. I made sure the *Coprates'* external cameras got images of both the layers and the talus slope.

We landed just short of the talus pile. Since this would be our stop for the night, I adjusted the ballonets to reduce lift. Then D.J. held the controls while I tied *Coprates* down fore and aft, driving the stakes into the ground and securing the ropes to them.

I had hardly finished when D.J. was bounding out of the ship, hands full of sample bags and boxes. I wasn't surprised. I knew she'd be eager to start collecting. But first she lifted her space suit camera from its chest mount and aimed it upward to get more images of the layering in the chasm wall. Once that was done, she took soil and rock samples from the chasm floor.

Then she stuck a couple of sample bags into her utility belt, and began to climb the talus slope.

"Diana, wait!" I yelled after her. "If you want some samples of the talus, why not just pick up some from the base of the slope? You shouldn't climb alone! We don't know how stable this pile is!"

Even though the rocks beneath her were slipping from time to time, causing her to slide back and lose ground, making her ascent laborious and far from efficient, she did not even turn her head around to answer me. I would not have seen it if she had, with her space suit on. "I want to get some samples from the cliff face at the top of the talus pile! Don't worry about me! I've been climbing all my life! I know what I'm doing!"

That was true. She'd been climbing, if not all her life, at least a great portion of it, in the mountains of New Mexico and Arizona in the area where she grew up. But I was still worried. The top of the pile looked at least a couple of hundred meters high, and it would be dark soon.

I stood at the base of the pile just beneath her, watching her move easily in the low gravity, despite the impediment of the space suit, wondering if I should try to follow her up. She was about seven meters up when the talus gave way, sliding down and carrying her with it. She scramble for footing, but none held.

I caught her in my arms as she reached the bottom, and was glad that the low gravity of Mars lessened the impact. "Have you cut your suit?" I cried with worry. Together we quickly checked her suit, but there were no cuts nor punctures. Not even any serious abrasions; just a few red stains from the rock and dust.

"That does it!" I told her fiercely. "No solo climbing! Whatever we do, we do as a team! If you want to do something risky, first you convince me it's worth the risk! Then, *if* I agree, we do it together!"

She completed collecting a few more samples from the base of the talus pile, and in a few more minutes we went back inside the *Coprates* for the night. But not before she'd put a couple of her soil samples from the chasm floor through a simple analysis. We didn't have the equipment to do as complete a job as the P.I.'s could do with the shipboard instruments back at the landing site, but she could get a first cut. And of course she put them through the PPTU. She announced to me that they were unusually rich in water of hydration.

We helped each other out of our space suits and began to prepare a simple supper. As we did, I said, "I don't like to pull rank on you Diana, but there are some risks I can't allow you to take. The two of us are on our own out here. If we get into trouble, no one can help us. If one of us is injured, or punctures a space suit, odds are we're goners. Think first before you act. And above all, don't go plunging into something on your own!

"You may be an experienced climber, but you are *not*

experienced climbing on Mars, and only a little experienced climbing in a space suit." We'd done some climbing in our lunar training, but not much. And lunar gravity was less than half that of Mars.

D.J. placed a hand on my arm. "You are right," she admitted. "I let my eagerness get the better of my judgement. Thanks for reminding me to get hold of myself. I am really glad you were there to catch me when I fell, even if you did yell at me afterward." She put a finger to my lips before I could reply, and went on, "I'm not upset with you. I almost was. I heard the anger in your voice. But I heard something else, too. I heard fear, and I realized that you were afraid for me."

"Very much afraid," I responded. "Afraid I might lose you. I...I just wouldn't want that to happen."

The expression in Diana's eyes softened, and she caressed my face gently with her hand. She didn't seem to know what to say. After several minutes of silence, we turned back to finish supper preparations. The Martian sunset had already given way swiftly to darkness. Twilight did not linger as it might have on Earth.

After supper, we prepared for sleep, swinging fold-out bunks into the tiny cabin space. We conversed for a while, holding hands as we talked over the wonders we had seen that day, and our general excitement about the whole Martian expedition.

After a time, I leaned toward D.J. and kissed her gently. I began to draw her into my arms, but she put a hand against my chest to stop me.

"What is the matter?" I asked her. "Are you afraid I won't be able to stop?"

"No," she shook her head, her raven tresses floating softly. "I am afraid *I* won't be able to stop. You are a temptation that is very hard for me to resist. I am still trying to make sure in my own mind that you are the man I want to spend the rest of my life with, before I give myself to you, and to my own desires."

I shook my own head, now. But I had learned from experience that if D.J. had her mind made up about something, it was hard to argue with her. Besides, I didn't want to argue her into something she wasn't truly ready for. If and when she did give herself to me, I wanted it to be with her whole heart, with no lingering doubts or reservations holding her back. If I managed to win her, I wanted *all* of her.

So I lay down on my bunk, within easy reach of hers, aching to reach across that short distance and take her into my arms. I wondered to myself if I would survive the frustration until D.J. convinced herself — or until the trip was over, or if I would go crazy from it.

— CHAPTER SEVEN —

NEXT MORNING we resumed our flight toward Coprates Chasma. When we reached it, I set the *Coprates* down near the center of the one hundred fifty-odd kilometer wide floor near the western end of her namesake.

D.J.'s first act, of course, was to collect more samples. Her second was to emplace the first of the automated meteorology and seismic sensor stations. Each station has two modules. One module has seismometers; the other takes atmospheric data: temperature, pressure, composition, wind speed and direction. They will relay their data to the landing site and to Earth via the ships in orbit and the satellites we had deployed.

Once D.J.'s sensor station was out and her samples were in, I took the *Coprates* aloft to an altitude of twenty-five hundred meters above the chasm floor and headed her 101 degrees true...straight down her namesake canyon. At this altitude, we could see the red walls on both sides beneath the butternut sky, stretched as far away as we could see ahead and behind. It was still early enough in the morning for the sun to cast strong shadows from the north wall onto the chasm floor. The shadows emphasized the vast depth and breadth of the canyon, and threw into relief the colors and layering on the south wall.

A sharp intake of breath as we reached cruising altitude and speed told me that D.J. was as much in awe at the sight as I was. "This planet continues to astound me!" she exclaimed. "I've hiked the Grand Canyon back home, but this...! I'm still overwhelmed! This is stupendous!"

I understood how difficult it was for her to find words. My own feelings were just as strong. The occasion called for superlatives, yet it was difficult to find any that had not been overworked.

D.J. seemed to feel a need to share her emotions. As close as her seat was to mine, it did not seem to be close enough to suit her. She unstrapped from it and stood as close as possible beside me, our bodies touching, accepting my right arm around her waist, placing her right hand on mine and her left arm about my shoulder.

I sighed with a joy combined from the awe at the sight of Coprates Chasma rolling past around us and the sweet warmth of Diana's touch. The fragrance of Diana's hair entered my nostrils. Not a perfume; simply her own warm, wonderful, natural womanly scent, adding one more pleasure to the moment like the perfect seasoning to a dish.

We made sure that *Coprates'* onboard cameras were operating to record the passing scenery, so that we would have both a scientific and a historical record of the trip. We expected that some of these images, relayed to Earth via the orbiting deepspace ships and satellites, would be seen on nightly news programs all around our home planet, just as many other images from our expedition already had been. We have been informed that news program ratings have gone up tremendously since we reached Mars.

I was glad that our communications enabled Earth's citizens to share, at least in part, what we were seeing. It was only fair, since many of them were supporting us as taxpayers, through the governments of the several nations that financed this expedition.

When we approached the ridge that rises from the floor mid-canyon, I followed the north or left-hand channel. About midday I brought the *Coprates* down to the chasm floor so we could have lunch. Immediately after we finished eating, we went out so that D.J. could collect more samples. She took some readings from her weather instruments and announced, "It's actually quite balmy today. Sixteen degrees Celsius. It would be shirt-sleeve weather…if the atmosphere had enough pressure and oxygen to breathe!"

We kept our space suits on, because I headed the *Coprates* to the north wall of the chasm, so that D.J. could collect samples to compare with those taken from the center. First we landed at the floor, next to a talus slope. Once D.J. had samples from there, I lifted the ship to the cliff top. D.J. collected samples from the very top.

Then, I made sure the winds were *very* steady, without gusts. Once I had convinced myself of that, I held the *Coprates* steady at the cliff edge and deployed a rope ladder. D.J. descended this about three meters. I feared for her safety, and had offered to do this for her. "Let me collect the samples, and you hold the controls of the *Coprates*."

D.J. had vetoed that. "No," she shook her head. "You could probably do it. But I am a more experienced climber, and you are by far a better pilot. I would much rather trust my life to your piloting skill, than yours to mine." She saw from my face that I was about to protest, and silenced me in her gentle way by lifting her hands to my shoulders. "I know it's a risk," she admitted. "But if we weren't planning on taking risks, not one of us would be on this mission. Somebody, sometime, is going to have to take the risk of dangling from a rope to get samples from the chasm walls. These samples will be important. I think so, and Tara and Fay think so, too."

"I don't know how to argue with three P.I.'s," I admitted, "but I am still afraid for you."

"I understand. I'll only ask you to do this once here, and once on the opposite wall of the chasm. Then I'll never ask you to do it again on this mission."

With that promise, I finally agreed. So here I was, holding the *Coprates* steady, while D.J. dangled on a rope ladder next to the chasm wall. She hammered off one rock fragment and placed it in a sample bag. Then she climbed back up about a meter or so, to what looked like a different layer, and chipped off a second. She decided those would be enough, and climbed back up into the ship. I reeled up the ladder and she closed the hatch. I let out a sigh of relief. She hear it and nodded. "Me, too!" were her words.

Hearing those words gave me comfort, of a sort. They reaffirmed to me that she was being thoughtfully courageous, not foolhardy. They told me that she would take chances, if she thought enough was at stake, but that she wouldn't take *stupid* chances. I'd had that opinion of her for a long time, but some of her actions on this air voyage had started to make me wonder. It always helps when you have confidence in the judgement of your teammates.

We repeated the exercise on the south wall of the chasm, first collecting samples from the base of the cliff, then from the top, then — with D.J. dangling once more from the rope ladder — from the wall about three meters down from the top. Having done it once, I was more confident in my ability to hold the *Coprates* steady. Even so, I was *extremely* relieved when D.J. was back on board.

I was doubly pleased, and so was Diana, that I'd managed to find a spot at the base of the south wall with very little talus. That had enabled Diana to get two samples directly from the chasm wall, near the base, from an identifiable layer in the wall rock and at an identifiable areographic location.

Between collecting samples from the canyon walls and flying back and forth between them, we had consumed the afternoon. It was time to stop for the night. We'd made a bit over seven hundred kilometers eastward from the point where we'd entered the Coprates Chasma. Early tomorrow should see us at the point where the Valles Marineris system splits into the Capri and Eos Chasmas.

After supper, we were scheduled to communicate with the landing site crew. *Xanthe* should be in an orbital position to give a good relay between us and there for at least ten minutes, and with luck and good tracking by the antennas at both ends, perhaps fifteen.

I switched on the comm panel, then our cameras and TV monitors. Diana handled the antenna controls, boosting the gain on the omnis and aiming the directional antenna toward the place in the sky where we expected the *Xanthe* to be passing.

"*Coprates* calling Redsand Landing One," I began. "Over."

The picture on the monitor wavered, then steadied to show a familiar face, grinning. "Hello, *Coprates*, this is Redsand Landing One. It's good to hear from you. I'm glad to know you're alive and well. Go ahead."

"Hello, Captain," I said to Kent Squared's image. I had a

smile of my own. "We're calling to report our progress so far." I gave him a brief summary of our activities and findings.

D.J. followed up with comments on the geology and the samples she had collected. "I wish Tara and Fay could be here with us. Some of the layering we've seen in the canyon walls looks an awful lot like sedimentary deposits, and some of the soil samples I've collected from the floors give me the same impression. And when I've run some of those soil samples through the Propellant Production Test Unit, they show unusually high water of hydration contents." Then she began to discuss her specialty, atmospheric measurements.

At that point, the smile left Kent's face, and he grew more serious. "If we're talking about the atmosphere, there's something you should know about. The cameras on our ships and satellites in orbit are picking up more and more blowing dust. Various places around the planet, but especially in the south, in and around Hellas basin. I'm going to switch you to a composite time-lapse video of today's weather images, from all around the planet."

Kent's face disappeared from the screen, and in its place was a side by side image of both hemispheres of Mars. The *Phobos* computer had taken the satellite images taken one by one of various local areas on the planet, and synthesized them into a combined globular view.

As the views moved forward through the day, I could see the spots of blowing dust here and there, as Kent had said. When my eyes picked out the region around Hellas basin, I whistled. I heard another, higher pitched whistle from beside me. It was D.J.

Kent responded to our whistles with just one word, "Yeah." His face returned to the screen.

"Looks like we'll have to forget about visiting Hellas this trip," I commented. A disappointment. I had been looking forward to exploring the giant impact basin. The comments I'd heard from the planetary science and geology P.I.'s had intrigued me.

"I think you'd better," Kent agreed. "In fact, I'm not sure but that we should recall you now."

D.J. argued strenuously against this. "We've come this far," she said. "We understood the risk when we planned this mission, when this airship was first designed. Overdesigned, in my estimation, Jonathan's occasional doubts notwithstanding. There is still no real indication that this will be a global dust storm year. There is so much we can do on this flight — don't cut us short yet."

I supported her. "Rerouting our itinerary to avoid Hellas makes sense. The first expedition doesn't have to do *everything*. But cutting this flight off *doesn't* make sense, at least not yet. The risk of undertaking this flight at all we've already accepted. The additional risk from the weather we've seen so far is not really very large by comparison. We'll keep a close watch on your weather reports, and be ready to make a run for home if things really seem to be closing down. But unless they do, let us do as much of our mission as we can."

After a bit more discussion, Captain Kent gave in. His own deep-down preference, in spite of his fears for our safety, was for continuing our exploration. And he knew perfectly well he could not force any decision on us. Not only did he not have the means, but he knew that we, on the spot, were in a better position to judge our situation than he was and had to be trusted with the responsibility to do so.

After Kent had switched off and we prepared for our second night of sleep, Diana said, "It's been an awe inspiring day, hasn't it? And an exciting one. It is hard to believe how much we've seen today, of an entire new world, seeing territory no one has ever crossed before! I can't help it. I still have a school girl's excitement about all this."

"I can't blame you." I placed my hands on her slim waist. "Some things are worth getting excited about."

Diana ran her fingers along the stubble of whiskers on my cheek and chin. Despite our cramped quarters, I had managed to shave this morning. I used an electric razor; a safety razor was out of the question — we can't spare the water. It was a bother, because all the whiskers had to be vacuumed up and stowed. We couldn't let them accumulate in the cabin; neither could we simply dump them — or any other waste — overboard. Until the existence of Martian life was finally proved or disproved — and according to Teresa Sola, that question was still not decided — the rule was to avoid jettisoning anything if possible. If circumstances did require us to do so, it must be in carefully sealed containers.

In spite of all that, I had decided that shaving was less bother than growing a beard. And if I'd thought that D.J. was ready for some amorous exploring, I'd have been glad to shave again this evening.

The whiskers didn't seem to trouble her, though. This time it was she who initiated a good-night kiss. Her hand slid from my face around my neck, and the other joined it. And when my arms slipped from her waist around her back, she stepped willingly into my embrace. Her lips parted slightly and met mine, at first softly, and then pressing eagerly as her hands caressed my back.

She held me closely and kissed me softly and gently on the cheek and then my throat. She accepted a few of my kisses to her neck before she hungrily tasted my lips again. Our embrace lasted only a short while, however, before she called a halt.

"You don't know how much will power it is taking me to stop!" Diana told me.

"I think I have some idea!" I answered, and I'm sure my voice had a grumble in it. I might not be certain of her state of arousal, but I surely was of my own!

Her gaze was warm, and she touched my face softly once more as we ended our embrace. I couldn't stay mad at her. I knew she was as frustrated as I was, and I knew that she was *not* doing this to frustrate me — or herself.

But while I could accept her behavior, at least for the time being, I didn't entirely understand it. During the day, while we were in flight, D.J. seemed to welcome — even to seek — expressions of affection. Holding hands, an arm around a waist or shoulder, brushing our bodies together as we moved around the cabin. Yet in the evenings, she seemed to be determined to keep things under careful control. Was that because she knew that in the press of duties during the day, nothing would develop that would get her in over her head?

And was her desire to keep our amorous adventures under such careful rein because she wanted to make sure of her emotions, as she said? Or was she *denying* her emotions? Was she being honest with herself about this? We'd both looked forward to this trip as an opportunity to renew our courtship. Yet now it almost seemed as though she was backing off from that.

I decided that now was not the right time to bring the subject up. We *had* only completed the second day of our journey, and perhaps the press of all our activities in that short time had distracted her from the idea of romance. But if this pattern continued for very many days longer, I determined that I would face her with the question.

The next morning, after a short breakfast, we were on our way once more, and shortly we reached the fork. If we weren't going to Hellas, we wouldn't be going southerly by way of Eos. I turned the ship northeast into the Capri Chasma.

By noon we'd passed the junction where Ganges Chasma joined Capri. Here we stopped for lunch, but before we ate, we picked up some more rock and soil samples, and planted another of the atmosphere/seismic sensor stations.

When we resumed flight for the afternoon, I decided on a tack with which to pursue my courtship. As we flew, we commented from time to time on especially interesting bits of the awe inspiring scenery below and around us. While we conversed, I began to remind Diana of how we'd both had dreams from childhood of flying in space and traveling to Mars. I reminisced about how when we found the chance to pursue those dreams, me through piloting and her through science, we'd been drawn to this program. And how learning of our shared dreams had drawn us to each other.

I continued this line of conversation throughout the afternoon, between stops for photography and sample collection. I resumed it when we stopped for the evening.

This reminder of how our mutual affection had begun seemed to soften D.J. and rekindle the flame of her emotions toward me. Tonight she allowed several minutes of kissing and caressing before she gently disengaged from my embrace. Dared I think she even encouraged it?

Her kisses and touches were not erotic, except for the fact that her mere presence is enough to stir my blood, but were extremely affectionate. I took my cue from that and responded the same way. It was her heart I wanted to win first anyway. If I could win that, and then her hand, there would be time enough for consummation.

Encouraged by this, I decided to continue this approach to my courtship. And it seemed to be working. Day by day, evening by evening, my conversational focus on our shared dream and the wonder of our surroundings, and a gentle, self controlled approach to kissing and touching seemed to open D.J.'s affections.

In spite of feeling frustrated at times by arousal I could not satisfy, I was enjoying myself. If possible, I was falling even more in love with Diana. I saw her affectionate nature that I had observed and grown fond of during our training reassert itself. And although she did not yet say so in words, I sensed that her fondness for me was also growing stronger. During the days, she spent more time close to me. Her touches were more frequent, and lingered longer. I noticed her glancing my way more often — or was it because I was spending more time looking at her? And when she did, I often observed a smile and a warm light in her eyes.

Each evening, our good-night embrace lasted a little longer, her kisses and touches a little more intense. I sensed that Diana was growing to trust me in closeness. Perhaps as important, she was growing to trust herself.

This courtship, so far as I could see, was going wonderfully. As wonderfully as our flight.

— CHAPTER EIGHT —

Early on the fourth day of our flight, we approached Galilaei Crater. Flying up to a major impact crater by air is very impressive. They're impressive from orbit, too, and from orbit you get a better overall view of one. But craters go by rather quickly at orbital speed. From the air the view is closer, and you have plenty of time for awe to build as you approach. We saw the rim first, of course, curving away from us for a very great distance to either side of our approach point. When we got close enough, we could begin to see down into the floor, deep enough below the terrain outside the crater to make us take a deep breath. As we crossed above the rim, we could see the far wall. But had we been flying much lower, we would only have been able to see the rim on the far side, not the floor. It would have been beyond the planet's horizon.

We weren't going to fly to that far, however, until we'd taken samples from the near wall and the crater floor. This was the first of several craters we meant to get samples from.

After that we visited the Sinus Meridiani region, then traveled north, stopping at the craters Rutherford, Becquerel, Curie, and Slodowska on our way to the Deuteronilus region. Then south to take samples and plant an instrument package at the giant impact crater Cassini. Did I leave the impression that Galilei was awe inspiring? Cassini is older, its rim much more degraded — which is part of the reason we wanted samples from it, too — for age comparisons. But it is more that three times the diameter of Galilei.

When we looked down upon Cassini's worn but massive rim as we approached it, extending out of sight to either side, then crossed over the rim to fly above the basin within, I once again found myself filled with powerful emotions, as I had when we'd flown down Coprates Chasma. This time we couldn't even see the *rim* of the far wall at first, at the altitude we were flying, because of the curve of the planet. Once again, I found myself at a loss for words to express my feelings. I glanced at D.J.'s eyes from time to time, and sensed that she was equally impressed. Yet she was as silent as I. Like me, she was struggling to find words that might convey the feelings this enormous planetary feature evoked.

Every day since we've landed I have experienced feelings of awe and wonder so powerful as to be almost overwhelming. We are, after all, exploring a whole new planet — the first humans to do so. No matter how busy, how preoccupied we are — and we have plenty of work to do, much of it the mundane, even trivial, housekeeping chores everyone has to do everywhere — sometime during each day, each of us has a spare moment to stop and think, and just take in what's around us. In those moments, every one of us gets hit with a sense of the history we're making, and with the wonder of this new world around us. This is work of a sort — an entire experience of a sort — we had only dreamed of before we launched from Earth.

For me, feelings like that have become even stronger and more frequent since Diana and I began our flight aboard the *Coprates*. You can imagine why. Every day, we two are going places where no human has ever been before, and seeing sights no one has seen — or only by remote, robotic probes from orbital distance, not close up with their own eyes, as we are now able to do.

Yet, a few experiences on this trip bring feelings that stand out even among these. One was our initial landing, and setting foot on Mars' soil for the first time. Another was seeing Coprates Chasma, and the other portions of Valles Marineris we'd flown down. Seeing Cassini crater was like that. The feelings it generated were not quite as intense, perhaps, as seeing Valles Marineris, but still strong, even for this expedition.

Ours was not the only excursion away from the base, even though we were the only *airborne* one. As we made our progress reports back to base, we heard their updates in return. The inflatable passenger modules had been put aboard both THOATs, and Terence Tarkhan was leading short four- or six-person jaunts. The first were to a few smallish (hundreds of meters across rather than kilometers), reasonably nearby impact craters.

The plan was, if all went well, and the THOATs continued to prove themselves as reliable as they had so far, to mount an expedition north to Kasei Vallis and from there westward to Tharsis Tholis. How much of that got done depended not only on the continued reliability of the vehicles and avoiding mishaps, but also on not finding any terrain the THOATs couldn't handle. If all continued to go well and there were time enough, there was even an option in that plan to continue on beyond Tharsis Tholis as far as Ascraeus Mons.

After we'd taken our samples and emplaced D.J.'s instruments at Cassini, we turned east toward Syrtis Major.

Trouble was, day by day, as our explorations bore fruit and D.J.'s and my courtship blossomed, the weather was growing worse. Each day's images from the orbiting satellites and deep-space ships showed more blowing dust and evidence of stronger wind. I was observing the increased wind as well from the flight behavior of the *Coprates*. Nothing I couldn't handle, so far. But the wind vectors were certainly enough to affect my heading to keep on course, and the time it took to cover ground. I even had to set the ship on the ground a couple of times to wait out blows when the dust obscured our vision, or when the wind was against us or across our path, and faster than the ship's maximum airspeed.

The daily satellite images seemed to indicate that the weather would not blow up into a global dust storm this year. It wasn't enough, yet, to make us run back for Redsand Landing. But it would certainly affect flight conditions regionally, and we'd have to keep a very sharp eye on things.

What concerned me most was that the two ships and two satellites made only four objects in orbit to monitor weather conditions. In low orbit at that. Which meant that they could not possibly cover all the planet all the time. No unmanned satellites from earlier scientific projects are still functional. We could easily be blindsided, hit by a local dust storm none of the ships or satellites had seen in time.

That realization was making me edgy. In spite of my growing affection for D.J., my concern about the weather occasionally put a growl in my voice.

The first few times that happened, D.J. snapped back at me. In these close quarters, we could have developed a real hostility, and seriously harmed the growing affection between us. Then D.J. began to understand that I was upset with the situation, not with her. After that, she responded to that tone of voice with a soothing caress of her hand over my back or through my hair.

That response was enormously helpful to me. It relaxed me, and helped me focus my attention on flying the ship and watching the instruments, where it needed to be, instead of on my worry. I did not know how to express to Diana how much I appreciated those calming caresses. I tried once, rather clumsily I felt. But Diana understood, despite my difficulty in finding words. She answered my stumbling remarks with a smile and another caress.

Our goal after Syrtis Major was to cross Isidis Planitia and then Elysium Planitia to visit the volcanic peaks Elysium Mons and Hecates Tholus.

One inconvenience is that we can't bathe. I mentioned I could shave only with an electric shaver, because we can't spare water for shaving with a safety razor. For the same reason, we have no bath or shower. All we have to clean our bodies is the equivalent of "wet naps", the treated paper napkins offered by some fast food restaurants. Every few days, we run some over our bodies. That seems to work, though. These particular "wet naps" have been treated with something that absorbs the substances that cause body odor. So once over, dry off, a little deodorant, and we smell fine.

Getting a modicum of privacy to use these napkins is difficult in the cramped quarters we have. What we've been doing is to withdraw to the corner of the cabin that contains the toilet, and draw the privacy curtain it is provided with.

    I judge our romance to be progressing. Slowly, but definitely, Diana is warming up. Her reserve is gradually melting. Like ice on a lake as spring approaches. I have not used that exact simile in our conversations, however. She might misunderstand.

— CHAPTER NINE —

WE WERE WITHIN SIGHT of Elysium Mons when the dust storm hit us. First came wind gusts, sudden, unexpected, batting *Coprates* about as a child would bounce a toy balloon. I found myself fighting for directional control with D.J. trying to assist.

Then D.J., in the right hand seat, tapped my shoulder and pointed to her two o'clock direction. Approaching from our southeast, from the direction of Cerberus, was a ruddy, billowing, airborne wall of dust.

As I had feared, this was a part of the weather pattern that had been missed in yesterday's orbital scans.

I would have preferred to set *Coprates* down and wait the storm out, as we had done before. But the ship was already in the grip of the storm's wind. As dust began to surround us and obscure our vision, an updraft took the ship high into the air, as I continued to fight for control.

So high that with the dust around us, we could no longer see the ground. I was grateful that our radar could still penetrate the dust, and give us our altitude that way.

I managed to get the ship aligned tail into the wind. I would have preferred to have the nose into the wind, but this was the best I could do. Perhaps we could run with the storm until it blew itself out, although neither of us had a clear idea how long that was likely to be.

Shortly the radar was telling me something I didn't like at all. No longer in an updraft, we were now in a powerful downdraft. And blown with the storm as we were, we had a very fast forward velocity. We were headed rapidly toward the ground. If we struck at this velocity, I didn't know if the ship, or we, would stand it.

"We're going down!" I yelled over the storm noise. "I can't control her against this wind! Secure your seat belt and hang on!"

The best I could do was apply reverse thrust on the propellers and work the pitch control to try to slow our forward motion and rate of descent. That did slow us, but only a little.

The wind speed was simply too high, well exceeding our maximum airspeed.

We reached a low enough altitude that we could see the Martian surface through the dust, even though it was obscured. I could see the ground going by swiftly below us through the swirling dust. And coming up at us, much too rapidly for my comfort. But nothing more I could do than I was already doing.

I felt a jarring impact as the gondola hit, throwing D.J. and me forward against our shoulder harnesses and snapping our heads forward and down in a reverse of the whiplash motion that occurs when someone is rear-ended in a car. The gondola was scraping forward along the ground, still moving very rapidly, friction gradually slowing it down. It was an extremely bumpy ride; we were running into rocks so frequently that I was scarcely aware of them as individual impacts, but more as a continuous, buffeting vibration.

Mars had one more trick to pull. A sudden downgust on the tail pitched the rear section of the blimp's envelope to the ground. I thought I could hear popping and tearing noises over the wind shriek as we finally came to a stop.

We unstrapped, still feeling shaken up. Still, I seemed to be all right. "How are you, D.J.?" I asked. "Are you hurt?"

She felt of the back of her neck, where it had bent as her head had been thrown forward. "I think I'm okay," she assured me. "That was a rough ride, and I may wind up sore in a few places. But I don't think I've sustained any injuries."

I looked out a rear port to see how the ship had come through. From what I could see through the still-blowing dust, *Coprates* had not fared as well as we. The propellers looked okay. But there was a limp place in the fuselage, about halfway between the gondola and the tail surfaces, that I didn't like the look of at all. And when I turned back to check my instruments, I saw that two of the gas cells were not holding pressure. Readings on those two were now matching external pressure readings, instead of slightly above.

But nothing I could do about that now. We had to wait until

the storm settled down before we could go outside to fully assess the damage or attempt repair.

Which meant I needed to lose more lift, to keep *Coprates* and us from being blown about over the surface. So I adjusted the ballonets and pumped half the hydrogen from the remaining six gas cells into the reserve high-pressure storage tanks.

It was mid afternoon, local Mars time, when we went down. The storm was still blowing strong when nightfall came. With the sound of the wind outside, and the knowledge of our situation, we munched our supper half-heartedly. Neither of us had much appetite.

It was another hour after supper before we had a ship — the *Hesperia* — in orbital position to pick up a message from us. Because we were now halfway around the planet from Redsand Landing One, there was no possibility of direct, two-way communication with our crewmates back at the base. If one or both satellites and perhaps the *Xanthe* had been in the right positions in their orbits, we could have made a two-way link. As it was, I had to send a message via *Hesperia* with a "store and forward" command. That meant it would record the message and play it back when its orbit next took it within broadcast range of the landing site...say in fifty minutes or so. I gave the basics of our situation and our location.

An ironic thought crossed my mind, and I mentioned it to Diana. "We'll probably make the headlines in tomorrow's news, back on Earth."

When it came time for sleep that night, Diana asked, "Could you hold me for a little while? I don't want to make love, but I'm scared, and I need your closeness."

"Here," I said as I gently took her into my arms. "As long as you want me, I'll be here. I understand how you feel. I don't mind admitting to feeling a little scared myself. But we're not dead, yet, and somehow I have the confidence that we'll think and work ourselves out of this."

"You are so encouraging!" D.J. whispered, and kissed me softly. I felt her relax, felt the tension in her body that grew out of her fear subside. I was glad for that. She needed to rest, and she would have had a hard time doing that if she had remained as tense as I had initially felt.

The next morning, the storm was still blowing, although with perhaps a bit less wind velocity, from what we could tell by the ship's instruments. By then, we had received a reply to our message, also by store-and-forward, in this case via one of our polar satellites. Captain Kent acknowledged our message, expressed deep concern for our situation, and wished us luck. Others at Redsand Landing One, especially Terence Tarkhan and Teresa Sola, added a few words of concern and good wishes of their own.

What no one stated aloud was what everyone knew. The others, back at the landing site, could hope and wish and pray. But they could not help us in any physical way. Win or lose, live or die, the only people who could do anything about the situation were the two of us. Just D.J. and me.

Even we could not do anything just yet. Not with the storm still blowing. Oh, we could have gone outside in our space suits, and could have stood up to the storm, too. But to open the door would be to let blowing dust inside the cabin, risking fouling our instruments and equipment, making a mess, and generally adding more problems to those we already had. There was no way to make any effective repairs to the ship as long as the dust was blowing, without letting a lot of that dust get into places that could be harmful to the ship.

As long as we remained in the cabin, we were in no immediate danger. We had plenty of food, and the air and water recycling systems were working perfectly. The radioisotope power plant was going strong; no shortage there. Nor would we freeze, even in the frosty Martian nights. The cabin was superbly insulated, and with two human bodies putting out heat, plus all the electrical power we needed, the temperature was actually on the warm side. Diana stuck to wearing shorts and thin blouses, and I dressed lightly as well.

It was two more days before the storm slacked off. We used

that time to check out everything about the ship we could with instruments and computer diagnostics. So far as we could tell, only two gas cells had leaks. Counting the cell furthest forward as number one, and the cell furthest aft as number eight, the leaking cells were numbers six and seven. We could not detect any other damage. I intended to do an all-around eyeball inspection as soon as we could go outside, however.

I also tried to use the time to further my romance with Diana. I thought perhaps that with some embraces, some kisses, some affectionate caresses, I might enhance her feelings toward me. I also hoped it might help ease her fears and help her relax by taking her mind off our predicament. She needed that relaxation, if she were to rest, and be ready to function at peak level when we *could* do something about the situation.

It helped, but not as much as I had hoped. D.J. was too tense. She simply couldn't get her mind off the situation we were in for long. But I discovered that with a gentle backrub or forehead rub at bedtime, I could ease her tension enough for her to get to sleep. Backrubs and neck rubs also helped with the soreness in her neck that had resulted from the inverse whiplash we had gotten in our landing.

I had some soreness, too, although not as badly. So she also gave me neck rubs. Her hands were very soothing; I discovered she was quite skilled at getting the kinks out of my muscles.

— CHAPTER TEN —

THE FOURTH MORNING, the storm subsided. The wind did not *stop*, but it was blowing at less than twenty percent of the speed it had during the storm's peak. Neither did the dust completely vanish, but it, too, was substantially diminished. It was now only a very light haze in the air.

We could go outside. I don't recall if either of us gave an audible sigh of relief, but I know we both felt that way. We rushed through a light breakfast and put on our space suits. I clipped a flashlight to the utility belt of my suit in case we needed to check for damage in any hard-to-see crannies.

When we went aft, we saw that each of the two cells that weren't holding pressure had tears in the lower part of the skin. Cell number seven had a gash better than half a meter long, roughly at right angles to the longitudinal axis of the ship. Cell six had two holes: one was a centimeter sized puncture; the other, about a meter to the left of it, was an L-shaped rip about ten centimeters each way.

Glancing about the ground, I could see plenty of rocks, several easily sharp enough to cause those tears, given the force of the downgust. It would be difficult to tell which particular rocks had caused the tears, but that was unimportant. What mattered was: what could we do about it?

What other damage might there be? D.J. and I made a complete walkaround of the ship. D.J. commented as we made the final turn back toward the cabin hatch, "I observed some dust abrasions on the tail surfaces and propellers. And the bottom of the gondola is terribly scratched up from all the rocks we went over as we slid in. I'm amazed that it didn't spring a leak. It's tougher than I thought. But I honestly don't see any damage that will require repairs other than the ripped gas cells."

I agreed with her assessment. Our main task now was to repair those torn cells.

We went to the supply locker and got out reels of plastic patching material, cans of adhesive, scissors, rolls of adhesive tape, and brushes. We needed two kinds of brushes, one to brush dust away from the repair site, the other to apply the adhesive.

We also needed clamps to hold patches in place while the adhesive set, and some poles, rope, and stakes. These would secure the skin of the gas cells (I hoped) against wind gusts while repairs were going on. More important, they would hold the surface being patched up off the dusty Martian surface while the adhesive was setting.

We got out a pair of short stepladders, too. Although the wind had slapped that section of the fuselage into the ground, in its normal position (such as now), the wounds in the skin were a bit too high for us to reach from the ground. Especially for Diana, who is a good foot shorter than I. Yes, in Mars' low gravity, we could jump up and reach the tears. But we couldn't work that way. Not fastening patches into place.

I decided that we would also need a folding work table. I'd first thought of the possibility when we'd done some early simulated repairs, during practice on the lunar surface. We'd tried it out, and it made some types of repair operations immensely simpler. It provided a stable work surface that was first of all within easy arm's reach for a crew member, and second up and away from dusty ground surfaces which we had in practice on the Moon, and which we knew we could expect on Mars.

What we'd evolved to during our lunar practices was a table about the width of a card table and twice as long, with a hinged center for more compact folding, but with a locking device to secure that center for a solid work surface. It was light and easy to stow, but quite strong and stable when in place. The legs had telescoping tips, so that we could adjust their lengths to get a stable, approximately level surface even on rough or sloping terrain.

It took a couple of trips to get everything we needed out to where we wanted it.

The first thing D.J. and I did, when we got our supplies and equipment arrayed near the torn gas bags, was to set up our stepladders side by side near the tears, and carefully measure the dimensions of each tear. We would have to size each patch to the hole or rip it was to mend. We wanted the patches big enough to close the gap, obviously, and to have a wide margin for the adhesive we would use to hold them. But we didn't want them too big; another thing we'd learned in lunar practice was that the bigger the patch, the more awkward the job became.

Once we finished those measurements, I reached in carefully with a soft brush and gently brushed out as much as I could of the dust that had gotten inside the gas cells through the gash in cell seven and the L-shaped rip in cell six. The circular puncture in cell six was too small for any brush we carried to reach through. We simply had to hope that whatever dust had entered the cell through that hole would not impede our repair effort. I expected it would not be a problem; our repair equipment was designed to allow for the presence of minor amounts of dust.

Our next step was to secure the ship's skin around each tear with framing clamps. These clamps are made of four rods of material arranged to form a rectangular frame. Ours are carbon fiber composite, but what they are made of is not important; what is important is that the corner links allow the length and width of the frame to be adjusted up to the maximum length of the rods. The other important feature is that the rods are equipped with gripping elements to hold the skin. What that allows is to hold a rectangular area surrounding a cut or puncture flat and slightly taut. Not tight, mind you, with the risk of causing the tear to grow worse…just snug enough to hold the area flat. You'd be surprised how much the mere fact of holding the area flat simplifies the repair procedure.

Putting the framing clamps in place took teamwork. Very much a two person job. I was immensely glad for D.J.'s presence. Especially because the job needed someone not only well trained, but a quick thinker, able to deal with the little unforeseen variations that always occur in the field. One of us alone *might* have been able to secure the clamps, but it would have been much more difficult. And neither of us alone would be able to put the patches in place, when we got to that part of the job.

We used a very large size framing clamp for the gash in cell seven, two much smaller ones for the holes in cell six.

Once the framing clamps were in place, we needed to secure them in an elevated position to keep them off the ground, accessible to us for the rest of the patch job, and steady against wind gusts. That's where the poles came in. We placed an extendible pole between the ground and each corner of each framing clamp. Once each was in place, we must secure it against toppling with ropes and tent stakes.

All of this work was simple, but none of it was easy. Especially while standing on stepladders. And in space suits, definitely not fast. Our suits are much improved over those of the early space age, and allow us greatly improved mobility. But it is still not the same as working Earthside at one atmosphere pressure, in shirtsleeves.

In addition, we took a midday break for lunch. We were both tempted to skip it, but I decided we needed to be properly nourished if we were to be at our peak performance. Skipping necessary activities in an attempt to rush things would probably slow us down in the end.

The result was that by the time we had all three framing clamps in place, it was mid-Martian afternoon, at our location. Did we have time actually to put any patches in place before sundown? I wanted to make sure a patch was well joined before the nighttime cold set in. Tests of this patching system had showed that if the adhesive we used had at least two hours of cure time at daylight temperatures, the bond would usually hold very firmly. But if the cure started at Martian nighttime temperatures, it would freeze up, and the patch would slough off easily.

I decided that we could probably fit *one* patch into place with a good margin of time before sundown. Which one? I decided on the L-shaped tear on cell 6 for a first try. Not too big, and it would make a good trial case to see if our techniques were working here as well as they had in the pre-mission tests. Or to see what corrections we needed to make, if anything *didn't* work.

We got another framing clamp ready. We had allowed generous spacing on the clamps we had put in place around the gashes, to allow room for what was going to happen shortly. But for this one, we made sure the frame rods were none too long.

Next, D.J. and I together unrolled a short length of plastic from a roll of patching material. This is not easy in space suits. Try handling your kitchen plastic wrap with thick gloves on, if you want a comparison. Thanks to our practice sessions on the Moon, we had the skill to do it. We measured off the length we wanted, then I held the plastic steady while D.J. scissored it off. I held the cut length again while she trimmed the width to the size we wanted.

Once we had our rectangle cut, and had secured the rest of the reel of plastic, D.J. held it flat to the table while I spread adhesive over one face of the rectangle with a paintbrush. Then I took the coated rectangle over to the ship while D.J. brought the framing clamp and a roll of adhesive tape.

In pre-mission preparations, someone had found an off-the-shelf brand of adhesive tape that worked perfectly well at low atmospheric pressure — even in vacuum. And did so in extremes of heat and cold. Our rolls were modified with a special large tab on the starter end that could be grasped easily with a space suit glove.

I was glad we'd put up the work table only a few steps away from gas cells six and seven. Carrying an adhesive coated sheet of plastic and making sure it doesn't come into contact with anything you *don't* want to stick it to is a good trick. Climbing the stepladder with my hands thus occupied was an even better one.

D.J. didn't have it much easier. She had to climb her ladder carrying the framing clamp, although she'd managed to hitch the roll of tape to a utility belt around her suit's waist.

Very carefully, I pressed the adhesive coated side of the patch to the gas cell skin around the L-shaped tear. I smoothed the patch carefully, making sure all lumps and bubbles were pressed out. Then I held it carefully to the skin as D.J. secured the edges of the patch with the transparent adhesive tape.

Once the patch was taped, D.J. and I reinforced that tape by affixing the framing clamp she had brought to those same edges, inside the boundary provided by the framing clamp that was already holding the gas cell skin in place. This was, if possible, even more awkward than placing the initial clamp, but between us, we managed to get the patch well secured in a clamp-within-clamp configuration. Between them, the inner clamp and the adhesive tape should hold the patch in place until the adhesive bonded.

The sun was just thirty degrees above the horizon by now. Just barely enough time before sunset for the two hours of daytime cure the adhesive would need. This would be all we could do until tomorrow. We secured our tools, supplies, ladders, and work bench against dust and wind gusts before we went inside for the night. This we did with covering cloths and tiedowns. We put back into the supply locker the items such as adhesive and tape that might be damaged by exposure to Martian nighttime temperatures.

A day's work in space suits had tired us both. The exercises I had done aboard the *Hesperia* on the voyage to Mars had kept up my endurance as well as strength, but still I was tired. I hardly noticed our brief supper. But tired as I was, I did notice the expression on Diana's face. I saw the drawn lines of exhaustion. Satisfaction, too, with what we had accomplished that day. She looked genuinely happy with herself. But very, very tired.

When we had cleaned up after our meal, I reached out my hands and placed them on her shoulders. My thought was to offer her encouragement. But when I touched her, I realized that her shoulders and back were even more tensed up from the day's work than mine.

We took turns massaging each other's shoulders, neck, and back, working out some of the tension. After about thirty or forty minutes of this, I began to relax, and I felt D.J. start to relax as well. The thought occurred to me to turn our shoulder massages into a petting session.

But when I began to caress D.J., she took my hand in hers and said, "Dear, sweet Jonathan...I'm just too tired."

That reinforced a decision I had already made. "We're going to have to pace ourselves," I told her. "Starting tomorrow, we take breaks at least every four hours. At lunchtime, if not before, we get out of our space suits and stretch."

We could afford to do that, because our space suits, unlike those of the old days, can be gotten into or out of in a matter of minutes, and do not require extensive "prebreathing" time with the small difference between cabin pressure and suit pressure.

But worry knit Diana's lovely brow. "But can we afford the delay? Will we be able to get all our repairs done in time to get back to the landing site before liftoff?"

"From our rate of progress already, we'll do it easily, with plenty of time to spare," I assured her, "*unless* we drop from exhaustion first. This is a marathon, not a sprint. If we want to win *this* race, we have to last long enough to cross the finish line."

Diana might have been lacking in energy that night, but not in affection. We'd been sitting next to each other while massaging each other's shoulders. She slid from her seat onto my lap and into my arms. She put her arms around my neck and shoulders, drawing me into a close, tight hug. Her lips met mine in a soft but very emphatic good-night kiss.

While it was night for us, daylight had started at the mission landing site. This was the morning the THOAT expedition was setting out for Kasei Vallis. Yes, they were concerned about us. Damn worried, in fact. Not only our fellow Mars explorers…all Earth was abuzz with the topic on the news channels, as we learned later. But there was absolutely nothing anyone on Mars *or* Earth could do to help us. And no point whatever in ceasing to carry out the other research and exploration activities that had been planned. Not after coming all the way to Mars.

So both THOATs started north: Terence Tarkhan and Teresa Sola in one, Carter Horace and Ruth Dean in the other. They also carried a few extra of Ruth's "little lion" robots that had been saved for this opportunity to set them loose at locations well away from our landing site.

The crew modules in place on the backs of the THOATs

can each easily provide space and life support for four people. If one THOAT breaks down, the other can get all four back to the landing site.

A much better situation than Diana and I were in.

The next morning, we were able to apply patches to both remaining gas cell tears. Because of the head start we had made with the framing clamps the previous afternoon, we were able to get the patches in place by mid-morning, about 1000 hours local Martian time.

I decided that this would be a good time to take a break. I wanted to check the cure on the first patch, but that could wait.

When we got inside and removed our space suits, Diana did not put her outer clothing back on. Rather, she remained in her underwear — bikini briefs and bra. Not that they made an unattractive outfit. Quite the reverse, especially with her figure. Perhaps *too* attractive…and that was the problem.

When I commented on her lack of clothing she responded, "What's the point? We'll have to get right back in our space suits. We have to see each other half dressed while we're changing into them anyway, and there's no one here but us to disturb."

('I'm disturbed enough for ten people'), I thought to myself. I tried to explain myself.

"The point is that the sight of you is so arousing," I told her. "You are so incredibly beautiful! A few minutes' glance at you while we're changing from clothes to space suits or back is one thing. But to look at your nearly bare figure constantly…it's very distracting!"

"I trust you to control yourself," she responded softly. "Surely you've seen women showing this much skin on the beach, back on Earth. You don't have difficulty controlling yourself on the beach, do you?"

"A public beach in crowds of strangers feels a lot different from being alone with the woman I want more than anyone else in the —" I almost finished the phrase automatically with the habitual word 'world'. Then I remembered where we were, hesitated, and substituted "— solar system. To be this close to you, and not be able to touch you...it's like torture!" I couldn't use the argument that women's underwear is usually less opaque than swimwear, because the styles she was wearing weren't sheer or lacy.

But she was right; she had me. I would control myself. I cared too much for her to betray her trust in me.

That set the pattern. From then on, when we took our breaks, D.J. did not put on her shorts and blouse when she removed her space suit, unless we were stopping work for the evening...and not always even then.

I could have used a commander's prerogative, and ordered her to dress when not in a space suit. But I had had enough experience as a commanding officer to judge when it is wise to press an issue and when it is not. We were isolated, alone, and confined in a small cabin, which we could leave only while wearing space suits. As much as we loved each other, normally petty issues could become irritants. I judged that throwing my authority around on this issue would be an irritant we didn't need. My arousal could be an irritant, too, but I decided I could handle it.

Rather than having a noontime lunch, I decided we should take a short snack now, during this break, then get back to work, and possibly take another break and snack early in the afternoon.

As soon as we returned outside, around 1100 hours, I inspected the cure on that first patch we had made the day before. It was looking good; I was confident it would hold pressure. We'd have to test that once all three patches had cured sufficiently. But for now, we could remove the framing clamps that surrounded it.

We made one more check around the ship for any additional damage that required repair. But our assessment was the same as before. Except for the gas cell leaks, the ship had sustained only nicks, scrapes, and abrasions that were very unlikely to develop into cracks. This meant we could begin putting away most of our tools and equipment.

I called an afternoon break partway through this, about

1430 hours, and we had our second snack of the day. Before evening, we had all the tools away except for a few items we might need to release the framing clamps from the two remaining patches, and the stepladders we needed to reach them.

The following morning, the remaining two patches were far enough along in their cures for D.J. and me to remove the framing clamps securing them. I estimated that in a few more hours, the adhesive on all the patches would be cured well enough to test them by attempting to inflate those gas cells and put some pressure on them.

At about 1600 hours, local Martian time, after a careful visual inspection of all three patches, I decided it was time for an inflation test.

I first set the ballonet volume so that total possible lift was less than our gross weight. The object was not to fly the *Coprates* yet, just to determine whether the gas cells would hold pressure. Then I very carefully began to let gas from the storage tanks back into the cells. I put the undamaged cells, numbers one, two, three, four, five, and eight, back up to full pressure. Then I started to fill cells six and seven, slowly...carefully...with D.J. helping watch for any sign of pressure loss or leak.

I got both cells filled to a pressure just above the outside atmosphere. I stopped filling, and D.J. and I both watched the pressure reading carefully for several minutes. It held, and showed no signs of dropping.

There was still one more test I wanted to make. D.J. and I put our space suits on. When we went outside, we took with us a hydrogen leak detector as well as one of the stepladders. The instrument is designed specifically to detect any significant source of hydrogen molecules. It looks vaguely like an old-style tank vacuum cleaner, since it has a hose connecting a gas-inhaling and instrument-bearing "head" to the "body" that contains a pump, vacuum chamber, most of the electronics, and the power source.

First we took readings of the open air, and adjacent to areas of the *Coprates'* envelope well away from the patches. That was to calibrate the instrument and find the background reading for hydrogen. Then I clambered up a stepladder. D.J. held the body of the leak detector and handed the head end of the hose to me. Once I was in place, she switched on the power.

I played the head of the detector all around the three patches we had put into place. If there had been a leak, the detector should have broadcast a sonic alarm which my suit radio would have picked up. Not a sound. I called down to D.J., "Any sign of hydrogen on the instrument panel?"

"Not a bit above background," came her clear answer. Even in this situation, concentrating on a task that could literally mean life or death to us, I was aware how pleasant and melodic Diana's voice was. Yet that awareness did not distract my concentration. Rather, in some way I cannot account for, it seemed to make focusing my mind easier.

— CHAPTER ELEVEN —

I THOUGHT WE WERE HOME FREE. But we'd left something out. D.J. called my attention to it after we'd returned back inside the cabin and gotten our space suits off.

"Take a look at this," she told me. She was beckoning me as she spoke, waving me to look at the instrument panel she was facing. She was looking at the readouts for our compressed hydrogen reserves.

She turned toward me with an extremely worried expression on her face. I could understand why, because I could read the display over her shoulder, from where I stood. The same worry was in her voice, when she spoke. "We don't have enough hydrogen left to lift us!"

I wondered if my face was as grim as I felt at that moment. We had been so caught up in the effort to fix the tears in the cells that we had not stopped to ask ourselves: then what? We had not carefully calculated the lifting gas reserves we had left. Now that we had, D.J. and I could see that even if we used the entire amount of the remaining hydrogen, there would not be quite enough to lift the weight of the *Coprates*. I was quite annoyed at myself for having failed to check what should have been obvious.

In a few minutes, the initial shock of the discovery had worn off, and I was beginning to think of possible courses of action, trying to find some solution to this difficulty. "Maybe we could jettison some things, and lighten our load enough to lift."

I had been speaking half to myself, but Diana caught my meaning, and nodded. "We may find a way out of this yet," she said. She had turned to me when she said it. She stepped into my arms and put hers around my neck and rested her head against my chest. There was nothing wrong with her courage, and her characteristic optimism had not evaporated. But she'd had a very rough shock, and she wasn't afraid to acknowledge that she needed comfort. And I think she sensed that so did I. "We'd better contact Captain Kent," she reminded me, and let him know the situation."

It was about 1700 hours, local Mars time. I checked the orbital positions of the *Hesperia*, the *Xanthe*, and the two satellites. According to the computer model, in another 30 minutes or so, *Xanthe* would be in a position to receive a message from us and relay it to one of the satellites. That satellite could store the message and get it to Redsand Landing within another half hour. It looked like our quickest link.

I began recording a message to Captain Kent. "The good news is that we've got our holes patched and sealed. The bad news is...."

While we waited to transmit our message with routing instructions up to the *Xanthe*, D.J. and I began to clean up and get ready for supper. After we transmitted, we continued. Neither of us was greatly enthusiastic about food; we were acting out of habit and sense of duty — almost on automatic pilot. Our food choices were probably reflecting our state of mind: plain, easy to prepare, and not especially flavorful. Crackers, bread, and beans.

We got a reply to our message only forty-five minutes after we sent it — before we actually sat down to eat. Just fifteen minutes after Captain Kent received our message, at 1816 hours our time, the two satellites and *Hesperia* were in one of those occasional orbital position arrangements that allowed a real-time relay. It would last for just ten minutes.

Kent's face looked as grim as I probably had earlier that evening. "Take an inventory of what you can jettison," he told us. "Find out if you can lighten the ship enough to fly. Keep me posted."

I decided he needed a little cheering up. "You sound as though we're goners. I thought you were Captain *Can*. We are still alive, and I intend to make every effort to stay that way. Don't count us out yet."

Kent's unhappy expression softened, and then he smiled. It was a faint smile, but it was a smile. "I see you haven't lost your courage or your confidence. If anyone can make it, I expect the pair of you can."

"My confidence has been shaken," I admitted, "but not obliterated."

"I'll be hoping for you — and praying," Kent added. "We all will. Kent out."

D.J. and I ate supper with little spirit. Neither of us had very much appetite, and in spite of what I had just said to Captain Kent, I was feeling somewhat down. Judging by what I could see on D.J.'s face, so was she. Neither of us spoke much. But we did reach hands across the table from time to time, and clasp them in an effort to lend each other emotional strength.

As we ate, my mind was already working on the problem of how to get the ship to lift, going over what we might jettison, and what I knew of Mars' winds and weather patterns, trying to think if there were any tricks of aviation or atmospheric physics that might help. While I was thinking about that, it crossed my mind that the news media back on Earth would have a field day, with this latest chapter in our cliffhanger.

Once we'd cleaned up after supper, I concentrated fully on the problem. D.J. was doing the same, seated at a computer console, looking at lists of ship's stores and equipment. I was seated at my pilot's chair, not using the instruments, just as a place to be while I went over in my mind what items we might leave behind.

Our accumulated waste was the first thing that came to mind. It made good policy not jettison it until we have thoroughly examined Mars for native life, present or past. But our present situation was clearly an emergency, and we had containers on board that could be sealed very well. With the tools we had, we could bury them to reduce the change of having them breached by a local meteorite impact.

Tools. My mind went over what we had on board, evaluating which ones we had to have, which ones we would not need again, and which ones we might take a chance on.

Scientific data and samples? I shook my head. D.J. glanced up at me, no doubt wondering what was on my mind to evoke the gesture. We'd taken too much trouble to gather them. They were the purpose for this entire flight. I would leave them behind only as a very last resort.

Scientific *instruments*. Now *there* were some possibilities! Some of them we would surely not need again, if we got the chance to run for base. We had one sensor station left, for instance. Before our crash I had planned, at Diana's request, to place it a bit closer to Elysium Mons. But we could emplace it right here. Not a perfect location, but it would be adequate. And adequate would have to do, under the circumstances.

What other scientific equipment? The Propellant Production Test Unit?

The PPTU.

"I just had a thought," I told D.J. "We use the TwoPeeToo! Check the local soil. Previous orbital surveys indicated some hydrated minerals in this general area, but I understand it isn't clear at what concentrations. If local material has enough water of hydration, we use the Unit to generate hydrogen. If not, we run atmosphere through it and generate carbon monoxide. That won't give us as much lift as hydrogen, but it's still less dense than CO_2. Combined with the hydrogen that we still have left, it should be enough to lift *Coprates*."

I stood up and took a step toward Diana as I continued, "I estimate from the production rate of the Unit that we'll be able to reinflate and get back to the landing site in time for liftoff for the return to Earth. If we have to use CO, we'll probably have to jettison some equipment and supplies. If we can generate hydrogen, we won't have to jettison anything!"

D.J.'s eyes were lighting up. "Jonathan, I think you're on to something." She was punching keys on her console in calculator mode, checking my estimate. "You're right, it'll work!" she confirmed as she turned back toward me, joy on her face. "Jonathan, you're brilliant!"

In the next instant, she threw herself into my embrace,

flung her arms around me, and pressed her lips to mine in an enthusiastic kiss. The reserve she'd forced upon herself and me to keep our passions from overwhelming us had evaporated.

As she drew back from the kiss, the expression in her eyes grew softer. The joy, the enthusiasm from knowing we could solve our problem and had a chance to live were still there in full measure, but something tender had been added.

"Let me do this right," she told me. She approached me again, this time more slowly. Her arms stole softly around me. When our lips met again, hers parted, and I felt the sweet pleasure of her tongue stroking gently deep into my mouth, as Diana gave herself wholeheartedly to the kiss. I responded by drawing her closer into my arms. Instead of resisting, she tightened her own embrace.

After a few moments that seemed like a sweet eternity, we drew back from the kiss, but not from the embrace. Diana was looking deep into my eyes. She began, "I made a big mistake not marrying you before we started. We've both missed out on all the time we could have had together. I was a fool not to trust my feelings then. And since we've been out on this airborne excursion, I've been trying to deny them, to keep them under control, instead of cultivating them as you've been trying to do." D.J. drew a breath. "Can you forgive me for my foolishness? And for all the frustration I've caused you?"

I returned her gaze. "Yes, I can forgive you. Making sure of your feelings is not foolishness. I just happened to be certain of mine before you were of yours. In the real universe of real people, people's feelings aren't always in perfect synchrony the way they might be in a romance novel. As for mistakes, this one can be corrected. We can have Captain Kent perform a wedding ceremony for us as soon as we get back to the landing site."

D.J. lifted her right hand from my shoulder to caress my face. "A good idea," she said, "but I've got a better one. We can have him perform the ceremony by radio as soon as we can raise him." She glanced over at the chronometer reading on the instrument panel. That readout on the *Coprates* panel has one extra feature that our deepspace craft and landers do not. In addition to Earth Universal Time, it has *two* Martian time readouts. One is set to the time at the landing site. The other tracks the local time for whatever longitude the *Coprates* happens to be sitting on at the moment. *Coprates'* inertial navigation system is supposed to update the second readout automatically, although I had been double checking regularly during our trip.

D.J. was looking at the reading for the landing site time zone as well as our local time. "It's just about 2000 hours here. Their work day should be getting started about now," she affirmed. "According to the orbital position data, *Xanthe*, one of the satellites, and *Hesperia* should be in position for a half-hour's worth of real-time relay starting a little more than an hour from now. We can do a store-and-forward that can reach him in fifteen minutes, to alert him to be ready."

She looked back to me and held me tighter. "I don't want to make you wait any longer," she told me. "The truth is...I don't want to wait any longer myself. I want you with everything I've got."

I was in much better spirits as I began recording another message to Kent S. Kent. "We'll be on our way home shortly, but you've got a job to do first. We've found a way, I think, to generate a new supply of lift gas." I described my idea to use the PPTU, inviting him to make any comments or suggestions he thought might be helpful. But I asked him to send those suggestions later, informing him of Diana's and my desire to be married. I ended with, "Be sure not to make the ceremony too lengthy. We will only have twenty minutes of connection time."

When we got the real-time connection, a few minutes past 2100 hours, our screen showed not only the crew at the landing site, aboard the *Phobos*, but on a split-screen relay, Terence Tarkhan, Teresa Sola, Carter Horace, and Ruth Dean. Captain Kent had managed to work a real-time relay via the second unmanned satellite to the THOATs, and Terence, Teresa, Carter, and Ruth had made it clear they didn't want to miss the ceremony. Neither Diana nor I were completely surprised. We had all become very close on this mission. That emotional intimacy sometimes had its problems, such as Fay Adair's infatuation with me. But despite the difficulties, we all felt a connection with one another.

D.J. and I both noticed Fay standing next to Xavier Buthelezi, one of her hands in his. We glanced at each other, and gave each other the faintest of smiles and nods. Our captain might have another wedding to perform, before too long.

"This ceremony is also going live to Earth," Kent informed us. "It seemed appropriate for the first Martian wedding in history. Terence Tarkhan will be your best man, Jonathan."

He worked the controls of his screen reader to access the computer file that stored a wedding ceremony, and began.

— CHAPTER TWELVE —

I woke to the feel of long, soft, black hair nestled against my chest. The subtle, pleasing scent of it permeated my nostrils. My eyes opened to the sight of satin-smooth red-brown skin, and I became aware of the woman in my arms, and of her arms around me.

I must have stirred slightly, because Diana seemed to come awake herself just then. She lifted her head and looked into my eyes. A smile of pure joy spread across her face. "Good morning!" she greeted me, and added, "It was certainly a wonderful night! More wonderful than I had imagined it could be!"

('More wonderful than *I* had expected, as well'), I thought. "I had not realized you would be so passionate, Princess," I told her. I had begun calling Diana that the night before as a pet name, and she was pleased with it.

"Nor I that you would be," she responded softly, "or that at the same time you could be so gentle!" With that, she tightened her embrace enthusiastically, and pressed the firm, perfect shape of her bare breast even more snugly against my chest.

I felt my arousal beginning to stir. "Oh, good!" was her response. She gently kissed my bare chest and heard me breathe an involuntary "aah!" of pleasure. "I want you!" she whispered. "Let me be your princess again!"

"I have a feeling I'm going to be late for work today!" I murmured. D.J. gave a joyous laugh at that, and then her mouth found mine.

Generating hydrogen for the *Coprates* with the PPTU wasn't *quite* as easy as we had supposed. The first major obstacle was that the outlet coupling from the Test Unit had a significantly smaller diameter than the couplings on the hoses used to fill the *Coprates'* hydrogen tanks. The two systems had never been intended to interface.

It was D.J. who figured an answer to that. "How about this?"

she asked, after we'd been puzzling over the problem for a few hours. She had disconnected the hose from the hydrogen leak detector. That hose, by happy chance, was just the same diameter as the tank fill hoses. Those two systems had not been designed to interface, either, but the designers had happened to select the same hose size, out of the range of standard sizes available.

That wasn't all D.J. was grinning about. She was disconnecting the instrument head from the hose, and while doing so, tapping her finger on the end of it as she did so. That action reminded me of a fact that had slipped my mind. Where the leak detector's hose met the head, it had an adapter that necked down to the same diameter as the outlet coupling on the PPTU!

"We'll make an engineer of you yet!" I told her.

D.J. cocked her head, her grin still wide. "You'd be surprised how much attention I can pay to detail when my life is on the line!"

The next question was…how much hydrogen content would the local soil provide? D.J. provided that answer, too, by running a few samples through the Test Unit. "The soil in our immediate vicinity has a high water of hydration content," she told me after running the first five or six samples. "This area is practically a swamp by Mars standards! We'll be able to get all the hydrogen we want."

Once we started hydrogen extraction, we still weren't out of difficulties. At the output rate of the PPTU, it was going to take days weeks to produce enough hydrogen to fill the reserve tanks to capacity. We were still in danger as we waited. And getting batches of soil and loading them into the Unit, then disposing of the leftover after the hydrogen was extracted, was a tedious procedure.

It could have been boring. But D.J. and I were still in awe of this new world. D.J. took advantage of the waits while batches of soil were processing in the PPTU to gather and analyze air and soil samples. She took me with her on her short walks and taught me what to look for. We all had some geology training while preparing for the mission, but now D.J. had time to take me beyond the rudiments. Back at the ship, she also showed me how to do the analyses.

Even though we were stuck within walking distance of one place, we didn't mind the scenery. The planet was still new to us, and beautiful in our eyes. Rather than being bored, we had a sense of growing at home on this world.

Nor did I mind learning from D.J. The new knowledge and skills were rather fun. More than that, I simply relished the opportunity to be with this lovely, brilliant woman. For we two were definitely not bored with each other. We made a treasure of the wait by making it our honeymoon.

D.J. put it very well. "I've learned from this experience how uncertain and how precious life really is. I won't waste opportunities for rejoicing again."

We conversed with each other on our field trips, in the lab, while waiting for the PPTU to complete a run, over supper, getting to know each other more intimately by sharing our childhood experiences, hopes, and dreams. We had begun this sort of personal exploration back on Earth, when I had started courting D.J. during mission training and preparation. We had continued on this flight, before the crash. Now we were taking things further, discovering even more of each other's hopes and dreams and memories.

At night, we would often step out of the cabin in our space suits to watch the light of the Martian moons. And we made sure we took plenty of time for loving. D.J. had her own thoughts on that, too. "I waited too long for you, and we don't know how much time life will give us. So I don't intend to miss the chance to be with you now."

Also, most evenings, we would make radio contact with Redsand Landing One. Live sometimes, other evenings by relay. We'd keep Captain Kent up to date on our progress, and keep up with activity and new findings they were making at the base. And check up on how the THOAT expedition was going on.

The members of that expedition decided not to go beyond Kasei Valles. We understood why not when they sent an image to base that Kent Squared relayed to us.

Diana let out her breath in a soft whistle when she caught sight of their camera's view of the interior of Kasei Valles. "Would you look at those erosional features? That valley was cut by water...I'd bet half the pay I'll have coming for this mission!"

That idea wasn't new. Already from orbital images, Kasei had been suspected of being formed by flowing water. But closer inspection, from the ground, was making the hypothesis a lot stronger.

The four of them on the THOATs decided it was so interesting to study the Kasei Valles system as a possible ancient watercourse that they would spend all the available time before they headed back to base on that, and not go on to Tharsis Tholis or Ascraeus Mons. One of the advantages of having people on the spot, able to decide on new courses of action in real time.

Once the THOAT expedition member got to poking around, they found some honest-to-goodness sedimentary rocks. Terence Tarkhan located a sandstone formation, and Ruth Dean dug some rock samples from what had once been a bank that looked very much like mudstones.

— CHAPTER THIRTEEN —

THE DAY CAME WHEN the *Coprates* was ready to lift into the sky once more. We'd called Kent Squared the night before, to let him know we were almost ready. Now, I switched our outside and inside cameras and microphones on "record". We would flash our recordings to one of the satellites, as soon as it was above our horizon, for a "store and forward". That way, whatever our fate, our crewmates and the people back on Earth would at least have a record of what happened to us.

The THOAT expedition was already back at Redsand Landing One. They'd returned from Kasei several days before.

Captain Kent had told us in the previous evening's conversation that our cliff-hanging adventure was still getting lots of coverage on news broadcasts back on Earth. The entire Mars expedition got coverage, but the human interest of a downed airship and two stranded crew members tended to get more air time than new scientific discoveries. I might wish it were otherwise, but even the long exploration expedition with the THOATs seemed tame by comparison to the newscasters. As impressive as that trip was to me, the THOATs never got more than several hundred kilometers from the landing site, not halfway around the planet! I suppose the sheer distance impressed some newspeople. And perhaps the idea that D.J. and I might die in our dangerous, isolated circumstance.

I hoped our return to base, if we were successful, would not disappoint them. Perhaps a few newspeople secretly hoped for a disaster that might earn them bigger headlines or a feature story. But "Captain Can" had informed us of reports of prayer vigils on our behalf. I had a feeling that those on Earth who wished us well far outnumbered any few who might feel otherwise. I was glad for any prayers, because *I* still intended to bring us back alive.

Now was a repeat of the start of our aerial trip. "Motor four on," D.J. read to me.

"Confirmed," I agreed.

"Propellers to vertical," came her next words.

"Check."

"Ready for liftoff," D.J. told me.

I took *Coprates* into the air and headed her east. From our present position, it would be slightly shorter to continue east and complete the circumnavigation of the Martian globe. We'd have to pass to the north to avoid the high terrain around Olympus Mons and the Tharsis region, but the distance would be less than returning west. And there was another consideration. From the satellite weather charts, it looked like there was less blowing dust on the eastward route. D.J. and I had had all the dust storms we wanted for a while.

Although I did not attempt to fly the *Coprates* up the slopes of Olympus Mons, I did get close enough for our cameras to get some impressive shots of the mighty cliffs that circled its base. I was in awe of the huge mountain, so broad that its top, nearly three hundred kilometers away, would have been beyond our horizon because of the curvature of the planet, were it not for its immense height. It would still have been beyond our horizon, but for our own flight altitude.

Diana did not try to put her emotions at the sight into words, but I felt her grip tighten as she placed a hand over mine.

Likewise breathtaking was flying over the face of Mars by moonlight. After a lot of discussion, Diana and I had decided that it was important to reach the landing site as soon as possible. One reason was to make sure of getting back before the launch date for the return flight to Earth. At *Coprates'* cruising speed, we had a comfortable margin of time to work with, and we wanted to keep it that way. There were still spotty dust storms blowing, even on this route back, and who could know if one might force us to land and wait several days on the ground before resuming flight? If we got back with time to spare, there was plenty of exciting work and research we could contribute to while waiting for the launch window. But if we missed the launch window, the rest of the crew could not wait for us. The planets wait for no one. You fly when they are aligned for the transfer trajectory, or you do not fly.

Another reason was that we did not wish to risk another mishap far from the landing site. We felt that would be pushing our luck.

Choosing to return rapidly meant using as much flying time as we could, allowing for rest stops to keep us refreshed and alert. So we decided to try night flying. We hoped that moonlight from Phobos, combined with *Coprates'* own lights, would give us clear enough vision to fly by.

It did. The first evening of our return, Phobos was already above the horizon when sunset came. Darkness came swiftly, as it normally does on Mars. The Martian atmosphere is so thin that twilight scarcely lasts any time at all. But we kept flying, and our eyes adjusted quickly and beheld the wonder of the ruddy landscape below us bathed in the soft glow from Phobos. Not as bright as full moonlight on Earth, but plenty to see by and fly safely.

That became our newest rule of operation. If Phobos was above the horizon at sunset, we would continue flying as long as it remained so. If we were flying when it went through its nightly eclipse, we reduced speed to one-third normal cruising speed, but remained in the air.

Flying was not the only use we made of moonlight. More than once, when Phobos was not up at sunset and we had to land, Diana would wait until it rose. She would switch off the cabin lights and approach me, wearing only her bikini style undergarments. The faint Phobos light reflected into the cabin by the ruddy Martian surface seemed to bathe her smooth, likewise ruddy skin.

I would usually be more than ready, because she had taken to the habit of wearing only the undergarments during the day, while we were flying, as she had while we were repairing the ship. It wouldn't have mattered much if she had worn clothing that completely concealed her figure, though. Any time she approached me, her presence could make me ready.

Diana and I both sought every opportunity we could for making love. We did not let a night go by on this trip back apart from each other's arms. And once or twice when we stopped for rest breaks during the day, we made time for a "quickie". We were very much in love with each other, and as we cheerfully confessed, very much in lust with each other as well. We wanted to make up for all the lost time when we had not been together. And we wished to take every advantage of the privacy that was now ours, but shortly would no longer be, once we were back at the landing site among the rest of the crew.

The third night, before Phobos was up, and before we had begun making love, we received a "store and forward" message via one of the satellites.

It was Teresa Sola's voice. She was so excited she could hardly she could hardly contain herself. "I took a look at a fragment of one of the mudstone samples Ruth Dean collected at Kasei Valles through a microscope! I am certain I saw microfossils! These are much larger than any fossils claimed for any Martian meteorites! Those are all still in dispute! These are more nearly the size of bacterial cells, or perhaps algae cells!"

Privately, I made a bet with myself that what Teresa had seen would *still* be disputed, at least until biologists and paleontologists back on Earth had a chance to look at those samples themselves. And maybe they'd still be disputed after that. But I made another bet with myself that the dispute would eventually be resolved in favor of fossils. Teresa Sola is not prone to make claims without very strong evidence. If she *was* right, it would certainly make history.

On the fourth morning after our liftoff from Elysium, the *Coprates* came over the horizon at Redsand Landing One. D.J. and I heard sounds of cheering from the radio speakers.

"Welcome back!" came Kent S. Kent's voice over the cheers. His image was on our monitor. "You understand, of course, that you are on camera, and that the feed is going straight to Earth."

"I'm not surprised," I told him. "This is a piece of history. I guess I wasn't hoping for *this* much attention on our arrival."

Then Kent switched the image he was sending from his face to one of the cameras trained on us. Suddenly I no longer minded the attention. We saw *Coprates* from a point of view we could not get while aboard her. A very impressive point of view. I hadn't been able to see her this way since the two of us had started our great aerial exploration trip. I heard myself speaking my thoughts aloud. "She really is a grand ship...even if she does have a patch or two on her now!"

You couldn't see the patches on the monitor, of course, because the cameras could only pick up the forward sections of the ship during our approach.

D.J. wasn't wearing just underwear today. We were back "in public". But from my point of view, her figure was still plenty devastating in blouse and shorts.

I decided that if the Earth viewing public wanted something worth seeing, she certainly qualified. I aimed our inboard camera to the center of the cabin, telling Captain Kent, "Maybe the people back on Earth would like to see a returning heroine!" I slipped my right arm around D.J.'s waist and drew her to the spot where the camera would have the best view.

D.J. glanced my way out of the corner of her eye, an impish grin beginning to play on her face. Before I realized what idea might be running through her mind, she surprised me by turning her body full to mine. Then, before I quite realized what was happening, she slid her arms around my neck, drew my face down to hers, and met my lips with a meltdown-level kiss.

In the days before we lifted off for the trip back, we carefully disassembled and deflated the *Coprates*, carefully folding the gas envelope. We put the components back in their packing boxes, which we had saved in a protected spot.

No, we weren't going to take *Coprates* back to Earth with us. We couldn't afford the mass on the return trip. We left the components in their boxes beside the beacon pyramid...for the next expedition to Mars. Even with her patches, she will be in flyable condition if reassembled, and we can expect her to remain so in the Martian environment for several years.

We will leave the THOATs parked alongside those boxes just before we depart, dust covers placed over critical components. They, too, will be left for the next expedition.

There was no difficulty rearranging crew assignments for the return flight. Fay Adair wished very much to return to Earth aboard the *Xanthe* with Xavier Buthelezi and make room on the *Hesperia* for Diana to fly back with me, for by this time Fay and Xavier were newlyweds themselves. They'd been married three days after D.J. and I had landed the *Coprates* back at Redsand Landing One. There had been enough cross training in crew skills by now that the shift meant no compromise in shipboard safety or operational capability.

We were two days out from Mars. We'd boosted out of orbit fifty hours before. Diana and I had undressed for our sleep shift, but we weren't ready to sleep yet. Diana nestled snug in my arms, her bare back warm against my chest, her dark mane of hair fragrant in my nostrils, and the two of us were gazing out our cabin viewport. Though we had turned out the lights in our quarters, the cabin was still very well lit by the light reflected in from Mars.

The Red Planet still showed a disk larger and much brighter than the full Moon seen from Earth. At this point in our Earth-bound trajectory, it showed a gibbous phase. Near the terminator we could make out the Argyre basin and Margaritifer Sinus. Further east, we could see Sinus Meridiani. And near the limb, Syrtis Major, and south of it the gigantic Hellas basin.

We could also see the sparks of light from Phobos and Deimos.

Both of us drank in the sight. Three months on Mars' surface had not drained us of enthusiasm. We were still filled with awe and wonder at this new world we'd touched, and we still thought it beautiful to behold.

Diana took my left hand in hers and placed it against her body to indicate that she wanted to be caressed. As I began, I heard a soft exhale of pleasure. Shortly Diana began to move against me.

"I want to make love in this light!" she whispered. "I want to savor this!"

"Gladly, Princess!" I murmured. I wanted to savor it, too.

As I caressed Diana, she asked, "Jonathan, do you suppose you and I will have the chance to return to Mars? There will almost certainly be more flights, but will we personally have another opportunity?"

I tightened my arms around her as I replied, "I very much hope so!"

Armor in Aristoteles

THE SUN HAD BEEN LOW on the western horizon when we left our base southwest of Cold Harbor, driving southeast, and it was not long before we had entered night.

You have a lot of time to think, rolling across kilometer after kilometer of lunar terrain. Especially when someone else is driving. You hear the voices of your driver and the other troopers aboard, the soft hum of your vehicle's motor, and the clank of its caterpillar treads. With no air to carry sound, other machines, even the ones nearest, are silent to you…but with more than one hundred together, you can sense the vibrations carried through the ground.

My thoughts drifted to what had brought this about.

The Caspian Islamic Union had started out well enough. First as a trade association between Syria, Iraq, Iran, Afghanistan, and Turkmenistan. A few years later, the trade alliance had become a loose political confederation. Economic and political ties had grown closer until, within a decade of its founding, the CIU was a unified nation in both practical and legal terms.

A prosperous and happy nation, at first. But unification of five nations, with Sunni Islam in the majority in some, Shiite in others, different political parties and their leaders each wanting a share of the pie, different populations wanting to focus on different problems, did not come without friction and some ruffled feathers. The rest of the world figured it was just growing pains, and that the people of the CIU would work their way through their problems. Not many years after the treaty of unification was finalized, some political unrest began, with legislators from Syria complaining that too much attention was being paid to the concerns of Iran and not enough to theirs. Civic leaders from Afghanistan began to quarrel with neighbors just across the border in Turkmenistan.

A new political party came to power by promising to settle the quarrels and satisfy the demands of each side. They spoke well, and their program sounded good. Too late, the quarreling parties discovered that the Blue Crescent had double dealt them by making conflicting back room promises to both sides. Too late, voters realized that the new party's method of "settling quarrels" and "bringing peace" was to forcibly suppress anyone who opposed them – even murdering key members of opposition parties. By the time people fully woke up to what was happening, the Blue Crescent was firmly in power, with a secret police and military establishment in place meant to keep them there.

We were in night, but not in darkness. About thirty degrees above the horizon at our right hand, at about our two o'clock direction, a waxing Earth stood nearly half full in the black sky, so bright that it washed out the dimmer stars, casting plenty of light to see by. We rarely needed headlights; shadows broad enough to require them are uncommon on a mare surface. So we used lights only when absolutely necessary, mostly when crossing occasional small craters. The few boulders we encountered we could easily route around, rather than show lights. We did not wish to be easily seen.

The Earthlight was not only dimmer but bluer than direct sunlight, reflecting from Earth's oceans. It lent a different mood to the scene than daylight. Shadows, though, cast by the rims of ever-present small craters and occasional boulders, were as inky black as by day.

If you're a bit vague about which of the several bases and settlements on the Moon Cold Harbor is, it's the one in northern Mare Frigoris. A reconnaissance satellite with a sounding radar located a lava tube that broke the surface a couple of dozen kilometers southwest of Timaeus Crater. Even better, the tube broke the surface at a slant: this wasn't just a "skylight", people could walk or drive right down to the lava tube floor. They had to pick their way around boulders and blocks of basaltic lava that had fallen from the tube's roof until those had been cleared away, but they could do it. Cranes and hoists weren't needed to bring down material and equipment to build a base.

Such a prime location within reasonable transport range of the north polar water deposits was irresistible. By now, Cold Harbor is home to more than two thousand scientists, technicians, construction workers, miners, etc., including representatives of several Earth governments and at least three major and two minor commercial Earth-based corporations that I knew of. That's not counting local Cold Harbor businesses: stores, restaurants, bars, or the like. And it's still growing.

The Cold Harbor Hilton hosts at least three dozen tourists up from Earth every month...even when business is slow. Most times, the number is more than twice that. The low cost launch vehicles that cut the price per kilo to Earth orbit by almost two orders of magnitude and made lunar bases financially feasible mean that those tourists don't all have to be millionaires, either.

Cold Harbor has a nice trade going with Shoemaker Station at Gioja Crater. Shoemaker Station's population numbers only a couple of hundred, most of them employed by the Clementine Mining and Refining Association. On second thought, "employed" isn't exactly the right word. The Association is a cooperative, and the miners and other workers are more like partners. The Clementiners are currently working two ice cold-traps and have filed claims on half a dozen more. Cold Harbor provides Shoemaker Station with mining equipment and electronic components shipped up from Earth, and with cast basalt pipe and electric wiring manufactured at Cold Harbor. In turn, Shoemaker Station sends Cold Harbor water. Although a pipeline is being laid north from Cold Harbor and south from Shoemaker Station, the two ends haven't connected yet, and tanker trucks still have to cover the gap.

The LunEarth Power Corporation is using Cold Harbor as a base from which to construct the Criswell Collection Complex in the highlands north of Mare Frigoris. Their fleet of roving robots have processing equipment to convert lunar soil *in situ* into crude solar cells with concentrator reflectors, connected to microwave antennas.

Those cells are far less efficient than the ones now made in factories on Earth. But with those construction techniques, making them is extremely cheap. And with enough of them, they don't *have* to be efficient. By now, LunEarth Power has nearly a hundred square kilometers in place. I don't mean one hundred square kilometers solid of silicon solar cells. There are spaces between banks of cells and rectenna elements for vehicles or people to move, to allow for repair and maintenance. But there is a ten by ten kilometer area just about ready to go into business.

I've been told that within a matter of weeks, LunEarth Power expects to make its first test of beaming power to Joseph's Jumpoff, the Lunar Merchants' Association L1 staging base. Up to now, the L1 station has beamed power *to* Cold Harbor (as well as to several other lunar surface settlements), augmenting the nuclear reactor. If the tests work, the power trade can start to go both ways.

If the beaming tests to L1 work, the next step will be to attempt to beam power to Earth. The plan is eventually to use geosynchronous relay satellites, but the GEO relays aren't in place yet, so early tests will be directly to Earth's surface, to clients who have volunteered to be initial customers.

Two armored battalions: the 125th tank battalion on the right flank, the 76th mechanized infantry battalion on the left. The tanks traveling in echelon right formation, the infantry in echelon left; together making an "arrowhead" spread out across a dozen kilometers or so. That formation gave us our best chance to avoid being flanked, and the easiest position from which to redeploy to meet an encounter from any direction.

Behind the tanks and infantry, a platoon of combat engineers and Special Combined Battery Bravo of self-propelled artillery: one platoon of battlefield rockets and one of self-propelled howitzers. Behind the artillery we had extra personnel carriers with drivers and gunners only...in case we wound up taking prisoners we had to transport.

Ahead of the engineers, just behind the point of the arrowhead, was our headquarters formation: two armored personnel carriers equipped with comm gear, displays, and computers, with two tanks as escort.

The CIU government is as ruthless as Sadaam Hussein's had been in his time. And just as hungry for expansion and regional domination. The Blue Crescent leaders were not religious zealots, the way the Taliban, for instance, had once been. The head of the party was called Supreme Leader, but his attitude was far from those of the one-time religious leaders in Iran. He and his cronies were more like the Italian Fascists of the 1920's and 30's: old fashioned tyrants with a taste for power and a hunger for more.

So far, the CIU's neighbors in the region, with support from the United States and the UN, have been able to discourage them from any overt moves against adjacent nations, aside from a few border skirmishes.

What worried almost everyone outside the CIU were indications that the new government is attempting to develop nuclear weapons. The good news was that before the Blue Crescent came to power, the CIU had become a signatory to the Comprehensive Test Ban Treaty and other nuclear disarmament treaties. By virtue of those treaties, the CIU is subject to random checks by UN weapons inspectors.

The Blue Crescent deals with weapons inspectors in a much more subtle manner than Sadaam Hussein's government ever did. They raise objections when UN inspectors visit the CIU, but very mild ones. And they make no overt attempt to keep them out of the country or to interfere with their activities while they are in the CIU. The new government's approach is simply to try to be so clever at hiding their weapons development that it would not be discovered.

They are darn good at it. But the UN inspectors are good, too. They managed to get wind that secret nuclear activity was going on. They didn't find enough evidence to prove anything. Not even enough, under the treaties, to trigger more frequent or more intensive inspections. But the U.S. and NATO, acting on their hints, stepped up their intelligence efforts. They focused more satellite attention on the CIU and attempted to infiltrate agents and to recruit CIU citizens who might be less than happy with the Blue Crescent government.

Success had been mixed. Satellite reconnaissance didn't reveal much. Some U.S. and NATO agents have been arrested and imprisoned, a few have been executed, others have simply never been heard from again. The same fates occurred to many of their local CIU citizen-recruits – or worse. A number of CIU recruits not only lost their own lives; their families were killed or imprisoned.

But not all were caught. U.S. and NATO agents, and CIU locals, managed to cobble together a network and get some solid information. Nothing that would stand up in the World Court. But enough to keep the U.S., NATO, and the UN alert, and to start some wheels quietly rolling.

The most significant information gleaned by the intelligence network was that the CIU is definitely attempting to develop nuclear weapons. But before long, the agents reported a new important fact. The CIU was moving its nuclear weapons development to a location where they believed UN inspectors would never uncover them.

A formation like ours would normally be commanded by a colonel, or maybe a lieutenant colonel. But I was along as Executive Officer, not CO. Whatever actions we took would have enormous implications not only strategically, but politically, and we needed a commanding officer with as much seasoning and good judgement as we could get. Our lunar post commander, Brigadier General Malcolm "Mac" McCormick was in charge. Just between us, I was glad the load was on his shoulders instead of mine.

No one was surprised that the Blue Crescent government had a lunar base program. The CIU had already started a settlement at Lacus Somniorum in its early years of exuberant prosperity, before the Blue Crescent party came to power. It was natural for the Blue Crescent to continue it. It is an important propaganda feather in their cap. In this twenty-first century, spacefaring activity is a must for a nation wishing to be considered in the front rank in technological strength and sophistication.

Knowledgeable people began to worry when the new CIU government developed its own launchers and Earth-Moon ferries, and stopped buying space on commercial space transports. Having the rocket technology for Earth to orbit and space to space transports means that the CIU has the capability to build ballistic missiles. Officially, the CIU has no ballistic missiles. But then officially, the CIU has no nuclear weapons program, either. With rocket technology in hand, the CIU could put ballistic missiles together in the blink of an eye. So CIU has missiles – or very shortly could have. If they get nuclear weapons to put on them...it's scary.

Using their own vehicles to ferry people and freight also means that there is no possibility for anyone to inspect what the CIU sends to the Moon. They even stopped staging their flights through Joseph's Jumpoff. When the CIU has a Moon flight, they rendezvous in lunar orbit with a surface-to-orbit ferry sent up to meet them.

The intelligence agents began sending hints that the CIU was moving its nuclear weapon program to the Moon. By international treaty, their lunar base is just as subject to weapon inspection as CIU soil back on Earth. We thought at first they might be banking on the extra expense it costs to send weapon inspectors up to the Moon. That they were figuring that the UN wouldn't want to pay that cost very often, and would inspect their lunar facilities less frequently than their Earthbound ones.

Three hours after we'd left base, we were passing Archytas Crater on our left. Another two hours, and we were beside Protagoras.

By then, Earth was three or four degrees higher in the sky than when we'd left, on account of our change in lunar latitude, and most of Africa and much of Europe had rolled into sunlight. Of Africa, only the western bulge was still in darkness. It was night in America, too, but President Dryer would be up. Or if he was catnapping, it would be with orders to wake him as soon as any word came from us. He'd been notified as soon as this phase of the crisis had started. The Secretaries of Defense and State, the Joint Chiefs of Staff, and the heads of the major intelligence agencies were on also alert. Unless I missed my guess, they were all standing by in what President Dryer liked to call the Situation Room at the White House.

But then the intelligence agents began to send hints that the CIU was setting up another, secret base on the Moon in southeast Lacus Mortis, north of their Lacus Somniorum base. Lacus Mortis. Lake of Death. How ironically appropriate. Word is, there is no surface traffic between the two bases, to avoid leaving any tracks that might hint to weapons inspectors that a second base even exists. Anything the CIU wants taken to the Lacus Mortis base, they land directly at that base; anything they want brought back, they launch directly from there.

It was a good trick. The bases are close enough together that our space tracking networks wouldn't necessarily pick up that a landing at the Lacus Mortis base *wasn't* at the Lacus Somniorum base unless they were specifically looking for it.

With a little nudging from the U.S. and NATO intelligence communities, the space trackers started looking for it. Very quietly, without publicity. And found it. Sure enough, there *was* a second landing site. After a couple of landings, the tracking networks pinpointed the lunar longitude and latitude fairly precisely.

Things cranked into high gear from that point. Very quietly, a set of reconnaissance satellites were put into orbit around the Moon. Officially they were for scientific observations. Well, they do that, too. But some of their instruments were selected with an eye to monitoring the Lacus Mortis base – and any other unannounced bases the CIU might have put into place.

Far out ahead was G Troop, our armored cavalry. They were our scouts. They were spread out with a kilometer between each ultralight tank, two kilometers – just barely within each other's horizon – between the tanks at the end of each platoon. Three platoons plus the tanks carrying the troop commander and his second in command were stretched out in a line almost fifteen kilometers wide, casting back and forth in a zigzag search pattern between the highlands bounding Mare Frigoris north and south, like a pack of hounds casting about for a scent. Or in this case, for a sight. They were urgently seeking a CIU formation we knew was headed toward Cold Harbor. We hoped they could find the CIU vehicles, or cut their trail, before the CIU troops found us, or worse, slipped past us.

The cavalry were making twice the speed of the rest of us, but with their search pattern, they were not making forward progress at twice our rate. So far, they had seen no vehicles, and no tracks.

Neither had the rest of us, once we got more than thirty clicks from base, except now and then coming across the tracks of our own armored cavalry, from their crisscross search pattern, at a diagonal to our own path. This was virgin territory, unexplored. Well surveyed from orbit; we had good maps. But no surface expedition had happened to come this way.

General McCormick had ordered a video record made of the territory we were traveling through, from the time we had left base. He knew the cartographers and planetary scientists would want to know what things looked like from ground level.

NATO had finally become scared enough to act. In secret council, NATO authorized the U.S. to act as its agent on the Moon. A U.S. Army contingent had been present from the beginning at Cold Harbor. Partly to do research on equipment durability in the harsh vacuum, radiation, and dust environment on the Moon. Partly to oversee more general lunar research the Department of Defense was funding. And partly in a law enforcement capacity, along with a U.S. Deputy Marshal. Because while members of the research and commercial communities came from all over Earth, Cold Harbor had initially been established by U.S. citizens and was by international treaty the legal responsibility of the U.S. government.

The United States began a very rapid expansion of its Army presence. We were in an arms race. Could we build up enough strength, quickly enough, to support a UN arms inspection of the Lacus Mortis base if the CIU resisted, and to put it out of action if weapons work was indeed found? We had reports the CIU was putting soldiers and weapons of their own on the Moon while we were doing this, to protect their base and possibly to test the nuclear weapons they were developing.

The rapid increase of the Army's presence didn't occur without some friction. To start with, our needs displaced a lot of shipping. Every tank or armored personnel carrier shipped to the Moon meant a civilian vehicle that couldn't be. A kilogram of military supplies took up space where a kilogram of scientific instruments or merchandise could have been shipped. Every soldier transported took a berth that could have been occupied by a scientist, a construction worker, or a tourist. Cold Harbor is self sufficient for life support. They recycle their air and water and grow enough food to sustain the population. But what we were doing was going to slow down development and expansion.

Part of the problem could be alleviated by increasing the number of flights to the Moon. But there were only so many Lunar Transfer Vehicles in existence. Even if they were all booked solid for 100% of their available time, there was only so much cargo tonnage and only so many people they *could* carry from Earth orbit to the Moon in a given time. It would take time to build more ships. Spacelines would only invest in more ships if they expected a *sustained* increase in traffic. A military buildup did not look like that to them. And while part of the load could be carried on ships of the U.S. Aerospace Force, those added only modestly to the total shipping capacity.

The U.S. Aerospace Force ordered more ships of their own to be built, anticipating there would be other occasions when a "surge" in space transport would be required, but those, too, took time to construct.

Suddenly adding several hundred military personnel in close proximity to the Cold Harbor civilian community was another source of friction. Some of the civilians, especially some of the scientists, simply aren't comfortable with a military presence. A matter of temperament, I suspect. For a lot of those not comfortable, their discomfort was amplified by the fact that the number of soldiers was now comparable to the civilian population. Fewer, but of the same order.

"The hell of it is," General McCormick commented to me in one meeting, "We can't tell the civilians the real reason *why* we're suddenly building up. If we could, things would be a lot less tense around here. But if we do, we'll be letting the CIU know exactly what we are up to. They realize *something* is going on. Our military buildup is simply impossible to hide. I'm sure the CIU has intelligence agents trying to find out American and NATO plans, just as we have agents trying to keep track of their activities. Hell, they could have agents right here at Cold Harbor for all we know. There are scientists, traders, and workers there from all over the Earth. But there is a big difference between *suspecting* what we're doing and why, and *knowing*. I don't want to make their task easy by spreading all our cards on the table."

"We can't tell *every* civilian the real reasons for the sudden military expansion, Mac," I agreed. "But I could brief a few selected community leaders. If key people are convinced, maybe they can persuade their fellow workers, scientists, and citizens to accept us, even without knowing all the reasons why. Not by their words so much as their attitudes toward us. When I pick people to talk to, I don't plan to pay much attention to formal security clearances. I'll base my judgements on my observations of individuals' characters. For instance, are they dogmatically opposed to military presence on the Moon, or are they open minded enough to listen to facts? Do they have the judgement and understanding to grasp the danger the CIU weapons base pose both to other bases and settlements on the Moon and to future peace on Earth? Can they keep their mouths closed, and not blab the information?"

"I like your idea," McCormick responded. "I'll check it with General O'Connell." That was his CO back on Earth. "And thanks for taking on this job."

"You have enough problems," I told him. "I can take this load off you."

McCormick got the go-ahead from Earth. They agreed that community leaders had a genuine "need to know", and our job would be made a lot easier if they were kept up to date.

I picked people like John Stanton, Mayor of Cold Harbor, and two Town Council members, Miles Drake and Virginia Franklin. Thomas Edwards, LunEarth Power Vice President for Lunar Operations. Mike Mailen, President of Lunar Mine Workers Local # 2. Dr. Madeline DeVere, Director of Tombaugh Observatory.

It would also ease tensions if we provided our own quarters, and didn't overcrowd the available lodgings in Cold Harbor. There was another lava tube about six kilometers west southwest of the one where Cold Harbor had been founded. Much smaller, and with much less room for expansion; it only extended a short way before it was blocked by frozen lava where a flow from an ancient eruption had stopped. Which was why Cold Harbor was built where it is, not in this smaller tube. But it was plenty large enough for us to put in barracks, a mess hall, maintenance facilities, storage depots, and so forth. So that's where the bulk of our troops are quartered.

Not only community leaders, but most of the people at Cold Harbor warmed to our troops once they understood that the soldiers weren't there by their own choice. They'd been ordered to the Moon, just like me. And not all of them had been briefed about the reason for their presence, either.

Local merchants and bar owners didn't mind at all when soldiers came to town to have fun on payday. When we gave 'em passes, we cautioned them to stay out of fights. We didn't want our soldiers getting a reputation as troublemakers. We didn't get completely silly about it; if someone *else* started a fight, our troops were authorized to defend themselves – but they weren't to start any fights.

For the most part, our soldiers obeyed those orders. Well...there were a few cases when our troops got into scraps with some of the miners and construction workers in bars. It'd be hard to pin down who started those fights. And it seemed like our soldiers were *more* welcome after a few of those bashes, not less. When I chatted with a few bar owners after some of these in the process of paying damages, I found out that a lot of miners, construction workers, and other "outside" labor occupations liked to get into fights now and then as a way of blowing off steam. It's why a lot of the bars catering to that crowd outfitted themselves with drinking cups of break resistance plastic or ceramic, not glass, and with padded furniture and walls. When our soldiers proved willing to give as good as they got, the local workers felt they fit right in.

Unattached civilian women of Cold Harbor seemed pleased to find a whole new set of single men around. Some of our soldiers are married, but most are not. It wasn't that single civilian girls were necessarily enamored of uniforms. But with a much enlarged masculine contingent on hand, they suddenly had more choice.

Unattached civilian bachelors were not so pleased. We have some women among our soldiers. Some of our artillerists, tankers, and mechanized infantry. Quite a few among our clerks, maintenance personnel, and working in supply. Most of them, like most of our men, are single. And they got plenty of attention from the Cold Harbor men. But the U.S. Army is still an overwhelmingly masculine organization. The odds were in favor of the civilian Cold Harbor women, but not the men. So in that way, our presence was still a source of tension.

But the most important thing I figured we could do to make ourselves welcome was to make ourselves useful. Was shipping military vehicles slowing the shipment of construction equipment? I had our engineers fit 'dozer blades onto some of our tanks. Then I put those tanks at the disposal of civilian construction and mining outfits who had dirtmoving (they don't call it "earthmoving" here) equipment delayed on our account. Our crews would drive the 'dozer tanks...but at the direction of the civilian crews who would have been operating the delayed equipment.

I also introduced some of our soldiers and officers to civilians with mutual interests.

"Thanks for showing me around, Dr. DeVere," Specialist 5th Class Robertson was saying. "I've had an interest in astronomy for a long time. Part of the reason I enlisted was to get some electronics training. When I finish my enlistment, I'm hoping to find a technician position at an observatory somewhere. Maybe even go back to school and get an astronomy graduate degree." He had freckles and straw colored hair sticking up and sideways that sprang back to its own directions five minutes after every combing. His front teeth seemed a little too large for his mouth. He looked like the class nerd, and even younger than he was. He did not look like the bright, very efficient technician I knew him to be.

We were in pressurized portion of the dome of Tombaugh Observatory's 3-meter Schmidt camera. Madeline DeVere brushed back the white blaze in the midst of her black hair from her forehead with one hand. "I enjoy showing off our toys to a fellow astronomy enthusiast," she commented. Then she added, almost in passing, "We've got one bug in this thing we still haven't figured out, though." She waved her other hand toward the telescope. "The maximum slew rate we've been able to get out of this mount is way slower than the design specs. At least an order of magnitude slower. More like a factor of thirty."

One blond eyebrow went up behind Robertson's glasses. "I wouldn't think a slow slew rate would be a big problem on the Moon, given its slow rotation."

"*Tracking* a target isn't a problem," was Dr. DeVere's answer. "But *switching* from one target to another seems to take forever. Causes us a lot of 'dead time' we'd rather do without. There's nothing wrong with the motors or the drive gears. We've checked for dust getting into the drive, and we haven't found any. And so far, we haven't found anything wrong with the command software."

Now both of Robertson's eyebrows went up. "You know, that sounds an awful lot like a problem we were having with the mounts of our antimissile laser artillery, when the system was first issued. We were getting slew rates a lot slower than they should have been, like you're describing. Turned out to be a hardware-software interface problem. We found a solution by modifying the computers' operating systems."

He, looked at me, then at Dr. DeVere. "Sir...Doctor...maybe if some of our techs took a look at the telescope drive system – and its software – we could find out something. Doctor, your telescope drive is a completely different system from our laser mounts, so the problems might not turn out to have anything in common. But maybe, just maybe, we could spot something that could help."

Dr. DeVere brushed a hand through her hair again. "Colonel Devaine, Mr. Robertson, right now we're willing to entertain suggestions from just about anyone. If you can spare Specialist Robertson, Colonel, and any other soldiers with appropriate expertise, we'd be glad to have them take a look at our system."

I smiled slightly. "Specialist Robertson, you are hereby detailed to assist Dr. DeVere and the Tombaugh Observatory. As of now, you are a Specialist *Sixth* Class; you'll be in charge of the team we send over. Who else would you recommend including on your team?"

Robertson's freckled brown wrinkled in thought. "I'd like to have PFC Snyder. He's probably our best hardware man. And Spec Four Tompkins is maybe our best programmer. I may wish to request additional personnel, sir, after we've had a chance to assess the situation."

I nodded. Then I said, "If you manage to find a solution to the telescope drive problem, you and your team will all receive promotions."

"And Dr. DeVere," Robertson added, "I'd like access to all the schematics and manuals for your drive system."

Dr. DeVere responded, "Let's plan on you and your team meeting me and Mandy Morgan here tomorrow morning. She's my chief technical assistant. She will give you a complete rundown on our system, the symptoms we've observed, and what we've tried so far to solve the problem. Shall we say 0930 Universal Time?"

Then Dr. DeVere smiled warmly. "One more thing. You may be aware that different groups in the Cold Harbor community take turns sponsoring and organizing a fortnightly dance. Well, this coming Friday, it's our turn – we astronomers at the observatory. We'd love to have you and your friends attend, Will. We'd be glad to teach you some sixth-G dances that have been developed here." Then she added to me, "That invitation holds for any of your troops and officers who may be off duty, Colonel."

I bowed. "I thank you graciously, for all of us."

Our vehicles looked a bit odd, if you were used to their standard Earthbound counterparts. We had to make some serious modifications to fit lunar conditions. Not just because the hatches had to form airtight pressure seals, either. Most obvious, the main guns on our tank turrets are all displaced to the right, not on the turret centerline. Think about it. Can you imagine venting propellant gases into the crew compartment after firing our cannon? We can't just open ports to the outside as we could on Earth. Even opening the breech to load the cannon would expose the crew to vacuum. Yes, we all wear pressure suits, but we normally keep our helmets open until just before going into action.

Instead of American battle tanks, we were using European Union Arachnids. Trace their history to the British Scorpion family of vehicles. I can see eyebrows go up among military history and tactics buffs. I can hear them saying: "You mean your main combat vehicle is a *light* tank?"

Shipping may be less expensive than a couple of decades ago, but every kilogram sent to the Moon still costs...and ships' capacities are still weight limited. As it is, we've had to ship some of our vehicles only partly assembled, and finish assembly on the Moon. But the CIU faced the same limitations. Their lunar transport vehicles are no larger than ours, and our intelligence reports were that they were only sending light tanks and other low-weight armored vehicles to the Moon themselves. So if we did get into a scrap, it would be a battle – at least to first order – among equals.

So the guns had been moved to the right side of the turret. An airtight pressure bulkhead separates the crew compartment from the gun and up to three "ready rounds" of ammunition. The main ammunition storage was in a starboard compartment of the tank's main hull, again separated from the crew by a pressure bulkhead. Automatic machinery loads the cannon from the ready rounds for each shot, and moves ammunition from main storage to the ready round volume when the turret is properly aligned. The ammunition is untouched by human hands, and the pressurized crew compartment is never breached.

For the same reason, each tank's coaxial machine gun has been moved to the far *left* side of the turret, together with all its ammunition, and placed in another separate, airtight compartment away from the crew.

The superlight "Ferret" tanks the armored cavalry were using had had their main guns moved to the right sides of their turrets as well, for the same reason. Two tanks in each armored cavalry platoon are equipped with antitank missile launchers fitted alongside their turrets in addition to the main gun, but that's a standard option. And with the need to keep vehicles light, our self-propelled cannons are 105 mm howitzers, not the 155 mm's that are standard for U.S. self-propelled batteries on Earth, so we can use a lighter chassis.

Some people wonder that we still use tube artillery, in this day and age, instead of going completely to rockets, guided missiles, and energy beams. The answer is that cannon rounds cost much less than guided weapons, and can still be given "smart" terminal guidance capability. And we can carry a lot more of them than rockets of the same range and warhead size, for a given weight and volume.

Another feature you might not see Earthside was that our vehicles – tanks, armored personnel carriers, artillery carriers, everything – all had nets slung on either side, supporting rows of sandbags loaded with lunar dust. For the infantry APC's, gaps were left at strategic spots in the sandbag coverage so that the riflemen could still fire through their usual ports. Our cavalry vehicles out ahead of us were also carrying banks of dust-filled bags.

The sandbags helped break up our outline. They made it a lot harder to spot our vehicles from a distance. More importantly, they gave us what amounts to a complete extra layer of armor. Performance cost to our vehicles? Under lunar conditions, next to nothing.

The conversation with Dr. DeVere had been just a few short months ago. Then about a week ago, the fertilizer hit the fan.

"Colonel, you need to see this report that came in this morning," Lieutenant Byrd was telling me. He's one of our intelligence officers. "Latest word from the US/NATO network in the CIU. Just finished decoding it."

When Lieutenant Byrd comes into my office in person and tells me I need to see something, it's serious. I looked away from the computer screen, where I had been scanning the monthly supply summary, and took the paper from his hand. I began reading it while he stood in front of my desk.

A few minutes later, I was exclaiming, "Holy shit!" I wondered if I looked as scared as I felt.

If this report was correct, the weapons researchers at Lacus Mortis had assembled an operational fission warhead. Worse, the CIU was planning to use it. According to the report, they were planning to send an armored strike force out from their Lacus Mortis base toward Cold Harbor. The warhead was to be mounted on a battlefield rocket (a short range rocket on Earth; on the Moon it has a range of at least two hundred kilometers), protected by a tank formation. The plan was, once they got in range, to knock out the soon-to-be-operational section of the Criswell Collection Complex. Heat and radiation from a burst at a few hundred meters altitude would ruin solar cells and fuse circuits.

If they weren't able to get within range of the Criswell Complex without being intercepted, a secondary target was Cold Harbor itself.

If they really had a nuclear weapon, the choice of target and timing made a lot of sense from the CIU's viewpoint. Once the LunEarth Corporation demonstrates that electrical energy can actually be harvested from the Moon, a lot of people on Earth may decide that they no longer need to depend so much on Earth's remaining oil reserves. And oil is a mainstay of the CIU's economy.

Economic blackmail was not the worst of it.

"Did you see this part?" I asked Byrd.

"Yeah!" he answered. "Looks like someone dug plans out of some old file for Scud III missiles."

"And did you see the part that they probably have some *on the Moon?*" I asked him. "Do you understand what that means?"

Lieutenant Byrd whistled. "Yep. Launch one of those from the CIU, basically you can hit any bordering nation, but nothing much beyond that. But those missiles can achieve lunar escape velocity. Launch one from the Moon, you can land a nuclear warhead anywhere on Earth. The CIU has its own Earth-Moon ships, so they have the guidance and navigation experience to land a warhead *precisely* wherever on Earth they want to. They can threaten the entire planet."

"Lieutenant, you remember I like to read some of the old twentieth century science fiction?"

"I remember," he answered. "I recall you lent me some of your collection to read. Some of the stories were pretty good."

"A writer named Robert Heinlein," I told him, "once commented that 'The nation that controls the Moon will control the Earth.' Maybe he had the right idea." Then I added, "Has General McCormick seen this, yet?"

"No, not yet."

"Then tell him right now. I'll issue orders to put all our troops on alert. Especially our antimissile artillery and armored units. And I need to get Mayor Stanton, Tom Edwards, Mike Mailen, and Dr. DeVere on the phone as soon as possible. On a scrambled line."

I managed to get all four of those individuals, plus Virginia Franklin of the Town Council, on a multiway video call within thirty minutes.

Once I'd explained the situation, Mrs. Franklin was first to speak. "Looks like we're going to need a contingency plan, won't we?"

"Yes, you will." I nodded as I spoke. "We are likely to have only hours of warning when the CIU start to move. Maybe less."

Dr. DeVere commented, "We'll have to shut down the observatory, close the domes, safe all circuits. But the lava tube roof should protect most of the Cold Harbor community from blast, heat, and radiation, even from a nuclear warhead, shouldn't it?"

"Yes, it should," I agreed. "Blast effects should be minimal if they use a high altitude burst, with no atmosphere to carry the shock wave. I would recommend sealing off the skylight access points you've drilled for yourselves, if you can. Your only real worries about blast would be if they land a warhead on the lava tube itself." I shifted the subject slightly. "I'm going to move Battery C of our antimissile artillery to a location near the mouth of your lava tube to help defend you. We'll keep Battery A here at our base. I will also arrange to send over some of our emergency rations. We have plenty to spare, and I don't know what your food storage situation is."

"I believe we're pretty well supplied," Mayor Stanton told me, "but we'll gladly accept the help." Then he added, more to the others than to me, "You know, what we'll need to do is a lot like what we'd need to do to get ready for a large solar proton event."

While the Cold Harbor community leaders made their contingency plans, we army types made ours.

And General McCormick consulted with the President of the United States. President Dryer already knew about the probable presence of an assembled nuke and Scud III's on the Moon. The intelligence agencies had informed him even before informing us.

"Do whatever you need to do," Dryer told McCormick, "and I'll back you."

General McCormick knew that if Philip Dryer said he'd back you, he meant it. McCormick thanked the God he believed in that in this time of crisis, the United States had a President who had had some military and foreign policy experience before being elected, and who had the moral courage to stand behind his decisions and his people.

President Dryer was continuing, "Keep me as well informed as you can, as quickly as you can. And I'll pass on as much information as I can. But you're the person on the spot. If you need to act quickly, don't wait for my authorization. You have it now. Use your own best judgement, and take whatever action you need to, unless I specifically countermand something. I've already gotten the NATO powers to put their authority for us to act on their behalf *in writing*. I've promised them I won't reveal that authorization until we actually have to act." The NATO heads of state would trust Dryer to keep that word. That trust was probably the only reason they were willing to put their names on paper.

Dryer concluded, "One thing: if you have to move against the CIU bases, make sure you make plenty of videotape of any evidence you gather, with narration by someone who can explain things clearly to a layman who doesn't know uranium from his underwear. We will want to make clear to the world the situation you were up against, so that no one can fail to understand it, and so that no *honest* commentator can twist the facts to blame you, or the United States."

Barely six Earth days after Lieutenant Byrd gave me that decoded report, the other shoe hit the floor.

This time Lieutenant Byrd was almost running when he came into my office. And I saw out in the hallway that General McCormick was only a short distance behind him, walking very fast. Byrd was almost out of breath. He stopped for a moment to gather himself together.

"This came in from RecSat Two just now! It picked this up on an overflight of Lacus Mortis about forty minutes ago!" He held out a digital image to me. He pointed with a felt-tip pen. "Here's the base."

I nodded as General McCormick stepped into the office. I'd become familiar with such images over the months. Either the CIU didn't suspect we knew of the Lacus Mortis base, or they hadn't managed to come up with any effective camouflage.

Byrd continued, "Now, do you see these shadows?" He pointed at the image.

I did. They were less distinct than they would have been by sunlight, but even in Earthlight, they were unmistakable. Those shadows had never been present on any previous image. Given their sizes and arrangement, there was only one thing they could be. A vehicle formation. Leaving the Lacus Mortis base. Heading northwest. Our way.

Several dozen tiny dark spots, each the shadow of a vehicle. Lieutenant Byrd said the best count he could come up with was eighty-seven.

"God help us all!" Later on, I could not remember whether I had murmured that, or General McCormick had.

"Inform the Cold Harbor community leaders immediately," General McCormick ordered, "and call down to Washington and get the President on the line. Then he asked, "Any chance of tracking these with the recon satellites?"

Lieutenant Byrd shook his head. "There's not another Rec-Sat overflight of the area due – by any satellite – for another nineteen hours."

Mac didn't ask if the vehicles could be tracked from Joseph's Jumpoff. We all knew that there weren't any instruments at the L1 station with the kind of resolution that would be needed. He sighed, "Then we'll have to count on our cavalry to find them."

The Cold Harbor leaders put their contingency plan into effect. They made the situation public to the Cold Harbor community. Secrecy was no good to us now. They moved people into the pressurized buildings furthest back from the mouth of the lava tube, and sealed off "skylight" access points. They also moved emergency food, water, and air supplies into the evacuation zone, plus fuel cells, in case the nuclear reactor was knocked out or power cables were cut.

While the Cold Harborites were putting their emergency plans into effect, we went into action.

The majority of our armored forces – the greater part of our combat troops – moved out in an attempt to counter the CIU unit. Armor is perhaps the most useful form of ground force to deploy in an environment like the Moon. Paratroop and helicopter units are of no use, of course. Tanks and APC's can be modified to hold pressure, and at the same time provide range and mobility. Their armor gives at least some shielding against solar proton events, should one occur while the troops they carry are away from base.

The history of armored combat on Earth has taught us that

tanks and infantry together are more effective than either alone. A pure infantry unit is terribly vulnerable if it runs into tanks. On the other hand, tanks without infantry support are easily ambushed by antitank weapons. So not only did we have a battalion of each, we had "cross-attached", just as we often do on Earth. One tank company from the 125th Battalion had been attached to the infantry, and one of the rifle companies from the 76th had been attached to the tanks.

Our two headquarters carriers were indistinguishable. A CIU gunner trying to take out our commanding officer would have no way to know which APC was his and which was mine. Not that it mattered. Either of us could command our troops without the other if we had to. Nor could CIU forces feel secure even if they knocked out *both* APC's. We could just as easily be riding our HQ tanks. They'd be more crowded than the APC's, but they, too, are equipped with extra comm and display gear, and we could transfer to them if we needed to.

Both the rockets and the howitzers of our self propelled artillery achieve astonishing range in lunar gravity. We also get extreme ranges for the mortars and the rocket launchers in our infantry battalion's heavy weapons company, and in each rifle company's heavy weapons platoon. We've needed a lot of practice to get used to our weapons' ranges on the Moon. Fortunately, we had a lot of unoccupied space west of our base where we could set up firing ranges. The great range of our "over the horizon" weapons was one reason why all of us, from private up to the CO, had been given extra training in artillery spotting since we'd reached the Moon.

The combat engineers would blast obstacles (large boulders, crater rims, etc.) from our path if we couldn't go around, or bulldoze slopes if any were too steep for our vehicles. They were also equipped with tow cables to recover vehicles that broke down, got stuck in difficult terrain, or became battle damaged. The infantry battalion had their motor pool platoon along to help repair such vehicles. The motor pool platoon also had a couple of APC's fitted out as tankers with extra fuel and liquid oxygen for our fuel cells, to make sure we had enough range to reach the CIU secret base – and back. We'd probably manage without refueling...but General McCormick saw no reason not to take out insurance.

And one other thing: if we managed to stop the CIU troops and their rockets, the plan was to go on to the Lacus Mortis base, gather evidence for the UN and the World Court, and eliminate it as a weapons base. The engineers, together with the mechanized infantry's headquarters company and our formation headquarters unit, had the radiation detectors and other instruments we'd need to identify fissionable materials, and demolition charges to destroy weapons or weapon labs we found.

We weren't up to full strength: Only thirty-six of the 125th battalion's forty-five tanks had been shipped to the Moon by the time we had detected the CIU vehicles moving with our RecSat. So we had reorganized with platoons of three tanks each instead of the usual four. And none of our infantry platoons had their command buggies. So the lieutenants and platoon sergeants had to ride in the APC's with the rifle squads. But with less than ninety CIU vehicles, maybe they weren't up to full strength, either. Whatever the case, we were going to have to stop them with what we had. Or try.

The armored cavalry troop was well beyond our horizon. So how could they let us know, if they spotted the CIU vehicles? We'd thought of relaying through Joseph's Jumpoff. Trouble with that was, the CIU could almost certainly listen in. We'd tip them off to exactly what we were doing. Then they'd know we were onto what *they* were doing.

So the plan was, when the armored cavalry made contact with CIU forces, for them to send up what we call a "Triple R": a radio relay rocket. Launched to a sufficient altitude, one or more of them would rebroadcast the cavalry's messages to us. In effect, it would give them an antenna tall enough to be above our horizon.

If the CIU forces slipped by us, we had left some troops in reserve. The antimissile artillery I've mentioned. Four companies of *non*mechanized infantry, two at our base, two posted at Cold Harbor for this emergency. A company of engineers. And a small mobile reserve: a company of mechanized infantry reinforced by a platoon of tanks and a platoon of self-propelled artillery, which could move rapidly to reinforce whichever position most seemed to need it. And every man and woman, whatever their usual Army jobs, would be carrying a weapon.

Some of the modifications to our vehicles were not so obvious as the starboard cannons and sandbags. Such as the fact that we had rebuilt the crew compartments of the armored personnel carriers as airlocks. That, plus the fact that we fitted our infantry with hard pressure suits, force us to reduce the number of soldiers per squad from nine to seven. We all have pressure suits, and they've all been made self-sealing, so a single penetration from a bullet or shell fragment won't necessarily be fatal. But the rest of us wear soft suits, so that we can move around more easily in the confines of vehicles. The infantry suits are hard because they are also meant to provide the soldiers with armor protection when they have to fight dismounted.

Then there were humble but important details, such as making sure our caterpillar treads, wheels, lubrication systems, and infantry weapons would all work in the lunar dust environment. And enlarging the trigger guards of our pistols, rifles, and submachine guns so that they can be fired by someone wearing a pressure suit glove.

It was amazing that the Army had been able to get the mods made to our vehicles and get them shipped to the Moon, in the short time we'd had to prepare. And without tipping off CIU intelligence about it. At least, we *hoped* the CIU did not know the numbers, types, and capabilities of the vehicles we had on the Moon.

In an army where promotion was based on performance, not connections, Colonel Kasim Ferishtah would have been a general. That wasn't just his opinion. Ninety-plus percent of the officers and soldiers who had ever served under him would have said so. He never asked his troops to take risks that he would not take himself, and units under his command had consistently been victorious in border skirmishes with Kazakhstan. The incursions into Kazakhstan had ultimately been a failure, and Kazakhstan had given the CIU a bloody nose, but that had been due largely to the fact that most CIU units were *not* under his command. Tactical blunders by the generals in charge of that operation had been costly for the CIU.

However, he was considered "politically unreliable". His first loyalty was to the CIU, his second to the men under his command. Not to the Blue Crescent party. No one had ever heard him say a single word against the Blue Crescent, and he obeyed the orders that came down through the Defense Ministry. But he was willing to talk back to his superiors, and tell them straight out if he thought a plan they proposed was a bad idea. Especially if it involved needless risk to his soldiers without increasing the chances for victory. He cared a great deal for his men's lives, and he wouldn't spend them for what some Blue Crescent official thought of as glory. For victory, if he had to, yes. But not just for show.

So the Blue Crescent party didn't entirely trust him. They wouldn't promote him. They liked the fact that he won most of his battles, and they didn't want to lose his talent. So they wouldn't fire him. But they wouldn't make him a general, either.

When it came time to staff the Lacus Mortis base, the Defense Ministry decided that with the number of CIU troops to be stationed there, the commanding officer should have the rank of colonel. And who was the most experienced colonel in the CIU Army? Who would be most likely to win, if they actually got into a scrap? Kasim Ferishtah.

So here he was, leading a force of armor escorting a rocket launcher northwest in the direction of Cold Harbor.

He had considered the plan to bombard the Criswell Complex a bad idea. Before he had taken command of the lunar contingent, he had gone all the way up to the Principal Military

Secretary. Next step up would be the Supreme Leader himself.

"I'm not saying this for my benefit, sir. I'm saying it for yours. If we attack the Criswell Complex or anything else on the Moon that doesn't belong to us the Americans and their allies will strike back. Not just at our bases on the Moon. I think they will hit our homeland, too. They'll be scared and they'll be angry. When they are that scared and that angry, they will fight for keeps...and they'll win. We are not strong enough to defeat them if they go all out, and you know it as well as I. The CIU will be seriously hurt, and a lot of our people will be killed. I and my family are citizens of this country; I wouldn't want to risk harm to them, nor have them face the chaos that is likely to follow a defeat. Oh and you and the Supreme Leader might want to think about this: They will probably hunt down every Blue Crescent member they can find, especially high ranking ones."

"Colonel, just between us, I think you are right. I've said as much to the Supreme Leader. But there is not talking him out of this. He is convinced the Americans and Europeans don't have the guts for a real confrontation. He believes their will to fight back will crumble once he announces we can attack any place on Earth from the Moon."

"Sir, I think he seriously underestimates President Dryer."

"So do I. But he calls the shots. Not worth your time to appeal to him yourself. At best he'll ignore you. At worst, you'll call unwelcome attention to yourself and your family. He is quite determined on this plan. You have your orders."

"And I will carry them out to the best of my ability."

Up ahead, our armored cavalry was just approaching the western rim of Aristoteles Crater.

"Heads up, everybody!" Major Jenkins spoke on the all-hands radio frequency. General McCormick had wanted an officer in command of the armored cavalry with plenty of experience and sober judgement, just as he did for our main formation. So here again, he had put an someone in charge who was a grade higher than you'd normally expect. "We're going to check out the interior of this crater. Once we get up on the crater rim, we should be able to see each other at greater range than we have been over most of this terrain. I'm going to spread us out so we can cover more territory…at least on the way down the crater wall. Lieutenant Carter," he called the CO of the first platoon, on the left flank of the company, "whose vehicle is farthest left in your platoon?"

"That would be Sergeant Rodriguez's tank, Major."

"And Lieutenant Nehru – " he was with third platoon, on the right flank " – who is on the right end of your platoon?"

"Sergeant Jones, Sir."

"As soon as we crest the rim, I want Sergeant Rodriguez to report the rightmost vehicle he can see, and Sergeant Jones to report the leftmost vehicle he can see. And everybody make sure to use your high gain antennas only, and point 'em at the vehicles next to you. If any CIU units happen to be within our horizon, I don't want them overhearing our radio chatter."

It took only a few more minutes for G Troop to reach the crest of the Aristoteles crater rim. The ascent was a bit steep, but not impossible in lunar gravity, and the troopers were well experienced from both Earthside and lunar training in scouting out the best ways up a slope. The troop adjusted its formation; no longer a straight line, it now matched the gentle curve of the crater rim.

Major Jenkins heard the surprise in Sergeant Rodriguez's voice. "Sir, from here I can see clear to the right hand end of the troop!"

"Same here!" came from Sergeant Jones. "I can see all the way to Sergeant Rodriguez's tank!"

"That's what I was hoping for," Major Jenkins said. "Spread out along the rim. I want to extend our line as far as we can, and still have everybody keep everybody else in sight. That should help us search this crater more quickly."

The line had spread to a length of about fifty kilometers – measured around the curve of the crater rim – when Sergeant

Rodriguez reported, "I can just barely see Sergeant Jones's tank. The problem isn't the horizon as much as being able to see something that size at this distance, even with the magnification on our scopes."

From his location at the other end of the line, Sergeant Jones concurred.

"Wait a minute," Sergeant Rodriguez came back. "Look down into the crater! Just short of the horizon!"

Everyone looked. From their vantage point on the crater rim, the cavalrymen could not see the far rim, but not the far side floor beneath it; the spheroidal curve of the Moon put that beyond their horizon. But they could see a bit beyond the center of the floor.

Just coming onto the center of the Earthlit crater were more than a hundred moving shadows, tiny at this distance, but clearly visible. Obviously moving in formation, they were spread out over an area eight to twelve kilometers across.

In his command tank, Major Jenkins studied the shadows, both by direct eyeball look and on a view screen that allowed him to enhance and magnify the images.

"Major," came a question from Lieutenant Carter in First Platoon, "how did we manage to get here before they did? They left base first, and we had a longer distance to go."

Major Jenkins answered rather abstractedly, as he continued to study the approaching force, trying to count vehicles and attempting to identify types, "Difference in distance isn't that great. And according to our maps, they had to cover rougher terrain than we did. Plus, we had orders to move as fast as possible; maybe they didn't. And don't forget: our whole force isn't here, yet; just us. I expect our main force is at least seventy clicks behind us, probably more like ninety."

The radio was quiet for the next few minutes, as the Major continued to study the moving vehicles. On the magnified images on his screen, he could tell that the CIU vehicles were using camouflage nets. But breaking up outlines wasn't enough to keep them from being seen...because the nets could not keep the vehicles from casting shadows. It wasn't even enough to disguise the vehicle types – not from the Major's experienced eyes.

There was no indication yet that the CIU forces had spotted the Americans... probably because the American tanks were sitting still on the crater rim, not moving. Since the troop was still using tight beam transmissions and high gain antennas only, their radio traffic had probably not been overheard.

Major Jenkins spoke on the all-hands frequency. "All right everybody, listen up! Once we send up Triple R's to notify General McCormick, the CIU forces are almost sure to spot them! We may have to try to keep them busy until the main force gets here! So if things get tight, and we have to regroup, if I say 'Checkmate White', it means rendezvous at the south rim of the crater. 'Checkmate Black' will mean to rendezvous at the north rim, 'Knight Fork' means rendezvous at the east rim, and 'Pawn Opening', means rendezvous at the west rim. And nobody move until I say so."

He paused. Then he continued. "Lieutenants Carter and Nehru: each of you launch one Triple R."

We saw the radio relay rockets against the dark sky above the horizon ahead. When they reach an altitude of five kilometers, they are programmed to trigger off a self-oxidizing flare, to call attention to themselves, so that the intended receivers – us in this case – know to turn on their radios, if they're not on already.

We heard Major Jenkins's voice. "CIU forces located inside Aristoteles Crater. Coordinates seventeen degrees, forty minutes east, fifty degrees, fifty minutes north. Estimate two tank battalions, each reinforced by one mechanized infantry company. Plus one rocket launcher and one vehicle which may be either an ammunition carrier for the rocket launcher or a second launcher. Looks as if each tank battalion may be a few tanks shy of full strength."

"Uh-oh!" The tone of his voice had changed. "They know they've been spotted! No doubt they've seen the flares from the

Triple R's. It looks like they're going to try to launch their rocket from their present position. The rocket launcher has come to a stop, and they're throwing off camouflage nets. Urgently recommend you fire an artillery rocket and try to knock the launcher out before they get theirs off! We'll pinpoint for you it with targeting lasers."

"Will do!" was General McCormick's reply. To us, he ordered: "Battery Bravo! Launch two rockets toward the coordinates Major Jenkins just gave us! Everyone else, increase speed!"

No need to ask why Major Jenkins had specified rockets. He had no way to know precisely how close we were until McCormick told him, but he did know that the rockets had longer range than the howitzers, so the chances were better that a rocket attack was at least possible. And while the howitzers could be loaded with "smart" warheads with terminal guidance, the rockets could be guided all the way from launch to impact, which meant a much greater chance of getting a hit.

Our artillery battery stopped in place, and one of the rocket platoon's three launchers elevated two tubes into firing position. Could we get a rocket to target before the CIU launched theirs? The battlefield rockets we were using were smaller than the type the CIU meant to use to bombard the Criswell Complex – at least according to intelligence reports. Also, according to reports, our equipment is more agile, quicker responding. So we should get ours launched before they even completed erecting theirs to firing position.

On top of that, it was probable that they were firing from their present position only because they had been spotted. They had probably intended to get to a much closer range before launching. That mean that they would have to reprogram the rocket's navigation and targeting coordinate data. That should cost them several minutes. Reports are that computer technology and software in the CIU are years behind most of the rest of the world, perhaps as much as a decade. Chalk that up to the fact that most of the rest of the world doesn't trust them and won't trade computer technology with them. They can get some stuff on the black market, but they're still behind almost everyone else.

On the other hand, the time of flight for our rockets from our present location to theirs would count against us. There was no way to know whether our rockets would be in time or not. But we had to try.

On board the CIU launcher vehicle, a rocket was beginning to erect, while Major Jenkins was giving orders to his troop. "Everyone hold your positions. Lieutenants Carter, Wu, and Nehru: keep your target identification lasers focused on that launcher. Everyone put their radios on scrambler setting Alpha Bravo Three. Switch from high gain to omni antennas."

The three platoon leaders beamed their lasers at the launcher as ordered. Not a tank in the troop moved.

The CIU tanks and APC's had increased speed and were spreading out, it appeared to be more a search than an attack formation. They knew there were American forces nearby, and they could guess probably on the crater rim. But it looked as if G Troop had not yet been spotted. The CIU troops apparently did not yet know *precisely* where on the rim of Aristoteles the American vehicles were.

The surest way to make it *easy* to be spotted was to start moving. Major Jenkins had trained his troopers well. The cavalrymen stayed right where they were.

Major Jenkins and Captain Turner, his deputy troop commander, were monitoring the frequencies the CIU usually used. Jenkins's driver could speak Arabic, Turner's could speak Farsi. They'd been picked with that in mind. There was an excellent chance one of them could interpret any messages intercepted – unless, of course, the CIU were on scramble, too.

Did two tank battalions, reinforced with infantry, have the advantage over our one tank and one infantry battalion? Hard to say. Most tactical textbooks say yes. Me, I'd say it's a tossup. Textbooks don't always account for differently organized forces: a CIU tank battalion only has 32 tanks – even if it were full strength – against our battalion's 38. (If we were at full strength, we'd have 45.) Further, the CIU formation didn't appear to have any armored cavalry, artillery, or engineers. And our infantry heavy weapons company has some pretty potent antitank weapons.

Textbooks don't always account for equipment differences, either. Our intelligence reports are that the CIU sent to the Moon tanks based on their LT-56 design. I'd much rather ride an Arachnid. The LT-56 armor is not as well designed, for my money, and Arachnids have much higher top speeds and better all-around agility.

On board Major Jenkins's tank, Staff Sergeant LeCroix was half chuckling under his breath. "I hear cussing!" he explained to the Major, referring to the Arabic voices coming from the radio speaker over the CIU frequency. "Seems like the rocket launcher's fire control computer is refusing to take the new navigation coordinates they're trying to put in for the firing solution. I'm pretty sure they'll get around the problem, but it may give our artillery rockets a few extra seconds to arrive."

Two minutes and fifty-five seconds after Major Jenkins sent the message asking for a rocket strike, his gunner, Sergeant First Class Morimoto, tapped his shoulder and pointed to the screen monitoring the up-pointing camera. The two rockets we'd fired were above them, made visible by intermittent flashes from their steering rockets, as they homed toward the ultraviolet energy being reflected from the three laser spotting beams being directed at the CIU rocket launcher. Two minutes and fifty-five seconds is not a long time in most situations, but it seems like ages when you're holding formation stock still, watching enemy vehicles move toward you, and racing to beat an enemy launch sequence.

Half a minute later, as the American rockets were still descending, Sergeant LeCroix said to Major Jenkins, "They've fixed their data input problem. If I read them right, they're about twenty seconds or so from launch."

Barely five seconds after LeCroix had spoken, the first American rocket struck home, making a direct hit on the CIU launcher vehicle. The second was less than half a second behind it, flying in through the debris of the first rocket's explosion for a near miss, half a meter from one caterpillar tread. Between them, the warheads of the two rockets turned the CIU launcher into an utter and unusable wreck.

"Now!" called Major Jenkins. "Captain Turner, take First Platoon and swing left around their flank. I'll take Third Platoon around right. Second Platoon, hang back until their attention is on us. Then try to dart in and knock out or capture that second missile carrier. Once you've done that, or if you can't find an opening, join up with First Platoon. If you can't get through to First Platoon, join up with Third Platoon.

"What we're going to try to do is get these people to chase us around in circles until our main force can come up. Okay, everybody, let's go!"

First and Third Platoons started downslope from the rims to the floor of Aristoteles, moving fast enough to fling up rooster tails of dust behind each tank. As they moved, the tanks in each platoon began to close up the distance between each other, shifting from a scouting to a combat formation.

The CIU forces spotted the motion of the First and Third Platoons, and their dust tails, and shifted the direction of their own forward motion. One tank battalion and its accompanying infantry company turned slightly northward to meet our First Platoon; the other battalion and its infantry support angled southward to meet the Third Platoon. As the CIU forces moved toward the Americans, they, too, closed up from search to combat formation.

However, one tank platoon from the CIU southern formation, and one mechanized infantry platoon from the northern formation, stayed back, apparently to escort the remaining missile carrier, which was withdrawing southeast. Their commanding officer was not so stupid as to leave the carrier completely unprotected.

Even though the CIU armor had already been moving forward before the armored cavalry started down from the crater rim, it would be a good fifteen minutes before the opposing forces came within effective weapon range of each other: Aristoteles is a *big* crater. The cannon and missiles on each side would carry far enough to reach each other before fifteen minutes had passed, but they wouldn't likely *hit* anything before then, not with targeting systems designed for Earth gravity and combat ranges.

Meanwhile, our main force was also throwing up rooster tails of dust. We had stepped up our speed to sixty kilometers an hour. Once they'd fired the two rockets Major Jenkins had called for, our artillery battery had started moving at seventy-five, and were catching up. And we, too, were closing distance between vehicles, the better to support each other in a fight.

Once the artillery had caught up to the formation, we all accelerated to seventy-five kilometers per hour.

Major Jenkins was counting on the superior maneuverability of his vehicles to keep ahead of the CIU forces in the deadly game of tag he was trying to play. His Ferret tanks had a mass of scarcely three metric tons. They were intended to be airliftable to support paratroops and airmobile forces, so lightness had been a must in their design. They were much faster and more maneuverable than CIU LT-56's or the APC's they were using. Even loaded with sandbags full of dust along the sides as they were, the Ferrets could literally run rings around the CIU forces.

And that's what Major Jenkins intended to do. His Ferrets weren't tough enough to slug it out toe to toe with LT-56's, even if they hadn't been heavily outnumbered – a single troop against two battalions. But he hoped to keep the CIU chasing his force until the rest of us got there. By having superior speed, his tanks could choose the range. With luck and skill, they'd keep far enough ahead so the CIU couldn't get many good shots at them. If the CIU were just a bit careless and left any gaps in their formation, Jenkins's men might be able to dash in once in a while and get a quick shot at the rear of a CIU vehicle – an LT-56's most vulnerable spot.

G Troop would have their work cut out for them, to try to keep the CIU occupied until we arrived, without getting shot to pieces in the meantime. Because even at seventy-five clicks an hour, which is close to our top speed, it would take at least an hour and a quarter for our main force to reach the scene. Maybe up to an hour and forty-five minutes, if the action drifted toward the east.

Had the CIU forces elected to withdraw toward their base, Jenkins would have followed, keeping contact with their flanks and rear, nipping at their heels as opportunity presented, and sending up radio relay rockets from time to time to keep us posted on CIU movements until our main force could rendezvous. Colonel Ferishtah had decided, however, that his best bet was to knock the armored cavalry out of action before reinforcements arrived, so that he could contend with any such reinforcements without distractions from the cavalry. I wonder if he would have decided the same way, had he realized how badly his vehicles were outclassed for maneuverability.

First and Third Cavalry Platoons continued to close with the CIU battalions facing them for another ten minutes. Then they swerved left and right, respectively, to begin circling the CIU forces.

Lieutenant Cavanaugh, commanding Second Platoon, watched the situation carefully from his vantage point on the crater rim, aided by his image enhancers and magnifiers. Each CIU formation had been advancing in a "box" formation: the tanks in each platoon line abreast, the platoons in each company side by side, each company in a battalion following the one ahead, leaving plenty of room for maneuver between one line and the next. The mechanized infantry company supporting each battalion followed the tanks.

He observed each battalion turning to keep facing toward its advancing platoon, not by swinging each line as a unit, but by the much more elegant mode of simply swerving each vehicle within the formation, leaving the lines in their initial formation. Thus the initial line abreast of each platoon was becoming an echelon, and if the CIU tanks continued to turn, would become a column. He also observed that as each CIU battalion attempted to close with the nearest American platoon, a gap was beginning to open between them. If it grew wide enough, that gap might just allow Second Platoon to get at the second CIU missile carrier, as the Major had instructed.

Twelve minutes after the First and Third Platoons swerved to begin their circle, Wu decided that the CIU battalions' attentions were fully focused on the other two platoons. The gap between the two battalions had begun to widen. The two platoons escorting the rocket carrier were concentrating on their southeast withdrawal; with luck, they might not think to watch their backs.

"Now," Wu ordered, "start downslope. Keep slow until we reach the crater floor: I don't want to send up any rooster tails of dust that might attract attention."

The four tanks in the platoon started down the interior slope of the Aristoteles rim. Instead of their top speed of eighty clicks an hour, they were moving scarcely thirty. As they descended, they converged on Lieutenant Wu's tank. Each tank crew was well aware that once on the crater floor, without the advantage of the rim's height, they would no longer be able to see each other at their initial separation, given the Moon's short horizon distance. They also knew they needed to be much closer together to give each other effective fire support in combat. By the time they'd reached the crater floor, the distance between adjacent tanks had shrunk from more than two kilometers to less than a hundred meters.

Once down on the crater floor, Second Platoon could no longer see any other vehicles, American or CIU. Another disadvantage of the short lunar horizon. Lieutenant Wu would have to guess what was going on. He figured that the two CIU tank battalions and their supporting infantry would continue to follow the cavalry platoons they were in contact with, that First and Third Platoons (and the Captain and the Major, respectively) would continue to lure the CIU tanks toward them in a circling motion, that the gap between the CIU battalions would continue to widen, and that the rocket carrier and its escort would continue to withdraw southeast. So he headed his platoon southeast at top speed toward where the rocket carrier ought to be.

Wu wasn't leaving everything to guesses, however, even educated ones. "Look sharp!" he ordered. "Keep an eye out for any vehicles, ours or theirs! Just in case the CIU do something we *don't* expect!"

First Platoon and Third Platoon were doing exactly what Lieutenant Wu believed. Captain Turner and First Platoon were circling the CIU forces clockwise; Major Jenkins and Third Platoon were circling counterclockwise. And the CIU forces were taking the bait. What turned out to be the CIU's First Tank Battalion were turning northward, trying to get within effective weapon range of First Platoon, their path swerving as they tried to keep pace with First Platoon's curving path and drive an intercept course. CIU's Second Battalion were turning southward, trying to get within weapon range of Third Platoon in the same way.

Rather than driving at right angles to the CIU vehicles, First and Third Platoons were keeping their paths angled about thirty-five degrees away. This, with their eighty kilometer per hour top speed, should just keep them out of range of the CIU's guns. At least, Captain Turner and Major Jenkins hoped it would. But it also kept the CIU troops *thinking* they might just catch them. If the cavalry got away too easily, the CIU might give up the chase.

First and Third Platoons also kept their turrets pointed back at the nearest CIU vehicles. Every cavalryman knew perfectly well that the little 25 mm main cannons the Ferrets carried would be no better than popguns against the CIU tanks' frontal armor, although they might do some damage to one of the APC's. But the two tanks in each platoon that carried antitank missiles would use them if the CIU got too close.

Meanwhile, Second Platoon was barreling up corridor the two CIU battalions were opening up for them, below the horizons of both, and our main force was continuing to approach Aristoteles. As they moved, they closed formation further for better mutual combat support, from one hundred to only fifty meters between adjacent tanks – about the spacing First and Third Platoons now had, could Second Platoon have seen them. But they didn't want to get *too* close together. They weren't yet sure whether the remaining CIU rocket carrier was a second launcher, or simply an ammunition transport, and they didn't want to chance getting two or three tanks knocked out by a single well-guided missile.

Eighteen more minutes, and Second Platoon spotted vehicles coming up over the lunar horizon. Three tanks to the right, four armored personnel carriers to the left, with the rocket carrier between and a bit beyond them. All eight vehicles were moving away toward the southeast.

"Sergeant Red Eagle!" Lieutenant Wu was addressing his Pawnee Platoon Sergeant, "take Sergeant Nguyen and try to keep those three tanks busy! If you get a chance for a shot at their rear armor, take it. I'm taking Sergeant Eisenberg with me. We'll try to break through the APC's and knock out that rocket carrier. If the tanks go after us instead of you, *you* go for the rocket carrier."

Jonathan Red Eagle understood the sense behind Wu's orders. The Ferrets' 25 mm cannons *could* penetrate an LT-56's rear armor, even though they had no chance from the front. And they had a reasonable chance to penetrate an APC's armor from any direction. Just as important, the CIU usually didn't equip their

APC's with anything more than heavy machine guns...which could *not* penetrate a Ferret's armor. So Lieutenant Wu and Sergeant Eisenberg could probably bull their way through or past the APC's if they were quick enough, and didn't allow the infantry on board the APC's time to dismount and bring antitank weapons to bear. And having a Ferret equipped with antitank missiles with each section – Sergeant Nguyen with him and Sergeant Eisenberg with the Lieutenant – meant they'd doubled their chances of someone getting through and knocking out that rocket carrier. They'd also doubled their chances, Red Eagle admitted to himself, of getting themselves destroyed piecemeal.

Red Eagle noticed that the turrets of the CIU tanks were all pointed more or less forward. The turrets of at least two of the tanks were turning back and forth as if their commanders were keeping up a search for incoming vehicles, but for the moment, at least, none were looking directly behind. This might present an opportunity.

"Charlie," Red Eagle radioed Sergeant Nguyen, "it doesn't look as if they've noticed anyone's behind them, yet. At least, none of the CIU vehicles have changed direction or appear to be preparing for action. Do you think you could get a hit at this distance?" Charles Nguyen and his crew were consistently the platoon's top scorers whenever gunnery contests were held.

"I'd want to stop to steady my tank at this range," Nguyen replied in the soft voice that told both of his Vietnamese family and his Texas home town. "And it's chancy, even so. But I think maybe I could."

"Okay, we'll both try," Red Eagle ordered. "I'll take the one on the left. Charlie, you take the one on the right. If either of us hits our target and has time for a second shot, that one goes after the middle tank."

Red Eagle's two tanks stopped. Lieutenant Wu and Sergeant Eisenberg, seeing what was happening, veered a bit further to the left. If Sergeant Red Eagle was going to provide a distraction, they'd take the best advantage of it.

Red Eagle's tank crews each focused their laser rangefinders on the rear faces of their chosen targets. No need to allow for windage in the firing solution here in vacuum, and their computers had already been programmed for lunar gravity. Within a five-second span, they had each fired a round from their 25 mm guns.

Red Eagle's shot hit the right-hand tread of his target. His round didn't put the tread out of action; the CIU tank continued to move. But it did damage the tread. It looked as if the damaged section of tread might work itself into a complete break given time.

Sergeant Nguyen's round made a clean hit on the right hand CIU tank. Although no one could see it, an invisible vapor cloud began spewing out of the hole in the rear of the hull. Nguyen had hit their fuel supply.

These CIU troops knew the Americans were around now! The three tanks began to swerve around to the right, to turn themselves about and face the Americans. Three quarters of the way through the turn, the tank Sergeant Nguyen had hit came to a stop. Looked like Nguyen had put them out of gas. The remaining two CIU tanks completed the turn and started toward Sergeant Red Eagle's section, although on his view magnifier, Red Eagle noted that the right tread on the tank he had hit was looking a bit ragged.

The CIU radio frequencies were filled with chatter.

"Probably trying to call for help," Lieutenant Wu commented to his crew, "but I doubt anyone can hear them. I expect everyone is below their horizon." There were no Arabic or Farsi speakers in his platoon, however, to tell him whether his guess was correct or not. It did not appear that the CIU had radio relay rockets to help them in their quest for aid. If they did, they sure weren't using any.

Two of the CIU APC's had stopped to let their crews dismount; the other two were moving to try to interpose themselves between Lieutenant Wu's section and the rocket carrier, which was fleeing southeast at top speed. Top speed for the carrier was not going to be anywhere near enough to escape a Ferret, Wu noted.

The dismounted CIU infantry were attempting to bring weapons to bear. Looked like one man from each APC carried a shoulder-mounted rocket launcher and two in each squad had grenade launcher tubes slung under their rifle barrels. Grenades of that type wouldn't be much of a threat to most armored vehicles, but they might damage a Ferret. Could blow a tread off, or something. The rocket launchers should be of concern to any vehicle light enough to be sent to the Moon.

"Sergeant Eisenberg!" the Lieutenant called, "let's not give 'em time to take a bead! Dust 'em with machine gun fire. I don't care whether we hit anything. Just keep 'em too busy to set up and take aim!"

"Roger!" Eisenberg replied.

Machine guns from both Ferrets blasted away. Too far for good accuracy, but not too far for the bullets to travel, under lunar gravity. And if they threw enough lead that way, they might hit something. Dust began spurting up around the CIU infantrymen. Wu saw at least three pressure suited figures fall before the others took the cue and threw themselves to the ground to make themselves as small a target as they could. He and Eisenberg kept firing as they drove past, closing with the remaining two APC's. Whether they got any more hits was impossible to tell, because the CIU troops were staying down.

Lieutenant Wu swallowed hard. This was his first actual combat, and he really had not wanted to kill anybody. He'd known he might have to, and he'd been prepared to do his duty. But killing was proving a hard thing for him, and battle wasn't pretty, even on the Moon. He could hope that the CIU soldiers were only wounded, not dead, but he knew he couldn't count on that.

He got his emotions under control. The remaining two CIU personnel carriers were close enough now to make out the blue crescent insignia painted on their sides, even through the camouflage nets, without any magnification or image enhancement.

There was a lot yet to do.

One of the lead tanks in the CIU battalion pursuing First Platoon opened fire. It was a clean miss. The round hit to the left of the end tank in the platoon (leftmost from the CIU's point of view), in the slight gap between First Platoon and Captain Turner's tank. The CIU had little chance of scoring a hit with any given round at this range, but if they fired enough rounds, statistically, they were apt to score hits now and then. Obviously some of them were going to try.

The Americans couldn't move faster; they were already traveling at top speed. But they could do a few things to make it harder for the CIU to hit them.

"Increase our angle away from them!" Captain Turner ordered, "and start zigzagging! Lieutenant Carter, you call the left and right swerves so we stay in formation!"

Before the Americans could put these instructions into effect, another CIU tank fired its cannon. The round hit the second-from-left tank in First Platoon. Fortunately it hit one of the dust-filled sandbags draped over the tank's side. The dust in the bag absorbed most of the force of the shaped charge round. The energy that got through scorched and pitted a small area of the tank's hull exterior, but did not penetrate through the armor.

The Americans could all feel a surge of adrenaline rushing through their blood. Especially the crew of Sergeant Nakamura's tank – the one that had been hit.

"Swerve left thirty degrees now!" Lieutenant Carter shouted.

Major Jenkins and Third Platoon were not experiencing such potshots. At least not yet. The commanding officer of the CIU battalion pursuing them apparently preferred to close to a more likely range before expending ammunition. And Major Jenkins and Third Platoon were seeing to it that the range stayed open.

Sergeant Red Eagle's section was close enough now to the two CIU tanks that were still moving to recognize blue crescent insignia, too. "Split up! " he radioed. "Charlie, go right! I'll go around them left! That way at least one of us will get a rear shot!"

Sergeant Nguyen's tank swung off to the right while Red Eagle veered left. Would the CIU tanks concentrate on Red Eagle's tank or the other? No, they decided to split their attention. The tank with the damaged tread swerved toward Red Eagle; the other turned toward Nguyen. The one turning toward Red Eagle was moving more slowly; perhaps the damaged tread was starting to slow it down.

Sergeant Nguyen got a good, clean shot into the rear of the tank facing Red Eagle. A gout of flame burst from the impact point. This time Nguyen's shot had ruptured both the fuel and oxygen tanks for the fuel cells, and some spark had set them off.

Sergeant Red Eagle's gunner likewise took a good aim at the rear of the tank facing Nguyen. The CIU tank fired, sending a 76 mm round at Sergeant Nguyen's tank. Scarcely a second later, Red Eagle's tank fired and scored a solid hit on the CIU tank. The effect was not nearly as dramatic as Nguyen's round had been, but the CIU tank stopped dead in its tracks.

But the CIU round had already hit the front left quarter of Nguyen's tank. The dust-loaded sandbags absorbed the worst of the impact, and the tank's hull was not breached, but the forward part of the left tread was broken apart and blown clear off its mountings. Nguyen's tank lurched hard left and came to an abrupt stop.

The crew of the CIU tank Sergeant Nguyen had hit were bailing out the hatches, trying desperately to escape the flame, although that was guttering out as fuel and oxygen dispersed into the lunar vacuum. Sergeant Red Eagle counted only two pressure suited figures. Where was the third crew member? A casualty?

Red Eagle had little time to worry about that, however. Sergeant Nguyen and his crew were also exiting from their tank.

They were pulling the limp form of their driver out after them.

"How is he?" Red Eagle asked with concern in his voice.

"Hit his head against the inside of his helmet when we stopped so suddenly," Sergeant Nguyen answered over his suit radio. "He's knocked out. His medical monitors say his breathing and pulse are okay, but he could have a concussion."

Much more slowly, the hatches on the CIU tank Red Eagle had hit were opening, and helmets were slowly poking out and looking around.

Sergeant Red Eagle moved his tank close to Nguyen's and stopped. Sergeant Nguyen and his gunner climbed onto the hull, carrying their driver with them. They hung on to the driver and to the outside of the hull. Then Sergeant Red Eagle's tank moved out to support Lieutenant Wu.

Red Eagle shook his head with disappointment. Too bad they'd lost one of the platoon's missile firing tanks. Glad the crew got out, though.

While Red Eagle's section had been engaged, Lieutenant Wu and Sergeant Eisenberg had been closing with the remaining two CIU armored personnel carriers. The APC's had turned to present their side armor to the American tanks. This gave them better protection than their rear armor, and the maneuver kept them between the Americans and the still-fleeing rocket carrier. As the Americans drew near, the APC's began firing their cupola-mounted machine guns at the U.S. tanks.

The American tank crews ignored the rat-tat-tat rattle and clang as bullets ricocheted off their front armor. The firing, they figured, had to be an act of desperation. A mere machine gun, even a .50 caliber, wasn't going to bother a Ferret.

Wu and Eisenberg had almost reached point blank range when they opened up with both their cannon and their own coaxial machine guns. The machine guns wouldn't do much to the APC's either, but they would discourage the soldiers they carried from dismounting. The cannons were a different story. The armor of a CIU APC wouldn't keep out even a 25 mm high velocity shell. And the Americans could scarcely miss at this distance. Holes began appearing in the sides of the APC's; whatever else was happening, they would rapidly be losing pressure inside. The explosive in the shells would be detonating once they passed through the armor. The Americans could imagine the havoc that was causing.

One APC veered suddenly to its left, away from the Americans, and came to a stop. Had its driver been wounded?

Then the Americans were sweeping past the APC's, dust flying up from rear of their treads. The remaining APC briefly attempted to pursue, despite the damage it had already sustained, but its commander quickly realized he had no chance whatever of overtaking Ferrets, and dropped back to help his countrymen.

Another three or four minutes, and Lieutenant Wu and Sergeant Eisenberg had closed the distance to the CIU rocket carrier. The CIU carrier was still headed southeast as fast as it could go, not because its crew expected to outrun the Americans but because it was the only thing left they could do. By this time, Sergeant Red Eagle had nearly caught up with them, the crew from Sergeant Nguyen's tank still clinging to the hull of Red Eagle's.

"Sergeant Eisenberg, I want you to fire one of your antitank missiles at that carrier," Wu ordered. "I want you to try to blow a tread off. I want to immobilize that vehicle, not destroy it. I have a hunch that this vehicle and what it's carrying may turn out to be mighty important evidence, when the United States has to justify to the world what we're doing right now."

Eisenberg understood. The current version of the Red Flame missile could be fired in either of two modes. One was "fire and forget", where the missile would home onto the target it first locked on to by itself. The other way was to command guide it all the way to the target, giving it a laser-illuminated spot for its aim point. The second mode made the missile a more precise weapon, enabling it not only to hit a target, but a specific point on a target. In this case, it would make possible what the Lieutenant wished: to disable the fleeing CIU vehicle without destroying it.

Eisenberg's gunner lined up the targeting laser and fired one missile. The missile streaked to the target with a white flash (whoever had given the missile its popular name had apparently never seen one in flight) and struck the laser-lit spot on the rear of the right caterpillar tread. The tread flew apart and the rocket carrier came to an abrupt stop.

The Americans heard an voice on the CIU radio frequency speaking Arabic-accented English. "If you can hear this, please hold your fire! We surrender! This is the Caspian Islamic Union ammunition vehicle."

Lieutenant Wu answered, "We accept your surrender. We will not fire upon you if you come out of the vehicle without weapons, and keep your hands where we can see them."

The top hatch of the ammunition carrier opened. A gloved hand appeared, waving some sort of notebook, probably a checklist, opened so a blank white page was showing. Probably the nearest they could improvise to a white flag. The crewman holding the notebook climbed the hatch and carefully lowered himself to the lunar surface and stood with his hands raised. Then a second crew member climbed out, and a third.

"Is that everyone?" Wu asked.

"Yes," came the answer via suit radio, with the same accented voice.

"Sergeant Nguyen," Wu ordered, "check it out."

Nguyen slid down from his perch on Sergeant Red Eagle's tank and climbed easily up to the CIU vehicle's hatch. He poked his helmeted head inside for a quick look, then climbed into the vehicle to search more closely. "It's clean. Also, this appears to be a cargo hauler only; I see several rockets, but no launch mechanism." Then he added, "Lieutenant?"

"Yeah."

"Could my crew and I remain here? There's plenty of room inside for the crew and us. Specialist Black" – Peterson meant his driver – "is coming around, but he says his head is hurting pretty bad, and it's pretty hard for the three of us to hang on to the outside of a tank when you're moving as fast as you have to. You can send someone to pick us up when dust settles."

"No guarantees how the fighting is going to turn out," Wu reminded him. "The situation could get sticky for you if we wind up on the losing side of this scrap."

Nguyen looked at his crew. They told him they were with him. "We'll risk it," he said.

"All right, then," the Lieutenant assented. "But first, I need to find out something." He spoke to the CIU vehicle commander on their radio frequency: "Does your surrender apply to the surviving infantrymen and tank crew members on your side?"

There was a quick exchange of Arabic on the CIU frequencies. Then the CIU rocket carrier crew commander replied, "Yes, they agree."

"Okay, then," the Lieutenant ordered, "Let's make sure that all the communication gear on the other CIU vehicles is disabled, and I mean *all*."

It took about ten minutes to make sure the radio gear on each CIU tank and APC was disabled. Those that weren't already knocked out from combat, they shot up with their small arms: the pistols, carbines, and submachine guns the cavalrymen carried aboard in case they had to bail out from their tanks. The Americans also made sure that the radio antenna from each CIU pressure suit was broken off.

Then, and only then, did Lieutenant Wu tell Sergeant Nguyen, "You can hold this vehicle for us until someone gets back. You didn't have a chance to bring out your small arms when you bailed, did you?" He produced a submachine gun and a pistol from his own tank and handed them out through his hatch. As he passed them to Nguyen and his gunner, Wu told them, "I don't think the CIU crew will give you much trouble, but just in case."

As the three CIU crew members and the three Americans climbed back in, Lieutenant Wu buttoned his Ferret back up and repressurized it. He then launched a Triple R. When its flare ignited, he radioed, "Lieutenant Wu, Troop G, Second Platoon reporting. We have disabled the CIU rocket carrier. Repeat, the CIU rocket carrier is immobilized." He saw no reason to mention that it was nearly intact and captured. If the CIU could overhear and break the scramble code, they might try to recapture it, which would put Sergeant Nguyen and his crew in needless danger.

Wu continued his report. "The vehicle appears to be a cargo carrier only, not a launcher. Any instructions?"

Major Jenkins's voice replied, "Move east by north and attempt to rendezvous with First Platoon." He was guessing – correctly – that Captain Turner and First Platoon had followed a path roughly symmetrical to his own, viewed from a northwest-to-southeast axis through Aristoteles Crater.

General McCormick took advantage of Wu's radio relay rocket to cut in. "We're about ten to fifteen minutes from reaching the Aristoteles rim. Major, can you give me a situation report?"

Major Jenkins gave him his location and briefly described the orders he had given and what he and Third Platoon had been doing. "Captain Turner," he added, "Can you give your and First Platoon's present coordinates?"

As Turner was doing so, Major Jenkins looked up at the Triple R's flare. It was still high enough to allow him to send one more set of orders. "Captain Turner, reverse course. I want you to start drawing the CIU troops *toward* General McCormick. We'll do the same. Lieutenant Wu, change your course to north by east. And everyone listen up for one of those special code calls I gave you. General McCormick, if I may request, please send up another Triple R and inform us when you crest the crater rim, or just before."

As we had been traveling toward the crater, our main force had changed formation. Not only had we closed up distance between vehicles; the tank battalion was now in the lead, with the mechanized infantry battalion behind and our headquarters between them. The artillery followed the infantry, then the engineers, and the auxiliary APC's last.

In twelve more minutes we were just at the foot of the outside face of the Aristoteles Crater rim. We could see the tracks where G Troop had climbed the rim. If it was a good route up for them, it should be for us. We started up the slope following their path.

General McCormick had a Triple R sent up. He sent the message, "Major Jenkins, we're on our way up the Aristoteles rim now! Should crest it momentarily."

Major Jenkins took advantage of the radio relay rocket to issue his own order. "All right, everybody! Knight Fork!"

The Major had drawn the CIU forces toward us for a time, to close the distance. Now he would be drawing their attention *away* from us, so that while the CIU troops chased the cavalry troop, we'd have the chance to hit 'em from behind.

As our lead tank platoons crested the Aristoteles rim, they could see shadows of vehicles streaming eastward in the Earthlight. Two clusters, at the moment less than halfway across the crater but moving away. One group south and a bit west of the other. The groups were separated far enough from one another that they were probably below each other's horizons, and thus out of visual and radio contact of one another, although both clusters could be seen easily from the vantage of the crater rim crest.

On the far edge of each cluster, well beyond anything else, were five shadows moving east at top speed. Those would be First and Third Platoons of G Troop, with Captain Turner and Major Jenkins. Following each platoon were forty or so other shadows, not doubt also moving at what would be top speed for them, but falling behind the American cavalry. Those would be the CIU tank battalions and their supporting infantry.

Between the two groups, and closer to the southeast horizon, were a scattered handful of shadows that didn't correspond to anything on our maps, but they weren't moving. The remnants, perhaps, of Second Platoon's scrap with the CIU vehicles escorting the rocket carrier? The three tanks from Second Platoon still moving weren't in sight. Likely they'd already moved beyond the horizon in response to Major Jenkins's order to rendezvous at the Aristoteles east rim.

Our tankers weren't stopping on the rim crest to enjoy this view. Their formation was continuing to flow over the rim and down the inner slope as they radioed this information to General McCormick.

The tankers also observed and reported that the paths of First and Third Platoons were converging slightly, so that by the time they reached the east crater rim, or maybe sooner. they would probably link up. The CIU battalions would no doubt link up by then as well, and become one combined formation.

An especially interesting part of their report was that in the heat of the chase, the CIU commander apparently had failed to detail anyone to watch his back. All the vehicles in both battalions were following the cavalry east; none were dropping back as a rear guard.

This gave General McCormick an idea. He wanted to issue Major Jenkins some new orders, but not to draw attention to his oncoming forces by sending up a radio relay rocket. But with Jenkins and most of his troop still above the horizon, at least from the rim crest, he didn't have to.

"Major Jenkins," McCormick radioed, "I expect I'm going to ask you and your troop to do some artillery and mortar spotting for us. Captain Howard " he was now addressing the CO of our artillery battery " I want you to stop as soon as you're in comfortable howitzer range of the far rim of the crater. Be ready to open fire with both howitzers and rockets when I give the order."

"In that case, General," Howard responded, "we can stop as soon as we reach the bottom of the inner slope of *this* rim." It was testimony to the huge ranges possible under lunar gravity.

"Colonel Higgins," McCormick went on, now to the commander of our mechanized infantry battalion. "I also want the mortar platoon from your heavy weapons company, and the mortar squads from the heavy weapons platoons in each rifle company, to stop and prepare to fire when they get within range of the enemy. Since the CIU troops will no doubt still be moving, make sure they leave themselves plenty of margin. Have them wait for my signal to open fire. And have the mortar squads from the rifle companies tell me when they are in position."

Lieutenant Colonel Higgins understood. General McCormick wanted to have all of his long range "indirect fire" weapons in position to give support when his tanks and supporting infantry hit the CIU forces from behind. He might even be planning a barrage before the American tanks made contact with the CIU. The other heavy weapons of our infantry battalion – heavy machine guns, recoilless rifles, and antitank missiles – were designed for closer range, direct fire. They were not very effective as "over the horizon" weapons.

The 60 mm mortars of the rifle companies had a shorter range than the 81 mm mortars of the heavy weapons company, and they in turn had less range than the howitzers or rockets. So the rifle company mortars would be the last to stop; when they were in place, all the others would be ready.

Against dismounted infantry, the mortars would use fragmentation ammunition. Against vehicles, we'd worked up a shaped charge round. Coming in from a high angle, as mortar shells do, they'd be hitting the tops of the tanks or APC's. Most armored vehicles have much thinner armor on top than in front or on the sides. Even a tank can carry only so much weight, so you put your thickest armor where you think you will need it the most. A shaped charge coming down from the top should be quite effective.

Our formation was a few hundred meters in from the bottom of the rim when Captain Howard stopped his battery, as he'd promised, and announced, "We're in position, General. You may call upon us whenever you need."

The rest of our troops kept moving forward at top speed.

Once G Troop's First and Third Platoon had stretched their lead over their CIU pursuers almost to horizon distance – about two clicks – they slowed down to the CIU's top speed. If they were to do artillery spotting as General McCormick had ordered, they would need to stay in visual contact with the enemy.

Seven or eight minutes later, Second Platoon linked up with Captain Turner and First Platoon. Lieutenant Wu had guessed correctly that First and Third Platoon would slow down to keep in contact with the CIU forces. This meant that Second Platoon could also dare to slow down. He also guessed correctly that if they did, and steered a course northeast, they were bound to encounter First Platoon. Wu was confident that if they encountered CIU units first, his tanks could easily keep ahead of them.

In another four or five minutes, First and Second Platoons had linked up with Third Platoon and Major Jenkins. The two CIU battalions had also rejoined each other to make up a combined formation.

Although we in the American main force could not see the CIU battalions now that we were down on the crater floor, we knew we were rapidly overtaking them. Top speed of our tanks and APC's is nearly twice theirs. But we had to get much closer before we dropped off our mortar teams. Even in lunar gravity, the extreme range of our 81 mm mortars is no more than twenty kilometers, our 60 mm mortars about twelve. And we had to allow for the fact that the CIU vehicles would still be moving away between the time the 81 mm mortar platoon stopped and when the 60 mm squads got into range.

We could have followed the CIU's tracks across the crater, but we took a more direct route, based on where General McCormick guessed Major Jenkins was leading them.

We were more than two-thirds the way across the great crater before the mortar platoon of our infantry heavy weapons company came to a stop.

By that time, we had encountered and passed the rocket carrier Sergeant Peterson and his crew were guarding. General McCormick detached one of our extra APC's, plus a squad from the mechanized infantry headquarters company with a medic.

They would help Peterson's crew guard the CIU prisoners, and the medic would treat Specialist Black's injury and do what he could for injured CIU soldiers.

Meanwhile, Kasim Ferishtah had begun to figure out that our cavalry troop was staying in his sight on purpose, that they were leading him somewhere. He also decided that even though the cavalry were at extreme range effective for his tank's guns, he should at least *try* to knock them out of action before any new threat appeared.

Easier said than done. It wasn't that CIU shells couldn't carry far enough. They had plenty of range. But their targeting systems weren't good enough to hit a moving tank-sized target reliably at that distance. At their commander's order, the lead CIU tanks began to fire at our cavalry. But as soon as Major Jenkins saw muzzle flashes, he ordered zigzags.

But throw enough metal at something, and you may eventually get lucky. Evidently what the CIU commander was counting on. Round after round went toward the dodging cavalry tanks. The CIU weren't firing rapidly; Kasim Ferishtah did not want to use up all his ammunition on a single troop of cavalry when other hostile forces might be around. But they kept it up. Most shells went wild, merely throwing up fountains of dust and shrapnel ahead, behind, and between the American tanks. The Americans could hear occasional clangs and clinks as shell fragments and occasional bits of lunar rock bounced off their turrets or the portions of their tanks' hulls not shielded by sandbags. After three or four minutes of these potshots, one hit a tank in First Platoon, but it hit the sandbags. They proved their worth again; the dust absorbed the impact and the shell's explosion.

Another three of four minutes of misses, and the CIU scored again. This time they hit one of Third Platoon's tanks, and this time the Americans weren't so lucky. The 76 mm shell hit the Ferret on the upper hull, above the sandbags, near the turret. The shell's fuse malfunctioned; the explosive went off slightly prematurely, while the shell was only part way through the Ferret's armor, instead of detonating inside the tank as it was designed to. Much of the explosion's force was spent warping the turret's mounting. The turret was now slightly off level and jammed in place, unable to turn.

Even with part of the explosive force thus absorbed, the shell still blasted enough shrapnel into to the crew compartment to wreck havoc. Cavalrymen in the other tanks could hear the explosion over the radio link, and the sounds of flying metal striking the inside of the hull before the air leaked out of the crew compartment. They could also hear cries of pain from the crew. Those nearest could see the puff of cloud as water vapor in the air froze out as ice crystals as the tank's air vented out through the breach.

Their fellow cavalrymen felt their guts tighten up inside them, and none more than Lieutenant Nehru and Major Jenkins. They were officers who cared about their troops, and they didn't like knowing that three of their troopers were being hurt, maybe killed. It was one of the hard facts of life about being in the Army, and they accepted it, but knowing that didn't make it easier to take when it happened.

Sergeant Klepacz's voice came over the radio through his suit connection, gasping in pain, "We've all been hit!" He took a ragged breath. "Our suits have all sealed, and we're all still alive, but we're bleeding badly. I don't know how bad we're hurt!"

Major Jenkins immediately radioed back, "Sergeant Klepacz, if you think you and your men are too badly hurt to stay with us, you may drop out of formation and surrender to the CIU forces. Maybe their medics can help you. Your call."

For a few seconds, Sergeant Klepacz's tank stayed in formation with Third Platoon, as he thought it over. The shell may have caused his tank to lose pressure, and injured him and his men, but it hadn't done any damage to the fuel cells or the drive mechanism. His tank could still move.

Would the CIU accept a surrender? Did they have medics with them? But as he had his men report their suit medical readouts, he realized they were growing weaker rapidly. They couldn't last. Probably neither could he. The rest of the troop couldn't help them; the CIU would cut them to pieces if they stopped. And his tank couldn't help the troop...not if his men died at their posts.

Attempting to surrender was the only hope he could see. He ordered his driver to bring the Ferret to a stop. He began broadcasting on CIU frequencies, in clear language, no scramble (and hoping they had someone who understood English), "This is the stationary American tank. We surrender! This is the stationary American tank. We surrender! We need medical help, please!" He repeated the message over and over, as G Troop kept retreating and the CIU kept advancing, firing from time to time as they came.

It took no more than three minutes for the CIU forces to reach Sergeant Klepacz's position. As they did, one three-tank platoon broke off and surrounded Sergeant Klepacz's tank. At point blank range, they began firing into it. At that distance, they could easily shoot around areas protected by sandbags, so that the full impact of their shells went directly into the Ferret.

While this was going on, G Troop was hearing rapid-fire traffic in Arabic on the CIU frequencies, in a tone of voice that sounded almost panicked. Staff Sergeant LeCroix was translating for Major Jenkins. "It's the CIU commanding officer. He's saying, 'Cease fire! Stop! They're trying to surrender!'"

The CIU tanks stopped firing, but too late. By then, Sergeant Klepacz's tank was riddled, and no one was left alive inside. Major Jenkins didn't know that, but he guessed. He gritted his teeth. No one's fault. Not even the CIU's. Not enough people on either side who spoke each other's language. One of those communication delays that can happen in battle. But there were still three men – his men! – dead.

Nothing he could do about it but continue to lead the CIU troops toward the east wall of Aristoteles; they should see its base in just six to eight more minutes.

But only two minutes later, the mortar squads from all the infantry rifle companies stopped, including the squad from the company attached to the tank battalion. General McCormick sent up a Triple R, and radioed, "Major Jenkins, give us firing coordinates!"

Jenkins radioed back coordinates for the leading vehicles in the CIU formation. He figured that allowing for their forward motion, by the time shells and rockets from the artillery battery started landing, they'd be hitting right in the midst of the CIU battalions.

McCormick gave the order to fire first to the units whose rounds had furthest to travel. "Battery Bravo, fire! Use the coordinates given by G Troop!"

Bravo Battery's howitzers would fire standard high explosive rounds. Lieutenant Cavanaugh had ordered his rocket platoon's launchers loaded with homing submunition rounds. It's a nasty device designed especially for attacking armored formations. The rocket is loaded with three separate warheads, each with its own, independent guidance system and a small rocket motor. When the rocket descends to an altitude of seven or eight hundred meters above a vehicle formation, the warheads separate. Each independently locates a vehicle and homes in on it, its rocket motor driving it onto the target vehicle at high speed. The guidance systems are smart enough that with one of these rounds, one rocket fired means three vehicles knocked out. Cavanaugh intended to fire these until he ran out, then switch to other types of warheads.

Howitzers and rocket launchers each fired their first rounds. Meanwhile, General McCormick was ordering, "81 mm mortar platoon, fire!" and then, "60 mm mortar squads, fire!"

Colonel Ferishtah had seen the American radio relay rocket. He could still see a Triple R: each time one went down, General Mc-

Cormick ordered another sent up. McCormick wanted the cavalry to be able to continually update firing coordinates for the mortars and artillery. Colonel Ferishtah could also pick up the American radio traffic. He couldn't decrypt it, but he could guess what the Triple R's and the traffic on the American radio frequencies meant: reinforcements for the American armored cavalry were close by, apparently behind him.

He had one company from each battalion drop back. They were to stay in contact with the other CIU forces, but if American reinforcements appeared from behind, they were to delay the enemy until the CIU could get their formation turned around.

Colonel Ferishtah could also see that the armored cavalry tanks were slowing down slightly. He couldn't know, but could guess, that any of Major Jenkins's cavalry tanks with antitank missiles were preparing to fire as soon as any CIU tank came within effective range. He guessed because that was what he would have ordered if he were the American commander. But two battalions should sweep aside a single troop once in weapon range, no matter how well the troop was armed. He knew that the American commander would understand that as well as he. *So why was the American cavalry slowing down?*

Less than half a minute after Colonel Ferishtah asked himself that question, American shells began raining on his formation. First 60 mm mortar rounds, because they had the shortest distance to travel. A few seconds later, 81 mm mortar rounds began landing as well.

The CIU lost a tank when a mortar round came down directly on top of it, shaped charge blasting right through the hull's top armor. Then another. A third tank was damaged. An armored personnel carrier had a tread blown off. The CIU were having a vehicle damaged or knocked out roughly every fifteen or twenty seconds.

A minute and forty-plus seconds after the first mortar rounds started landing, the first howitzer shells began coming in.

The American artillery rockets began to strike, their homing submunitions stabbing down from the black sky like white lances, wrecking three CIU vehicles for every rocket. One howitzer round made a direct hit on a CIU tank and blasted it to a wreck of bent metal. Another landed beside a tank and blew it over onto its side.

Colonel Ferishtah's force was being cut to pieces, and he had no one he could shoot back at! Even the cavalry was still too far away for reliable shooting. His tanks were still taking occasional potshots at the teasing American cavalry, but the Americans were dodging too effectively: his men had only gotten a couple more hits, and those were only on sandbags, which prevented penetrating the Americans' armor. He could have screamed with frustration, but he would not vent his emotions in front of his men. It might cause them to lose confidence.

Not every mortar or howitzer round hit a vehicle; most were misses. But so many were coming in, and so rapidly, that some were bound to hit. Colonel Ferishtah saw his forces being whittled away. It was like a cut that he could not bandage, that just kept on bleeding.

After about three more minutes of this, the companies he'd assigned to rear guard reported sighting the leading American tanks.

Our range finding and targeting systems were much better than the CIU's, enough better that we *could* get hits reliably, even at extreme range. At two kilometers, which is about where we and the CIU forces began to come up over each others' horizons, we could expect fifty percent hits. CIU tanks would average less than ten percent at the same distance.

As soon as our lead tanks sighted the CIU, they opened up. The CIU tanks in the delaying force replied. Our 76 mm main guns had no trouble penetrating the armor of the CIU tanks and APC's. Their guns were the same size, but by far the majority of their shots went wild, while we were knocking out tank after tank. They did score one lucky hit, and destroyed one tank of ours, but by then, they'd lost most of four platoons. Each of the two companies detached to delay us had lost nearly half its force. And all the time, our formation continued to close with theirs.

While this was going on, mortar shells, howitzer shells, and rockets were continuing to rain down upon the CIU formation, coming down on coordinates supplied by the cavalrymen of G Troop.

Kasim Ferishtah reached a decision. He was not going to win this battle. If he continued to fight, his forces would be chewed up at a rate of eight or ten of his vehicles lost for every American tank or APC. He couldn't touch the artillery or mortars that were raining destruction from above; at the moment, he didn't even know where they were. He was caught between the main American force and the armored cavalry troop. The cavalry couldn't do him much damage by themselves, but they could pin his forces and keep them from evading the Americans.

If he continued to fight, he would lose anyway, and the longer he fought, the more of his men would be killed. And he cared about his men. Inwardly he sighed. Not out loud. Another thing he would not do in front of his men.

Some of his troops were members of families well connected to the Blue Crescent party. If he saved some of their lives, it might keep him from getting cashiered – or worse. But losing this battle...he'd never be a general, not after this.

Colonel Ferishtah switched on his radio and spoke to his men, "Cease fire! Everyone, cease fire!" Then he switched to the frequencies the Americans used, and called in English, "This is Colonel Kasim Ferishtah, commanding officer of the Caspian Islamic Union forces. We surrender! If anyone can hear me, please cease fire! Repeat, we surrender! Please cease fire!"

General McCormick sent up a Triple R to make sure everyone heard him, and answered on the American and CIU frequencies at the same time, "We accept your surrender. All American units, cease fire! Repeat, all American units, cease fire!" He added to Colonel Ferishtah, "Some of our mortar and artillery rounds are already on their way. It'll probably take a minute or two before they all land."

"Understood," the CIU commander responded in a resigned tone of voice.

It took a couple of hours for McCormick to get all our troops reassembled and get prisoners organized, in some of our auxiliary APC's and in CIU APC's with American guards. Meanwhile, medics from both sides started to treat the wounded. They made little distinction about the nationality of the soldiers they treated. Didn't matter if the medic was American or CIU, nor which nationality the wounded soldier was. If you were hurt, they tried to help you. Colonel Ferishtah expressed his thanks for the help, because there were a lot more wounded CIU soldiers than American.

When the engineers checked the rockets on board the CIU ammunition carrier Lieutenant Wu's platoon had captured, they reported, "There are seven rockets on board this carrier. They all *look* alike. But one weighs different, and it gives significant readings on our radiation counters. The other six have conventional chemical explosive warheads. This one has a nuclear warhead: U-235, according to our gamma spectrometers."

So...they had had *two* nuclear warheads: the one we'd knocked out, and this. A backup, or perhaps they had meant to hit a second target.

General McCormick's driver saw him looking stern. This was the proof we needed to go before the UN, and to convince the rest of the world. Or part of it. Then we got another break. Four of our technical specialists – three computer whizzes and a fellow who could read Arabic and Farsi – managed to hack the computer in Colonel Ferishtah's tank. And I mean "hack" in the literal as well as the computer slang sense: they unbolted the machine from its mounting and brought it with them. On the hard drive they had found orders to bombard the Criswell Collection Complex. If circumstances made that infeasible, there was a list of secondary targets, in order of priority, starting with the Cold Harbor settlement.

McCormick radioed me. "How does it feel to help save the world?" he asked. "Or I should say, to save the world *and* the Moon?"

I don't know how a man's voice could sound glad and grim at the same time, but he managed it. And I knew why.

Grim because we'd taken casualties. McCormick hated losing men, and he hated having to write letters of condolence to their families. And grim because we'd had to inflict casualties upon the enemy. He hated that, too. He knew that by and large, the CIU soldiers didn't want to be there any more than ours did.

Glad because our casualties had been so light. The bloodshed could have been far worse. We'd been good, but we'd also been lucky. And glad because we had kept a nuclear weapon from being used.

"I'll let you know later," I told him. "When we're done."

Because we weren't finished yet. We still needed to capture and occupy the base at Lacus Mortis. To check for additional weapons and for weapon assembly and research facilities. We'd pulled the fangs from this snake, and cut off its head. But we needed to make sure there were no more uranium eggs waiting to hatch back at its nest...and to make sure there never would be.

We needed to take evidence of everything we found, to show the world the danger it had faced. To confiscate or destroy whatever weapon-related equipment we found. And to take into custody every scientist, engineer, and technician we could identify, along with military officers. Because if we left the equipment and the people, what would keep the CIU from simply starting again somewhere else?

Even that wouldn't be enough. We would have to go on to the civilian CIU base at Lacus Somniorum and occupy it, too. Not because we expected to find weapons activity there – not with the effort the CIU had put into separating the bases. But it was a possibility we couldn't ignore. And even if no weapons activity were taking place at the Lacus Somniorum base *now*, the CIU would almost certainly shift to that location as soon as their Lacus Mortis base was occupied, *unless* we occupied the Lacus Somniorum base, too. If we left any CIU lunar base unguarded, we could bet diamonds to beach sand that the Blue Crescent leadership would immediately begin weapons work at the unwatched base.

But McCormick was right. Our victory here at Aristoteles had knocked out the bulk of the CIU combat forces on the Moon. That made the rest possible.